THE NUMBERS KILLER

An Agent Victoria Heslin Thriller

Book 1

JENIFER RUFF

The Numbers Killer

An Agent Victoria Heslin Thriller

Book 1

Copyright © 2019 Greyt Companion Press

ISBN-13: 978-1-7339570-0-7

ISBN-10: 1-7339570-0-6

Written by Jenifer Ruff

Edited by Dan Alatorre

Cover design by Tim Barber, Dissect Designs

Visit the author's website for more information.

www.Jenruff.com

Chapter One

In the dark, decaying woods behind the Sonesta Hotel, fierce gusts of wind cracked brittle branches, and Beth Dellinger's trembling hand tightened around a 9mm Glock. As she pulled the trigger, something snapped deep inside her brain. Two terrible incidents occurred. A murder—the end of one life—and the inescapable new beginning of another.

Twisted brambles tore into her skin as she fled down the narrow path toward the parking lot, her heart pounding a frantic rhythm. Only one instinct fueled her movements. *Get away.* With ragged breaths, she counted her hurried steps in fours.

Four, eight, twelve, sixteen, twenty, twenty-four, twenty-eight, thirty-two.

She slipped on the incline at the edge of the woods and her bare feet flew out from under her. Windmilling her arms, she hit the ground with a thud and slid down the wet earth, dirt smearing the back of her bare legs, filling tiny scrapes with grime. She scrambled up, looking back over her shoulder, stumbled, and kept moving. Pebbles and beer caps littered the rough pavement and a broken bottle shard sliced the edge of her dirt-caked foot. She had yet to register the pain.

A nearby train barreled down the tracks with an overbearing whoosh and grind, its horn blaring, intensifying the pulsing blood in her eardrums.

Four, eight, twelve, sixteen, twenty, twenty-four, twenty-eight, thirty-two.

When she reached her car, she stared blankly at a tube of lipstick she was carrying. She had no idea why it was in her hand. With a violent shudder, she hurled the lipstick back toward the woods as if she'd been clutching a hot coal.

Fumbling for her keys, she yanked the door open, and plopped down behind the wheel. She tossed her purse on the seat beside her, struggling to catch her breath. With a death grip on the steering wheel, she stared through the windshield, seeing nothing.

What did she remember? Fleeing the hotel. A beautiful woman holding the back door open for her. She remembered screaming, and a fiery pain erupting from her cheek. Nothing more. What had happened next? All she knew was that she had done something bad, something she couldn't undo. *Had anyone seen?* She slumped forward on the edge of her seat, hung her head, and covered her face with her dirty hands, wincing when she touched the bruised skin around her eye. A burned stench emanated from her hands—the smell of gunfire. Blood dripped from her foot onto the floor.

Two, four, six, eight, ten, twelve, fourteen . . .

A sudden noise made her jump in her seat.

"Beth, Beth, Beth. What am I going to do with you now?" Danny bent over and stared from outside the car, his blood-shot eyes level with hers.

Beth shook her head, squeezed her eyes shut, bit down on her bottom lip between her teeth. A tremor coursed through her veins. When she opened her eyes, he was still peering in at her. He rapped his fist against the glass. "Roll down the window."

She turned on the ignition and lowered the window half-way. He glowered at her as wheezy breaths constricted her chest.

"Are ya happy now?" He pounded the roof of the car with his hand. "What you just did, it's a whole lot bigger than one of your

2

little identify thefts. You might not get away with it. This time, you might really pay for what you've done. As in going to jail for the rest of your long life."

Beth clutched the neck of her shirt, gripping it tight.

"They saw you. You know that, don't you?" His harsh whisper made his words all the more terrifying.

She didn't want to answer him. She didn't want to have this conversation. But she couldn't help herself. She had to know what he meant. A lump had formed in her throat. Struggling to swallow around it, she leaned farther away. "Who saw me?"

"All of them. They all saw you." He made a sweeping gesture toward the windows lining the back of the Sonesta Hotel. Most were large blackened squares. Some had light peeking out around the edges of the blinds.

"No. They couldn't have." Her voice shook. She studied the windows for a shadow or a flicker of movement, any sign of life behind them. *What did they see?*

He gritted his teeth. "Yes, they did." Each word was like a slap, punching through the air and smacking her in the face. He shifted his weight, still towering outside her window, seeming larger than he really was. "They know because you were screaming like a . . . like a . . ." His face flushed red. Vocabulary was never his strength. "Like a damn crazy lunatic. You know what you have to do now, don't you?"

She stared out the window, away from him and the sadistic grin he was sure to be sporting.

"You'll have to take care of them before they betray you, too."

Her heart picking up a rapid rhythm again. "Ta—take care of them?"

"What part don't you understand? For someone who thinks she's so clever—."

3

Beth cringed. Shoulders hunched, she gazed through the front windshield toward the creepy hotel. She hadn't liked much about the place since they checked in earlier that evening. It was all dark shadows and ugly carpet. And now, she didn't think anyone had seen her. But they must have. For a long time, starting soon after their honeymoon, Danny had been dismissive to her, sometimes even cruel. When he was in one of his moods, his brutal honesty—words that seared her soul—delivered more pain than any kick or slap. It had been a long time since she'd seen the once charming man who made her believe she was special. But she didn't believe he had ever outright lied to her. At least not to her face.

"I see you've still got my gun. And you know how to use it." He laughed and threw his head back.

She glanced at the brown metal grip just visible at the top corner of her purse. Another shiver rocked her body.

Danny spit on the ground. "Now, you have no choice. Unless you've got a better idea. Which I wouldn't bet on. And for Christ's sakes, don't do it here. Wait for them to leave or you'll draw the police right to us."

"If I don't do it here, then how will I find them?" she whispered.

He laughed, a crazy, maniacal sound. "Use your head. You're supposed to be the expert hacker. Figure it out."

Clenching her fists, she tried to think.

He pounded on the roof again and startled her. "I have to tell you everything, don't I?"

If I'm so unbearably incompetent, how come it's my hacking jobs that pay for everything we do? Our apartment. This vacation. Your new business venture with its many expenses and no income. Huh? Jamming her finger on the window button, she rolled it up and yelled, "Just let me think!" She squeezed her eyes shut again and covered her ears with her hands. Another train rolled by, drowning out anything else Danny may have said.

4

What am I going to do? What should I do? And then, after taking a deep breath, another option occurred to her—*what do I want to do?*

One thing she knew for sure—the prospect of jail terrified her. But was she strong enough? What would it take? She straightened in her seat and glanced at the gun again. She would do it. She'd show him once and for all. And more importantly, she'd show herself. She couldn't be pushed around. She wouldn't be caught by surprise. Not anymore. This was the new Beth. And she sure as hell wasn't starting off by going to jail.

She opened her eyes again. Danny was gone.

Yes, she could do this. She'd go after them one by one until she was safe again.

She climbed out of the car and rummaged through her purse for her phone. Hunched over and almost walking on her tiptoes, she crept around the parking lot with cold, dirty bare-feet, taking furtive pictures of each license plate, as good a way as any to get started. There were only twelve cars. The Sonesta Hotel was no one's dream destination.

When she finished, Danny was waiting at the car. "We have to get out of here. Now. Before *you* get caught. Go get our stuff and meet me back here."

"Why can't you—"

"Just go! Now!"

Beth hustled inside the hotel. She returned only minutes later with drops of sweat rolling down her temples, lugging two small stacked suitcases, one with a broken wheel, and a cooler. They climbed in their "borrowed" Honda and sped off, driving past the nearest hotel, *too close,* and parking at the second one they saw. The Vista View sat just off a busy road without a vista worth mentioning in sight. But even before entering, she knew it would be a step up from the Sonesta, which Danny had chosen.

"Get us checked in," Danny grunted.

Beth trudged through the automatic sliding doors and inside the quiet lobby. A man in a navy suit walked in through a door behind the desk. "Checking in?" He couldn't have been older than twenty-five and his smile indicated he had the energy to be charming despite the late hour. His name tag read, "Ahmad."

"If you have a room available." Beth adjusted her large dark sunglasses. "We don't have a reservation."

Ahmad narrowed his eyes, looked at Beth and then toward the door.

"My husband is with me." She cupped her hand around her chin, self-conscious of her tear-stained face, blossoming bruise, the dirt on her clothes.

"Okay. I'll be right back. I have to finish . . ." He wiped his nose with the back of his finger. "Just one minute."

Ahmad disappeared through a door behind the desk, leaving Beth to shift her weight from one leg to the other and twirl pieces of her hair.

"You didn't get a room yet? What's taking so long?" Danny had apparently grown tired of waiting for her outside.

Ahmad returned. Beth let out a loud sigh.

"Sorry about that." Ahmad dropped his head and tapped on his computer. "How many nights?"

How long will it take? One day? Two? Can I even go through with it?

"Better do three," Danny said, standing too close for her comfort.

"Four days." Beth lifted her chin. She scratched at the raised bump protruding on her arm. Had to be a bug bite, although it was too late in the year and too cold for mosquitoes. Something had attacked her in the woods and her body was just starting to react.

6

"You're in luck. We do have a room and it's available for four nights." Ahmad smiled at Beth, but his eyes were traveling elsewhere, and she recognized the judgment in his smug expression.

She frowned and squeezed her fingers into the flesh around her bug bite, simultaneously experiencing pain and relief from the itch. "What number is it?"

"Two twenty-seven." Ahmad smiled.

Her face twisted as if she'd just been bit again. "Do you have something with an even number?"

Ahmad stared at her for a second longer than necessary, but his forced smile had returned before he dropped his head again. "Let me see." He poked at his keyboard and leaned closer to his screen. "You could have two thirty-four. It's across the hall. Would that work for you?"

Beth let out a sigh. "Much better. Here." She handed over a new credit card, not the same one they used at the Sonesta. It should work for at least a few weeks.

Ahmad took her card. "Thank you, Mrs. Malone. And by the way, if you were planning to use the gym, it's closed. Leaks. Too much rain the past few days. I'm wondering if it's ever going to stop."

Once inside their room, she scrubbed her hands and gently washed the dirt off her face, dabbing at the crust of blood on her lip. What a sight she had been. Staring into the mirror, she tilted her head at different angles, killing time before she emerged.

With his head resting in the cradle of his hands behind him and his boots on the coffee table, Danny leaned far back on the worn pull-out sofa. Beth stood between the window and the bed, as far away from him as possible. She peeled back an edge of the curtain panel and stared out. A cloud of specks flitted around under a hazy floodlight and the wind tugged at tree branches. More than a dozen cars were parked between painted lines, their flat roofs stretched out long below her. What kind of person owned each of those cars? Grandmothers and grandfathers? Mothers and fathers? Waiters? Salespeople? Assistants and executives? No—not executives, not at this place. And, more importantly, what kind of people owned the cars in the Sonesta parking lot? With a bit of internet research, she was about to find out.

I can't do this. "What if I just go to the police and turn myself in?"

"Ha!" Danny tipped his head back further. "Like I said, you won't survive a day in jail. But if you do go to the police, I'll pay a visit to your sister's house. Have a little private chat with her kids."

She scratched the back of her head. Her sister complained incessantly about those kids. Maybe he would be doing her a favor by scaring the crap out of them.

"Don't believe me, eh? Remember what happened to her little dog when she crossed me? What was his name? Cootie? No, Coobie. Poor little Coobie. Ha!"

She shrugged, her shoulders moving the slightest fraction of an inch. *It was just an animal.*

"If you don't do this, you'll have to spend the rest of your life in a filthy prison. And don't count on me for any conjugal visits. You'll be alone forever. Cuz who else would visit you?"

Beth kept her mouth shut and didn't respond, even though it was killing her to be quiet. Threats toward her sister's kids could be rationalized—they'd survive. But she wasn't going to prison. Prison meant being surrounded by meaner, crazier people than the ones she already knew.

Danny rattled on. She almost couldn't bear the sound of his voice, each word dripped with his imagined superiority. She hated him. She also loved him. Didn't she? She could strangle the life out of him with her bare hands if she had the strength. How she would enjoy watching him struggle and gasp for air until he finally shut up for good. But then she would be alone, and she didn't want that either. She stormed back into the bathroom and locked the door. She began counting the diamonds on the wallpaper. *Four, eight, twelve, sixteen, twenty* . . . The tension across her forehead intensified until she reached ninety-six at the top corner of the wall. She pivoted around and opened the bathroom door.

The room was quiet and empty.

He was gone, leaving her to pace around and pull at long strands of her blonde hair, coarse from too much coloring. She pulled open the small fridge. A laminated sign stuck to the front said, "You use it, you pay for it." Her hand shook so hard, a mini-bottle of liquor slipped from her grasp and fell to the floor. She picked it up, opened it, and tossed it back. It probably cost more than a whole six-pack, but she didn't care. Not tonight. Not when she was using someone else's credit card number. Not with what she was about to do.

After emptying two more mini-bottles, she opened her computer and got down to business, somewhat surprised by her determination. Danny wasn't going to leave her alone about this situation until she did what needed to be done. She'd think of it as an opportunity to finally show him who she really was. If she could kill once, she could do it again.

And again.

She *would* survive this.

Chapter Two

And now it begins.

Morning drizzle coated the windshield. Beth started the car to let the wipers clear the glass. After four noisy swipes—they needed replacing—she turned the car back off and drained the last of the hotel lobby's burnt coffee. Three sugar packets and five containers of fake creamer made it barely palatable. Too bad it hadn't helped shut off the throb of her hangover.

Eyes on the young couple, she turned her key in the ignition as soon as their car began to move. With one hand, she reached underneath her seat and felt the metal of the gun, making sure it was where it was supposed to be. This was it. Game on. She was really doing this. Her stomach cramped and demanded a trip to the bathroom, but she had to ignore it. Knew it was just her nerves.

Kelly and Jason Smith. Twenty-somethings. Married for just over a year. Kelly was petite and curvy with thick, wavy, light-brown hair right out of a shampoo commercial, big brown puppy-dog eyes, and a beautiful smile full of perfect white teeth. Her pink sweater looked soft. Jason wore wire-rimmed glasses, had neat short hair, and didn't look much older than one of those prep school boys who wore striped ties and navy coats to school.

Aren't they just adorable?

It had been easy to figure out which hotel room they occupied.

Beth sneered as she followed their candy-apple red Jeep onto the main road. Their heads bobbed. Kelly's long hair swung from side to side. What was going on inside their car? Oh, for God's sake—seriously? They were dancing in their seats. Probably lip syncing too. Beth rolled her eyes. A clever, mean thought entered her mind and she almost shared it aloud for Danny, before remembering she was alone.

She trailed behind the Jeep, maintaining a respectable distance. The drizzle changed into a steady rain. She flipped on her lights and wipers. Following all the rules. Not attracting attention. There was too much at stake.

Jason was on his way to make a sales pitch to a company in town; his wife came along for moral support. Beth knew this because she was *that* good. Of course, it helped that people were so willing to share their lives on social media with whoever might be interested. And Beth was very interested in the information Kelly Smith had to share. Kelly's propensity for posting made Beth's task of tracking them so much easier. Their every activity was announced online. "Business trip with a side of pleasure because I'm coming with!" is what Kelly wrote on her very public Facebook site. She might as well have hung a sign on her door: "We're both out of town. Come rob us!" Because it was a simple feat for Beth, or anyone, to find the Smith's home address. And if they didn't have anything worth stealing, well, a frustrated thief might vandalize their place for wasting their effort. Beth knew this from experience. The time she and Danny broke into a house and found absolutely nothing of value—nothing they needed, nothing they wanted, and nothing they could resell—they'd taught those homeowners a lesson all right.

What would Beth's posts look like if she shared her daily life? "Great day! Hacked into an online account and opened three new credit cards with the info! Whoopee! Oh, yeah, and then Danny smacked me and broke a tooth because he was wasted and I didn't know where the TV remote was. Can anyone recommend a dentist?" Ha! The world would love knowing her dirty little secrets. She never made her comings and goings public and never would. People should know better, not be so trusting. Otherwise it served them right if someone made off with their flat screen TV, spread toothpaste over their walls, syrup on their furniture, or borrowed their identity until their credit was maxed out.

After a couple of minutes, Jason's right blinker light began flashing and he pulled the car into a complex with stores and restaurants: a Target and Best Buy, but mostly small franchises, the kind that lined most strip malls in America. Was this where he would make the sales pitch? Beth's heart beat a bit faster, like it was warming up for the main event.

Cars chugged along slowly in every direction, up and down the crowded parking lot lanes, no one wanting to make the trek from the empty spaces farther from the stores, not now, with the steady rain approaching a downpour. Beth prayed Jason would drive behind the stores where the trucks unloaded their cargo and there wouldn't be any people. And then what? Shoot them in the shopping mall's parking lot? How was that going to work? Maybe she hadn't thought this out as well as she could have. Until that moment, identifying her targets and following them had seemed like a big enough accomplishment.

With so much traffic meandering through the shopping center, and some of them being damn aggressive—*it's not Black Friday, lady!*—Beth had no choice but to stay close behind or risk losing the Smiths. Jason steered right up to the curb and stopped. Beth hit her brakes behind him, just in time. The Jeep's passenger door swung open and Kelly's shapely legs appeared, clad in tight yoga pants. With her head down, Kelly made a run for the nearest store, the Plush Nail Salon. It didn't look very plush. The H and the N hung sideways off the sign. One fierce gust of wind would send them flying away. So, Kelly wasn't going to the sales pitch with Jason after all. She was going to get herself all pretty while her man did the hard work. Beth frowned, rolling her bottom lip into her mouth. That wasn't good. Not good at all. She needed them to stay together.

Inside the doorway, Kelly blew her husband a kiss. But it wasn't aimed toward the driver's seat of the Jeep. Beth jerked her head back, following Kelly's gaze, knowing she'd missed something.

Jason was out of his car. Covering his head with a magazine, he hurried straight toward Beth, staring at her through the windshield, his face a determined grimace. A spike of adrenaline edged Beth toward a full-blown panic attack. What was he going to do? He must have recognized her. She yanked the steering wheel to her left, but a line of barely-moving bumper-to-bumper cars prevented a quick escape. Her eyes flew to the rearview mirror as she jammed the gear shift into reverse, but behind her, another car boxed her in.

Jason was only a few steps away.

Heart racing, she doubled over and grabbed the Glock from beneath her seat. Her stomach lurched. He was probably at her window now. There were too many people around. This wasn't the right place! She'd be caught for sure if she tried to shoot him here. She shoved the gun under her T-shirt, wincing in terror. Her hands were shaking so much she didn't trust them on the gun, especially not with the weapon against her own body.

A knock on her window made her bolt upright, still gripping the gun under her shirt.

"Hey." Jason stared right at her.

No choice. She eased the gun out from under her shirt.

Hunched over in the driving rain, Jason pointed toward the front of her car. "Just wanted to let you know that your right headlight is out. Didn't want you to get a ticket."

And then he trotted away, still covering his head with the sodden magazine, the shoulders of his coat dark from the drenching rain.

Beth sat stunned, staring into but not seeing the sheets of rain, not hearing the incessant hammering of drops on the roof. Danny was right. She couldn't do it. And right then, she didn't even have the wherewithal to drive her car, never mind follow anyone and do what needed to be done without being caught. But that wasn't all that had her freaked out. Something else about the brief encounter bothered her. Jason didn't act like he knew her. Not a bit. Unless he was playing some sort of game to screw with her head. Maybe that was it. Maybe her headlight was working fine, and the broken headlight story was just a ruse to get her out of the car. She whipped her head to her left and to her right but didn't see anyone else.

Jason was already pulling out into the slow-moving traffic.

She drove back to the hotel, below the speed limit, her breath coming in fast gulps, murmuring a rhythm to herself, counting every fourth scraping swipe of the windshield wipers.

"Four, eight, twelve, sixteen, twenty, twenty-four, twenty-eight, thirty-two. Four, eight, twelve, sixteen . . ."

#

"I knew you couldn't do it." Danny sneered. "Your screw up only made things worse for yourself. You're kinda . . . noticeable, you know. Ya stick out like a witch with the dark roots in your hair and that purple bruise."

Witch? She wasn't ugly. She'd always thought she was sort of attractive—average height and maybe she could have been in better shape, but it's not like she was overweight—until Danny started making a point of telling her otherwise. "The bruise—whose fault is that?" She sunk down into the corner of the hotel room couch and grabbed a pillow to protect her face, just in case. Danny always found a way to reason that everything was her fault. Like if it weren't for her he'd be living-it-up in luxury, driving a Mercedes, sitting in the front row ordering beers at the Wizards games. As if.

"So now he got a good, close look at you. He knows exactly what you look like. It will be real easy for him to pick you out of a line up once the police come for you. Set you up there with four other chicks past their prime—"

14

"He didn't act like he knew me. I mean, he—"

Danny grunted. "Have yourself a good time in jail. Not sure how you'll manage. You can't stand to be alone, can you? Makes you all freaked out and you start counting stuff like a fricking nut case. You're really a piece of work." He sneered and threw his head back. "They won't give you a pen because you might poke your eyes out, but you can use your own blood to make tic marks on the cement walls, one for each day. Ha! You'll have plenty of those, you'll be counting them tic marks until you're an old hag. One, two, three, four, five . . . no—not five! I can't end on an odd number because I'm a psycho! Unless . . . unless they hang you, shoot you up with electricity, or whatever it is they do to get rid of bat-ass-crazy killers these days."

Clenching her jaw, she faced away from Danny. She'd been counting the up motions of her bouncing leg. She pressed her hand down hard against her knee and kept it still, but the numbers didn't stop, they only grew faster and louder inside her head.

I'm not going to prison.

The day was only just getting started. She would wait until the Smiths were together again. In the meantime, there were more people on her list. She knew exactly how many—seven. She'd been counting them over and over again.

Next time, she wouldn't fail.

15

Chapter Three

Victoria Heslin's skin tingled in the cool October air as she walked the wet trails. She inhaled deeply and stepped over a rushing stream on a newly constructed bridge of logs, heading towards the mountain trails. There was no place she would rather be than outside, hiking with her dogs.

The rain had ceased, although the clouds were determined to keep out the sun. At the end of a pink leash, Izzy trotted down the path with her head up, alert for any movement or rustling in the bushes. Like a stealthy hunter searching for prey, the Spanish greyhound never stopped scanning her surroundings. Eddie, a large retired racing greyhound, lagged behind, nose toward the ground, sniffing and marking every few yards with a casual lift of his hind leg as if it was his sworn duty.

"Come on, Eddie. Keep up." Victoria gave a gentle tug on his leash. The big dog tore off a mouthful of grass and ambled after her.

Victoria's phone buzzed, an unwelcome interruption that made her grimace inside. She pulled the device from her hip pocket, glanced at the screen, and sighed. It was her boss calling. It was Saturday, but that didn't matter with her job. She answered. As she expected, it quickly became clear her walk would be cut short.

"Oh, no. And he's definitely dead?" she asked, already turning around to head back the way she came. "Okay. I'm just out on my property. I'll be there as soon as I can. I have his address."

She jogged home with the dogs, unlocked the heavy iron gate, and let them loose in her backyard. Inside the mudroom, while she pulled off her hiking boots, the rest of her pack of Greyhounds, Galgos, and Podencos surrounded them, wagging their tails, snorting, and sniffing Izzy and Eddie as if they had been transformed into brand new creatures during their walk.

"Hey. Hey. Calm down everyone." Laughing, Victoria wove through their wagging bodies and into the house. "You act like we've been gone a week." Their tails smacked back and forth against the entryway walls in response. "I'm so sorry to tell you all this, but I've got to go out again."

Seven wagging tails followed her into the master bedroom, Eddie and Izzy leaving faint traces of mud in their path. Victoria tore off her shorts and T-shirt and hurried into the shower. Less than three minutes later, she was putting on a white camisole that covered her sapphire necklace, her mother's birthstone. She ripped open a dry-cleaning bag and pulled on gray slacks, a blouse, and a jacket in a fast, rehearsed manner. Amidst strokes and head rubs for the dogs, she hustled into the kitchen and handed out treats and apologies. She checked the dogs' bowls, grabbed the prepacked bag of human snacks, slipped a water bottle into her backpack, locked the doors, and then jumped in her customized Suburban. Cruising down her long driveway, she hooked up her phone to the car and dictated a text message for Ned.

"Hi. It's Victoria. I had to leave on short notice and I'm not sure when I'll be back, so definitely plan to come around dinner time to feed my dogs and give them some attention. I'll keep you posted once I know more. As always, thanks for your help. And text me that you got this."

A soft chime indicated an incoming text. Victoria read Ned's reply at the next stoplight. *Got it. Monday still good for our dinner?*

She pressed the speaker button on the steering wheel. "So far so good." Victoria sighed. Was that apprehension she was feeling, just a little, or was it possibly a hint of nervous excitement? She wasn't sure. It wasn't a real date, was it? After all, Ned was her employee. She rarely dated. She'd been attracted to a few men, and recognized when it was mutual, but . . . then she kept her distance. Somewhere deep inside her subconscious, not getting romantically involved with anyone felt like the right thing to do, at least right now. A long time had passed since she'd given anyone a chance. She barely remembered her last awkward dinner. She'd been called away right in the middle of it. Should have shut her phone off, and she knew it, but maybe she wanted to have a possible excuse to bolt. She shook her head, remembering, and not impressed with her behavior. Perhaps it was time to give it another go, give someone a try. Maybe it wouldn't be so bad if the dinner with Ned *was* a real date. Or almost like one.

Ned sent another message. *Good. So we can talk about what I should bring when we go to the shelter in Spain next month.*

She dictated again. "Yes. I'm glad you're going with me. It's going to change your life. And you'll make a big difference there." After sending the message, she dropped her phone into the center console.

She was definitely nervous about having a back-up dog walker for so many days. She'd really learned to count on and trust Ned, finding him was nothing short of a miracle, but everything would work out. The trip to Spain was important. She had a long list of things to check on while she was there.

She pressed the home button again. "Send Ned a text."

"What would you like to say to Ned?"

"I can't remember if I told you this, but Myrtle seems to despise the new herbal toothpaste. Use the poultry one in red tube or she might snap at you." That was her subtle way of reminding him to brush their teeth after dinner.

Ned responded with a thumbs-up.

Thirty minutes later, thanks to non-existent traffic, she parked behind three police cars and an SUV. A chilly wind hit her as she

18

stepped out of her Suburban. She pulled her jacket tight around her chest. A uniformed officer approached. He held up a hand. "This is a crime scene, Miss, you need to get back in your car."

Victoria lifted the edge of her coat and looked down at her waist. "I'm Agent Heslin with the FBI."

The officer followed Victoria's eyes to the badge attached to her pants. "Oh. I didn't—"

"Not your fault. I'm not wearing my jacket."

The officer rocked back and forth on his feet, then turned toward the small, ramshackle house behind him. "We've been keeping the scene secure for you. The other agent just arrived."

Victoria moved her badge from her waist to the collar of her shirt where it would be more visible, in case any of the other authorities had any initial doubts that she belonged there. "Thank you." She smiled, walking past the yellow crime scene tape, toward the home that was currently the center of attention. Paint peeled off around the windows, gray mildew coated the exterior, and a broken gutter pipe hung loose at an odd angle. Aside from the weeds, the small yard was mostly dirt. Puddles of muddy water filled the ruts and depressions. An empty yellow potato chip bag and a blue ice cream sandwich wrapper provided the only color. Everything about the property shouted shoddy construction that had seen better days, except for a gleaming black Range Rover that just barely fit under the rusty carport.

The neighbors' homes all conveyed the same message—those living there had either given up caring or never cared much at all. They might not even be aware of the neglect they were loudly advertising—almost abandoned but not quite.

Agent Rivera stood inside the open doorway, one hand running over his short dark hair. His FBI coat was also absent. He wore a crisp white tailored shirt under a charcoal suit jacket and pants. His outfit was nearly identical to Victoria's, male and female versions of the same colors and materials. Oops. Someone at the office was bound to make a crack about their matching attire.

19

As she walked toward the house, he saw her and his eyes lit up.

"Hey, Tory." He stepped outside the splintering front door and let it creak closed behind him. "Forensics aren't here yet. Busy day for them."

"First off—nice to be working with you again. I didn't expect it to be so soon."

"Yeah. I'm not complaining."

"So, what have I missed?" Victoria bent down and pulled on shoe covers.

"Well, the state's best witness took a bullet to the head. No sign of a gun, so not likely his own doing."

"There's going to be a lot of angry agents and prosecutors." She pulled a pair of latex gloves from her pocket and put them on. "What do we know?"

"Shot to the temple at close range. Bullet went in and out. Cops found it under the counter."

Victoria opened the door and stepped inside. "Really?" She frowned. "A bullet was left behind?"

"Yep."

The agents walked into the house along the edge of the hallway. A trail of dark red partial shoe prints stained the tile floors and led outside.

She bent down to get a closer look at the narrow tread marks. "Who stepped in the blood?"

"According to the neighbor who found him—she's still inside—the prints were there when she arrived." Rivera lowered his voice and leaned toward Victoria. "We'll have forensics get shoe prints to make sure, but at a glance, they're too small for any of the officers here."

Still crouched, Victoria clasped her necklace through her shirt. "Whoever it was left during the day, out the front door, where they were more likely to be seen."

The agents entered the living room from the hallway. Three uniformed officers, all men, stood together in the room. A tall man with broad shoulders lifted a hand in greeting.

"Hey, Sully." Rivera gave his friend a half-smile. "You've met Agent Heslin?"

Detective Sullivan nodded, his expression slightly grim, as appropriate for a crime scene. He was a big guy who used to spend a lot of time at the gym, sometimes with Rivera when the agent was in town. He'd had his share of troubles and heartache, and Victoria hoped he was doing well. With his skin looking as flushed as deli ham, she wasn't sure. His eyes were a little bloodshot, but that could be from working a double shift and not getting enough sleep.

The detective introduced the other two policemen and said, "I just got here a few minutes before you."

The officer with glasses stepped forward. "No sign of a break in, although the doors might have already been unlocked. He was obviously dead, so we didn't touch anything and called forensics."

"Yeah." A very young officer with red hair nodded. "Only thing we touched was the microwave. It was beeping, so I opened it to shut it off. He was cooking something when he got killed."

Rivera smirked. "So you didn't touch anything except what you touched. Got it."

Sully snorted, repressing a laugh.

The young officer spoke again, his face now almost as red as his hair. "We were told to wait here until the Feds—until you came—because this guy is special."

"Yes. He was." Rivera headed toward the small kitchen and the reason they were all huddled inside the small home—the victim—Todd Meiser.

Light filtered in through a dirty window over the sink, casting a ray of dancing dust specs over the kitchen table and two chairs. The Range Rover key fob sat in plain sight on a small Formica topped island. The smell of cigarettes mixed with the smell of the meal that was still sitting in the microwave.

Victoria scanned the room, taking in the sad, gory scene. Wearing jeans and a long-sleeved T-shirt, Meiser was lying on the worn linoleum, legs bent to one side, as if he'd been on his knees praying before he was knocked sideways. Dark stubble coated his chin, and his mouth hung open in the shape of an O with his lips pursed, a shocked grimace. A blood-soaked woman's silk scarf, black with gray and pink flowers, covered his right eye and drooped down across his nose. A chunk of his skull was missing on the left side of his head, exploded into the mess of bone chips, brain matter, and blood now covering the kitchen floor, with bits plastered against the cabinets.

Victoria tiptoed around the perimeter of blood and pulp, studying the victim and his surroundings. "The last time I saw him, he was a nervous wreck, wringing his hands and pacing around the FBI office, when he wasn't excusing himself for another cigarette. But his behavior was understandable. He was a key witness for the prosecution of Raymond Butler."

"I know we've been after Butler and his organization for years." Rivera's eyes moved slowly and carefully over the corpse.

"Not sure how you missed out on all that fun, but now is your chance to get in on the messy tail end." Victoria placed her hands on her hips. "This is not what I expected to see."

"I know," Rivera answered quietly. "Someone got the job done . . . and dead is dead, but this doesn't look like a professional hit."

"Right." Victoria frowned. "Looks like the scarf was used as a blindfold. Strange to blindfold someone if you're going to kill them, isn't it?"

"Maybe the kill started out as just a threat for him not to testify."

Victoria crouched close to the body. "And what's this about?" The number two was scrawled in black ink above Todd's left eyebrow. Directly below it, the word LIAR. "Written after he was shot. And whoever wrote it must have stepped in his blood while doing so." Balancing as she squatted, Victoria used her phone to snap a picture of Meiser's head. She leaned forward to study the shoe track marks in the blood and took another picture. "Let's keep that info from the press and public for now. About the writing."

"Good call." Rivera walked into the next room. Sully was on the phone but covered it with his hand as Rivera addressed the officers. "Hey, guys. Don't say a word about the number or the writing on his head. Make sure no one else does either. That will be the thing we keep under wraps."

Sully nodded. "Got it. We were thinking the same." He returned the phone to his ear.

One of the officers followed Rivera back to the kitchen and waited until Victoria glanced up. "So, this guy is involved in the Butler case? That's why you guys were called in?"

"Yes. Well, he was."

"What'd he do?"

"He unwittingly helped the Butlers traffic illegal goods for over a year. He was key to putting Butler away." Victoria sighed. "Poor guy. He couldn't wait to get through the trial, start his new job, and leave his past life behind him. Only a few more days and it would have happened." Victoria dropped her head and stared at what was left of Meiser's face.

"Hey. I know what you're thinking." Sully shook his head. "But it wasn't you who got him into the whole mess and it wasn't you who murdered him while he microwaved his lunch."

"I know." Victoria offered a sad smile. She also noticed the slight tremor in the detective's hands, the flush on his light skin. "Who found him?"

Sully gestured back toward the living room. "Neighbor. She's in the next room. Hope you don't mind smoke."

"Let's go talk to her." Rivera walked past Sully toward the living room but stopped after a few steps to wait for Victoria.

An old woman in sweatpants and a sweatshirt sat on one end of a ratty couch. She wore white slip-on shoes. Purple rollers wound her gray hair into tight cylinders around her scalp. Her wrinkled cheeks sunk inward as she pulled long inhalations off her cigarette and stared with a blank expression at the stained carpet. On a side table next to her sat an ashtray overflowing with butts.

"Ma'am, I'm Agent Rivera and this is Agent Heslin. We're with the FBI. Can you answer a few questions for us?" Rivera took a small leather-bound notepad out of his pocket.

The woman's cigarette dangled from her mouth. She mumbled, "You're the Feds?" Her gaze traveled from agent to agent, up and down their bodies.

"Yes." Rivera nodded. "And your name, ma'am?"

"Shirley Woodard."

"Ms. Woodard, please tell us how you came to find the deceased."

She took a drag on her cigarette, turned her head, and blew a long white stream toward the window. "I heard a gunshot, so I came over here. The door was unlocked."

"Just one gunshot?" Rivera asked.

"Two. One right after the other." Shirley fidgeted with the hem of her sweatshirt.

"And you came over here and entered the house by yourself after hearing a gun go off?"

Shirley's eyes darkened. "Guess I ain't got much to lose no more."

"And what did you see?"

"I saw him . . ." she cocked her head toward the kitchen, ". . . on the floor, just like he is now. I didn't touch him. Didn't touch nothin'. Doesn't take a rocket scientist or a special agent to figure out he was dead. I called 911 and I sat here until the cops came. Helped myself to his cigarettes, they was right here on the table. He won't be needing them now."

Rivera jotted something down with his pen. "Anything else you saw or heard?"

"No." She blew out another lungful of smoke.

"A car driving away? Someone running down the street?"

"There weren't nothin' else I heard or saw to tell ya. He was just lying there dead and I expect whoever it was killed him was long gone."

Victoria clasped her hands together, elbows tucked by her sides. "How much time elapsed between when you heard the gunshot and when you left your house to come over here?"

"I don't know." She took another puff of her cigarette, her face growing even more haggard.

"An estimate." Victoria shifted her weight. "A few minutes? Ten?"

"I was getting out of my shower when I heard a bang. I came over to have a check on things after I got dressed."

"After you put your hair in rollers?" Victoria asked.

The woman patted the rollers above her temple. "I have to go out this afternoon." She frowned at Victoria. "I came over, didn't I? We got other neighbors younger than me. I don't see any of them here, none of them came rushing over."

Rivera put his notepad away. "Could you lift your shoes up off the floor, so we can see the bottoms?"

Shirley rolled her eyes but leaned back against the couch and lifted one foot at a time. There was no sign of blood on her scuffed, smooth soles.

Victoria leaned forward. "Ms. Woodard, sometimes the authorities need to keep certain pieces of information about a case from the public. The information we withhold can be critical in helping us identify the killer. We'd appreciate if you wouldn't share any of the details about Todd Meiser's death. You can say you found him, but that's all we'd like you to share until we've found out who shot him."

Shirley nodded. "I know. Cops already said so. I got it. And I can keep my mouth shut real good."

"Thank you for being a good neighbor." Victoria reached into her pocket and withdrew a business card. She handed it to the woman. "Please call us if you think of anything else that might be helpful in finding whoever killed Mr. Meiser."

"That mean I can go now?" She stood up, pinched her cigarette between two fingers, and dropped it on top of the other butts.

"Yes, you can go home now." Victoria walked back to the other officers. "Can one of you escort Ms. Woodard back to her home so she won't be bothered on the way?"

The young red-haired cop stepped to her side. "Right this way, Ma'am."

After Ms. Woodard left, the agents scanned the outside area through the grime-streaked living room window. A small crowd of onlookers stood on the edge of the muddy lawn, blocking the sidewalk. "Let's go talk to some of those other neighbors," Rivera said. "See who else might be out there."

The police activity had attracted attention beyond the neighborhood. A local news van had parked behind Victoria's Suburban. Amanda Jones, the ubiquitous young reporter from Channel 14 News was putting on a sweater. The tall brunette looked like she'd just stepped off the beauty pageant circuit. Her equally young cameraman stood next to the van, scanning the area. Amanda spotted the agents, alerted her cameraman, and rushed forward. As the agents walked down the front path, Amanda met them, holding her microphone outstretched. "We heard there was a murder and FBI agents were called in. Can you tell us who you are and what the FBI is doing here?" She spoke in such a rushed tone; her words almost ran together.

Instead of waving Amanda from their path, Victoria stopped to answer. "I'm Agent Victoria Heslin and this is Agent Dante Rivera."

"Thank you for speaking with us, Agent Heslin." Amanda's tone was more relaxed, like she'd just realized she didn't have to spit out all her questions in one burst. "We know this is the home of Todd Meiser and that he was dead. Murdered. Can you tell us what happened here today?"

"We can't share information at this time. But, if anyone has information that could help us with this case, please call your local police department."

"We've also learned that Todd Meiser was a—" Victoria raised her hand, but Amanda continued. "—witness for the prosecution against Raymond Butler, a notorious drug smuggler and money launderer. Did you know Meiser's life was in danger? Shouldn't he have been in witness protection?"

Rivera approached the cameraman. "You're not going to air that yet," his voice was low but authoritative, a voice that people were used to following. "Give us some time before you include that. We'll make it worth your while when we can. We still have to notify his family."

The cameraman lowered his equipment.

"But—" Amanda frowned.

"Thank you very much for your cooperation." Victoria held the reporter's gaze and then the cameraman's. "We'd appreciate a copy of your footage, so we can check out the crowd."

Chapter Four

Beth held her shoe upside down under the bathroom faucet. Diluted trails of blood ran in pink rivulets from the treads down the sides of the white sink.

"Damn, woman. I really didn't think you'd do it. I didn't think you had it in you." Intruding on her personal space in the small bathroom, Danny snorted, the way he did when he begrudgingly said something almost nice. Like when he called her kitten—*go to the store and pick up a case of Bud, kitten.* How long had it been since he called her kitten? Didn't matter anymore. She didn't have to be his errand girl any longer.

She felt his rough hand patting her on the back. "You might have more guts than I thought. Or you really, really can't bear the thought of rotting away in jail. I gotta say, you've surprised me."

Yes, she had. She most certainly had.

Meiser had been easy to find. He only lived a few miles from the Sonesta Hotel. People locked their doors at night, when they went to bed, but not always during the day. That was her advantage. And yet, Todd Meiser didn't seem all that surprised when she entered his back door with a gun. Terrified—yes. Surprised—not so much.

When he was on his knees, his features contorted with shock and disbelief, a surge of power coursed through her veins. Now she knew how Danny felt when he knocked her to the ground and watched her crawl under a table, apologizing and begging for him to calm down and back off. Too many men from her past had made her feel that way, starting with her own alcoholic father—*get your ass out of my sight before I make you sorry, Beth*. It was long past time she turned the tables.

And she had to admit, she liked how it felt once the tables had been turned. She couldn't help it.

But she didn't like all of it. Meiser's fear and raw vulnerability were all too familiar. They crept in, poking away at the armor she erected for the big moment, ruining her power trip, reminding her that she'd spent more of the past years cowering in fear than she ever intended. She couldn't look away from Meiser, but she couldn't bear to see those pleading eyes another second. She'd yanked her scarf off her neck, threw it at him, and yelled—*tie this around your eyes! Do it now!* And because she'd been weak, her scarf got ruined, sodden with the horrific mess that exploded from his face. She'd had to leave it behind.

Danny rubbed her mistake in. "You left something of yours behind at a murder scene? You know that show about stupid criminals? That's going to be your claim to fame, Beth."

She desperately wanted to shower and wash away the disconcerting sensation gnawing away inside her, the lingering image of Todd Meiser's terrified face, his desperate eyes. But Danny was in the next room now, still going on about the scarf, everything she still had left to do, and how she better hurry. She tried to block out his voice. She wasn't going to let him ruin everything for her. She had done it. And despite Danny's recriminations, he was impressed. And that, in itself, was something. A big, fat, huge something to be proud of.

But can I do it again?

"I'm going out to take a walk. I need to. It will help me concentrate." She edged past him to grab stretchy pants and a T-shirt from her bag. Danny was all for telling her to exercise, practically every day, while managing to ignore his own steadily expanding gut. *You got to get rid of that damn cellulite, those ugly dented cheese holes, before it spreads and takes over your whole*

30

ass. At home, he insisted she walk on the treadmill. The tiny Vista View gym had water dripping through the ceiling and yellow tape across the door. She'd have to go for a walk outside.

"Make it fast." He pointed. "You have to take care of the rest of them. Tick tock, Beth. Tick tock. You're running out of time."

"I know that." She was just procrastinating, putting off the inevitable, but she didn't care. Shouldn't the small milestone moments be celebrated too? Like their three-year anniversary? Ha! Some vacation it was turning out to be. She deserved a break to settle her nerves before she had to go out there and eliminate another name from her list.

She scurried out of his reach and back into the bathroom. If he was trying to drive her crazy, it was working. She changed her clothes and studied herself in the mirror. Lifeless eyes stared back, like there was nothing behind them. She patted concealer around her bruise; she didn't need to advertise the deep purple ring. Her lips were pale gray, like a cadaver. They desperately needed color. She rifled through her stuffed purse for her lipstick, pulling out tissues, a wallet, pens, receipts, a comb, pain pills, tossing everything to the side and yanking the inside of the lining forward.

Where was it? Where was her damn lipstick?

A jolting current shot through the center of her brain then branched out in alarm-inducing tendrils. She froze, overcome by a wave of unexplained terror. Her knees grew weak. A dark cloud swelled around her sight, closing in, squeezing her vision smaller and smaller, down to nothing. She grasped the corner of the sink, but her hand slipped off as she sank to the floor. "Danny," she moaned as her head smacked the edge of the bathtub.

She woke moments later on the hard tiles, covered in a sheen of sweat, aware of a painful lump above her ear. Crawling up the side of the tub and then the wall for balance, she stood and exited the bathroom with cautious steps in a cloud of confusion. Her head felt foggy, her body shaky. "Danny? Are you here? Danny?"

She walked on unsteady feet toward the window, stopped and started again, focusing on the bit of space between the curtain panels and the floor, searching for shoes, socks, or toes. She cautiously pulled the curtain all the way back to one side, bracing her body for a blow. Ridiculous, but she had to make sure.

No one was hiding there. Her shoulders relaxed a bit. "Good riddance," she whispered, in case he could somehow hear her, like if he was hiding in the closet, which he did once to spy on her. Who did that, right? Danny did. She should have checked there first. But when she slid open the closet door and jumped away from it, she found it empty.

She straightened, managed to push her shoulders back, feeling stronger. He was gone, and that was good, mostly, except for the all-encompassing loneliness. Like she didn't quite know what to do next without him around to tell her. A glance down at her T-shirt and exercise pants rekindled her plan to go for a walk. She'd feel better after a walk.

Outside, it was no longer raining, but the air was still nice and cool. She tried to pretend everything was normal. Walking down unfamiliar streets toward the town center they had driven through earlier, she absentmindedly rubbed her forearms. They had cramped earlier from the recoil of shooting Meiser, or maybe just from gripping the gun so tightly.

She tried to free her mind of all the stress building up around her, focusing on counting each division between the sidewalk squares. But without warning, Todd Meiser's desperate pleas came rushing back, filling her mind. Up until the last minute, she wasn't sure if she would go through with killing him. Even as she parked her car a block away and snuck into his backyard, even as she crept into his kitchen, she still wasn't sure. But then he convinced her she had no choice.

As soon as he saw her standing in his doorway with the gun, he knew exactly why she was there. And he didn't want to die. He begged her not to kill him. "Please. Please don't do it. I didn't see anything," he insisted. And when she came closer, gripping the

32

gun with all her might lest it drop from her shaking, sweating hands, he kept on pleading with her, sounding more desperate, more stricken with each second. "I won't testify. I promise. I'll just forget everything I saw, and I'll disappear, somewhere far away, where no one will ever find me. I won't tell. I promise I won't tell."

Yeah, right. As if she believed him.

Danny hadn't been lying. Todd Meiser *had* seen her. He knew what she had done. Which meant they all did. And it sounded like he'd already formulated a plan to tell the authorities.

Beth shivered. Thank goodness she had gotten to him first.

She was so freaked out when she left his house, she didn't even think to steal anything. She'd barely noticed her surroundings and couldn't even recall anything about his home. But the image of his desperate eyes and the sound of his begging—those were seared into her memory.

Her thoughts were jerked back into the present when a man and woman around her age blocked the entire sidewalk by holding hands with fully extended arms. Instead of walking around them, Beth stopped to watch. The woman peered into a furniture store window without letting go of him, then laughed as he twirled her around and into his arms. They kissed. It seemed to happen in slow motion, like a scene from a movie. The couple reminded Beth of Jason and Kelly Smith. Those foolish lovebirds now had every reason to appreciate their last few days. Too bad for them, they didn't know those days were numbered, but it didn't seem to matter. They'd acted unrealistically happy every time she saw them.

Beth pretended she was also interested in the strange contemporary art chairs in the display window while she thought about the Smiths and spied on the hand-holding couple out of the corner of her eye. A pang of jealousy struck her, followed by a deep sadness, a hard pit forming inside her stomach. Her life could have been like that of the smiling woman in front of her. Wait—it still could be. It wasn't too late. But it was never going to happen if she went to jail.

The door to a café opened and a family exited together. A little girl held her mother's hand, both wore matching yellow sun dresses. Beth wove around them, past a souvenir shop, a coffee store, and a donut store. In front of her, someone held the pink, brown and orange waxed bag she remembered from when she was young. Her father used to bring home bagels and coffee for him and her mother and donuts for Beth and her sister. Strawberry frosted with sprinkles used to be her favorite. Every Sunday he did this, to make up for his binge drinking the night before, until he left them for good.

Without thinking, she stopped and backtracked into the store, looking over her shoulder. Brightly lit bins of colorful donuts filled the shelves. She scanned each neat row. Blueberry cake, nine of them. Double chocolate, eight. Boston Krème, seven. Powdered Sugar, thirteen. There were no strawberry frosted donuts on the shelves. Maybe the donut store didn't make them anymore.

"What can I get you?" asked the unsmiling, acne-ridden boy behind the counter.

"Two double chocolate." She peeled a folded bill out of her jacket pocket and handed it over in exchange for the donut bag. She moved to a corner booth and sat down with her back to the rest of the store. Removing the first donut from the bag, she stared at it before finally taking a small bite, savoring the sweet richness. The next bite was bigger. She chewed faster, counting. Four chews, a swallow, and a bite. Four chews, a swallow, and a bite. All of it happening with a mechanical efficiency as if she had been given a maximum amount of time to consume the food.

The second donut didn't taste as good as the first. She gulped it down with a furtive glance toward the door. She was almost finished with it when Danny's barking smashed her reverie. "What the hell are you doing here?"

The remaining donut dropped from her hand and onto the table. She stared at it as heat flooded her face. "You're following me?"

"Do you have any self-control? You have a job to do. Get to it. Before they get away and you can't even find them."

"I know what I'm doing," she hissed. A fat man in a navy-blue T-shirt with Munchkins and a large coffee stared at her, one eyebrow raised.

"Oh, yeah?" Danny laughed, a mean sounding huffing noise. "How long do you think a body can stay in the woods before it starts to smell?"

An uncomfortable electric current shot through her brain again, just like it had in the hotel bathroom. Beth jumped out of her chair and ran toward the ladies' restroom, counting her strides. The fat man watched her run past.

"Don't run away from me," Danny yelled after her.

She locked the door and crouched down on the dirty cement floor in front of the toilet. She gagged once. Twice. The third gag released a hot lumpy torrent of brown processed carbs.

She gasped and tried to catch her breath. Wiping her mouth with the back of her hand, she slumped down on the dirty floor, her face hot and clammy, an irritating vibration occurring inside her, like she'd drunk one too many Red Bulls. Her breath came in hitching gasps. She shuddered and dropped her sweaty head back against the wall, letting her knees rest against the toilet. Her esophagus burned, and the taste of vomit repulsed her.

I hate you, Danny.

Chapter Five

Beth hurried back to the Vista View hotel, focused on what she needed to do next. Danny wasn't there. She brushed her teeth and rinsed her mouth before her stomach acid ate its way through her tooth enamel and she needed to visit the dentist again. So much for the walk making her feel better. She hadn't set out to eat donuts and vomit, but hey, she hadn't set out to become a killer either. *Look at me now! Ha!* She laughed aloud, without the slightest sense that anything was funny. *I may be a killer, but I'm not going to jail.*

After a bit of research on the internet—two YouTube videos on how to load a gun—Beth took the weapon apart. She filled the magazine with new bullets, painfully pinching her finger somehow during the process. Seeing the gun in pieces made her temporarily vulnerable, but it had to be done to make sure it was full. She wasn't going to be like the dumb asses in horror movies who walked away from their kill before it was really dead. Those who didn't or couldn't finish the job almost always ended up being sorry. The magazine slid back into place with a loud click. She sighed with relief. *Good work.* Using a tissue, she scraped a sticky dark splotch from the muzzle. Danny's gun was quickly becoming her good friend.

Without changing her clothes, she grabbed her laptop and keys and hurried back to her car, hoping to avoid Danny. She drove back to the same spot they had parked in last night. She would wait. It would only be a matter of time before someone came out. Had to be. She'd done her research.

Only a few empty spaces separated her from the Smiths' shiny red Jeep, waiting dutifully and somehow looking as irritatingly cheerful as its owners. Kelly Smith hadn't posted anything else yesterday, not since sharing a picture of her fresh manicure, a deep dark purple, almost black, with tiny silver moons on two of her nails. Maybe Jason had bombed his sales pitch and Kelly just wasn't in the mood to pretend their life was one big, happy, romantic adventure. Because no one's was. But from what Beth had seen of the Smiths, they were doing a commendable job fooling everyone. And it had to be an act, didn't it? Or were they still in bed, holding hands, legs intertwined, snuggling under the covers after making love? Was Jason whispering in a sexy voice that she was the only woman for him? The only woman he needed? The only woman he would ever love? Were they so happy they didn't even notice that the hotel was a dump?

Beth cringed, scrunching up her nose in disgust. Even with the windows down, the pungent smell of her unwashed body wafted through the car. Wishing she had showered, she gnawed at her cuticles one finger at a time until she drew blood. She frowned and closed her hand into a fist, as if that could repair the ragged mess. Danny would find something nasty to say about it. Oh yeah…she didn't care what Danny thought any more. To hell with him. She stretched out her fingers, the flaking pink polish in dire need of a fresh coat. She smiled. Killing each witness may have been his idea originally, but she was the one doing it now.

Lucky for her, the Sonesta Hotel hadn't been booked to capacity and the back side was barely occupied.

What's wrong, people? The Sonesta isn't your cup of tea? Was it the ugly carpets? The lobby from the seventies? Afraid you'll go the way of Jack Torrance in the The Shining when you get there? No reason to worry…it's only me following in his footsteps. Just me. Jason and Kelly Smith are having a fricking second honeymoon in there…I'm the only one sitting alone in my car, counting the seconds, counting the future corpses, and waiting to kill the next person on my list.

One down, six to go.

She viewed her surroundings. The parking lot was quiet. She was still alone. Sighing, she woke up her cell and pressed the news icon. Her feed contained mostly national headlines—politics and more politics, Russia, China, trials for people whose names she recognized but nothing more, food recalls, accusations against politicians—articles she'd never cared about and never would. She read about one celebrity's suicide and another's overdose, then moved on, tapping and swiping and occasionally looking up, until a story grabbed her undivided attention. She stopped chewing on her nails and bit down on the tip of her finger, holding it tight between her teeth as she read the headline written to grab everyone's attention—*Homicide in broad daylight, victim shot inside his own kitchen!*

Todd Meiser had been found.

Beth smiled, and wished Danny was there to witness her achievement. She played the accompanying video, staring intently at the image of Meiser's street lined with police cruisers, a television station van, two black SUVs, and a crowd of spectators. The scene was jumping with activity, a whole lot busier than earlier in the day.

The camera honed in on two people wearing gray suits and white shirts. They were walking away from Meiser's house. The woman was very pretty, but there was also a steely determination in her eyes, a seriousness that said, "don't mess with me or you'll be sorry." Her eyes drew Beth in like magnets. She was slim but muscular with flawless skin, perfect eyebrows, and a pert nose; one that had never been broken like Beth's. Her silky, shoulder length blonde hair parted to one side.

The handsome man beside her had short dark hair and a chiseled chin. If he tore off his shirt and posed, he could grace the cover of one of Beth's steamy romance novels. The couple stood a few feet away from each other while the female reporter asked them a question. The blonde introduced herself and Mr. Sexy as Agent Victoria Heslin and Agent Dante Rivera.

Agents?

The reporter asked them what they had found inside the house. She looked excited and sounded almost breathless. And all because of Beth.

Beth leaned forward, absorbing every bit of the scene. This was all about her! They were all gathered there because of her. The reporter wanted to tell the world what she'd done. What would the agents say? What did they think about Todd Meiser's death? Did they find any clues? That last thought wiped a bit of the grin from her face.

The agents said nothing about what they had discovered inside, nothing at all, although they were professional and polite and sure looked damn good doing it, and then it seemed the interview was cut short as the reporter asked another question.

That was it? Really? That was all they had to share? Perhaps they just needed more time before they could tell people what they found. And anyway, why was the FBI there? Didn't they only get called to work special cases?

Beth watched the video again, this time focusing more on Agent Rivera. He had a tough edge to match his hard body and projected a comfortable confidence in his suit, but it was something about the way he watched his partner that caused a stir deep inside her. A pang of . . . what was it . . . longing? She recognized what she'd seen in him. Something that was sorely lacking in her life, but she still knew it when she saw it. He cared about that woman. It was obvious. Did Agent Heslin feel the same about him?

She played the short video clip two more times, scrutinizing the agents. FBI agent—that was an unusual occupation for a woman. Beth felt a kindred spirit with Heslin. They were both special. Even if Beth didn't have anyone to tell her so. Even if Danny sometimes went above and beyond to tell her otherwise. She and Heslin even looked a little alike. They both had blonde hair. Beth's came from a box at Walmart, but that didn't matter.

Beth unzipped her purse and fished around for her comb. After combing her hair forward, she changed her part from the middle to the side. Turning her head right and left, she studied herself in the rear-view mirror, eventually tucking her hair behind her left ear just like Heslin. With one last glance at her new look, she settled back against the driver's seat and shut off her phone. But images of the agents replayed in her mind.

The air inside the car was stagnant and stale. She opened the windows to let in some cold, fresh air, started the engine and the heat to counter the chill, and plugged her phone charger into the cigarette lighter. She fiddled with one of the studs on the top of her ear, twirling it until it started to hurt. Bored, she typed Agent Victoria Heslin into her browser and opened the FBI profile and headshot. She was really beautiful. And obviously smart. You could see it in her eyes. No wonder Agent Sexy respected her. And a Georgetown grad. Fancy, fancy. There wasn't much else in the profile. She closed out and returned to the other links, opening one that intrigued her.

Well, what do you know! Who would have thunk it!

Victoria Heslin, the lovely FBI agent, was also the daughter of Gardener and "the late" Abigail Heslin and heir to the massive Heslin family fortune. Beth huffed at their elegant picture, a beautiful family with one of those tall skinny hounds on each side. The mother, daughter, and the son all had the same golden blonde hair. The father was handsome, with a strong jaw and an air of importance to him. His thick silver hair had probably been cut and his face shaved in one of those salons for rich guys. Their smiles were relaxed and self-assured. Like it was nothing to be part of this strikingly beautiful family, dressed and groomed to sophistication, perfectly posed, right down to the dogs. Nothing at all.

Beth sneered. Agent Heslin was damn lucky.

But now the mother, Abigail, who didn't look very old, was dead. Why? But even more interesting than that question, she wondered what compelled Victoria Heslin to track down criminals if she didn't even have to work. Earlier that very morning, when

40

Beth fled through Todd Meiser's front door, doing her best to choke back the overwhelming urge to vomit, Todd had looked like something straight out of a gory horror flick. Who would choose to visit dirty, disgusting crime scenes day after day, buzzing with flies crawling on corpses and stinking of blood and puke and urine? Who'd do that when they could be sipping a piña colada on daddy's yacht in the Caribbean?

Beth shook her head and stretched out her fingers, gazing through the window. What would she do if she were rich like that? If she could do anything at all and didn't have to scramble to make ends meet? Inhaling deeply through her nose, she let her imagination run wild. First, she'd make up a new identity. Disappear completely. And once she got there—massages. Definitely. Swedish massages every week, maybe every other day. And facials. And vacations at luxurious resorts surrounded by celebrities. She'd get a new nose, a perfect nose like Victoria Heslin. And a new car. One with valid license plates so she didn't have to constantly worry. She slapped the steering wheel. This piece of crap would be the first thing she'd leave behind. After Danny, that is. Unless he wanted to come with her.

An older man and woman exited through the front entrance, jolting her from her daydream. The Cossmans, room 383, on their way to an afternoon hike with their two mangy little fur balls. They'd told their families and friends as much on Facebook, right above yesterday's image of them smiling with a waterfall as the backdrop. Hands full with bags and water bottles, they crossed the parking lot, their faces animated as they alternated speaking and smiling. At least they would die happy. If they really were. Who really knew just how many times Robert Cossman had betrayed his wife when they were younger. Beth didn't know he had, but she didn't know he hadn't.

After both dogs walked in ridiculous circles and peed, and after the couple took their sweet time arranging stuff inside their Subaru Outback, they were on the move. Beth started her car and pulled out of the lot after them.

As expected, after a few miles, their little SUV made a left from the business road, onto a long, winding country road with gradually increasing elevation. They drove past picturesque farms, and rustic barns, and fields of fat cows grazing on grass made exceptionally green by the recent rains. How far away *was* this National Park place? Beth grimaced. All of it smelled like manure. She'd never been an outdoorsy person.

Would Agent Heslin and her handsome partner be the ones called to the scene once someone found the Cossmans? Beth sure hoped so. Perhaps she should leave a message for Heslin. The idea intrigued her. But what should she say?

Beating a red light by a fraction of a second, the Cossmans drove straight through a small-town intersection. Beth flexed her foot, about to ram the gas, noticed the police cruiser on the other side, and slammed on the brakes instead.

"Damn it!" She drummed her fingers against the dashboard. *Two, four, six, eight, two four, six, eight* . . . "Come on. Come on. I can't lose them."

She had to keep herself from going to jail, she had something big to prove, and now she had a new, added purpose. If she wanted to get to know Agent Heslin better, she had to hurry up and create another crime scene.

Chapter Six

Victoria and Rivera walked toward their boss's office. The Butler case constituted years of work and it was almost over, or so Victoria had thought. Figuring out how to keep it from going under with one less witness would become one of her boss's priorities. Victoria wasn't looking forward to briefing him.

"Don't you two make the perfect couple." A fellow agent smiled at them.

"Yeah, well, I called him this morning to see what we should wear." Victoria laughed, but inside she was doing her best to be tolerant. Her colleagues' attentions sometimes bordered on immature. Maybe that's what stress did to them.

The only door with an embossed plaque—Larry Murphy, Special Agent in Charge—jerked open. Head down, wearing cowboy boots under his jeans, Murphy and his military posture marched into the shared space in the middle of the building, carrying his ever-present Georgia Bulldogs insulated thermos. Victoria wasn't sure if the thermos ever got washed but attempts to replace it at Christmas with a newer model had not fared well. Murphy claimed his conviction rate went up to ninety-five percent after he got it. He wasn't messing with that sort of luck.

"I don't need this right now." Murphy pushed his rolled shirtsleeves up over muscled arms as he paced around the other agents' desks, speaking to no one in particular. A former drill sergeant, he liked to think out loud and he wasn't particularly considerate of others' space or concentration. He spotted Heslin and Rivera. "In my office, please." He slapped Rivera on the shoulder and corralled them forward.

Rivera and Heslin entered his office and stood on one side of his large desk. "Tell me Todd Meiser isn't really dead. Because that's what I want to hear. I want you to tell me that he's in the ICU right now and pretty soon he's going to be able to think and speak even if we have to wheel him into the courtroom on life support."

Rivera shook his head. "Isn't it still a crime to lie to FBI personnel?"

Murphy chewed on his lip. "Too many people are already breathing down my neck about this." He ran a hand over his buzz cut like he was pressing his scalp into place. "We've got too many other things going on for this case to implode after years of putting it together. It's not going to happen." He stared at each agent. "We're going to make damn sure it doesn't."

Every time Murphy opened his mouth, Victoria caught a distracting glimpse of dark green on one of his front teeth. Lettuce? That meant he was eating greens, even if it was just a few leaves on top of his hamburger, and something she didn't want to discourage. Not that he wasn't fit, he kept himself in great shape, but he was known to ignore the fruit and vegetable food groups. She wouldn't mention it. Somehow, it would disappear on its own. When Murphy paused to breathe, she seized the opportunity to get a few words in. "Meiser's death didn't seem like a professional hit. There were a few things that didn't feel right about it. It was careless, for one. He had the word 'liar' and the number two written on his forehead and—"

Murphy interrupted her mid-sentence. "The Butler case goes to trial in three days. Three days. Of course it's a hit. Writing 'liar' on his head—the Butlers are sending a clear message that Meiser's testimony is fabricated. Which is BS." Murphy wrung his hands, his eyes roaming from the pile of papers on his desk to the agents.

Rivera opened his mouth, but Murphy cut him off, too.

"So, do we want to know exactly who pulled the trigger on Meiser?" He pushed some papers aside and snatched one.

"Yes—"

"Of course we do. But is it more important than making sure the rest of the witnesses are safe?"

"No—"

"Of course it's not. I've already put protection on them. That's the first thing I did when I got the call on Meiser. Would have had it on them all along if the damn budget had allowed. Believe me, I asked."

"So—"

"But the rest of them, we're not going to let any of them even take a crap alone. I want eyes on all of them. Local PD is going to lend us a few bodies." He lifted his eyes toward the ceiling. "We'll see if they actually do." He pointed his finger from Rivera to Heslin. "And the two of you will split up and do a shift tonight. I already made a schedule." Murphy narrowed his eyes at the paper in his hand.

Victoria rushed to share her thoughts. "The reason I think Meiser was—"

She wasn't fast enough. Murphy went on as if she'd never spoken. "For now, go inform Meiser's family. That brother. The only one who seems to have his head on straight. Get a sense of how angry he might be, see if he blames us. See if he knows anything we should know—about anything. Threats, that sort of thing. I want evidence to add this murder to the charges against Butler."

Victoria nodded. They would need more proof before speaking to Murphy again about something he didn't want to hear. He was definitely stressed out. In the meantime, it wouldn't hurt to have law enforcement watching the other witnesses.

45

On her way back to the parking garage with Rivera, she reviewed her mental notes. Sometimes, with hits for hire, the victim's body disappeared, never to be seen again. Other times, the body was left on display, arranged as a brutal message of what happened to those who fell out of favor or displeased the wrong person. Professional hits were often executed with precision and grace, a testament to the killer's skills, because practice made perfect. Todd Meiser's murder was devoid of skill and caution. Yet . . . every hitman had to start somewhere. And if the killer was a novice, they had a good chance of catching him or her with forensic evidence. But . . . if the killer was a hitman, he had more than likely been contracted by Raymond Butler or one of his associates. And if anyone had options that included experienced hit men, Raymond and his guys did. Victoria rubbed her chin, bothered by the apparent contradiction. If it was a hit, it didn't appear to be ordered by Butler. And it wasn't a robbery, not with the keys to a luxury vehicle sitting in plain view on the counter. So what was it?

Rivera slid behind the wheel of a black sedan and dropped his container of spearmint gum in the center console. Victoria slid her leather backpack off her shoulder and lowered herself into the passenger seat next to him. "Lots of things are odd about this." She waited until Rivera put the car in gear and backed it out before continuing. "The blindfold for one. Like the killer felt guilty and didn't want Todd to look at him. Professional hit men don't usually feel guilty, do they? The woman's scarf, that was odd, too. Someone is trying to confuse us, or . . . they have no idea what they are doing."

"Or both." Rivera flipped his sun visor down as they exited the garage, even though the sun wasn't shining. "Hope James Meiser hasn't listened to the news yet."

Todd's older brother owned his own accounting practice. They located his office inside a brick building full of small, professional businesses and waited for ten minutes until his client left before gently breaking the news of his brother's murder.

James Meiser leaned back in his chair as the wind went out of him, his shoulders slumping as he closed his eyes and slowly shook his head. His voice shook as he spoke. "I guess I shouldn't be surprised, but . . ." He swallowed hard. "Butler." His eyes went to Victoria's. "You have to stop that guy."

"It's possible Butler was involved."

"Possible! Come on. Who are we kidding here?"

Rivera leaned forward in the office chair. "We'll explore all angles. The Medical Examiner and a forensic team will look into everything. We'll let you know what they find."

James placed his elbows on the desk and buried his face in his hands. "Toddy." Reaching for a tissue, he coughed then wiped his nose. "I guess you're saying you want me to wait to make funeral arrangements."

"Yes. Do you mind if we ask you a few questions now?" Rivera removed his notepad from his coat pocket.

"Of course not." James closed his eyes and pressed his lips together. "But you catch the bastard who did this. Butler or not, you get this guy."

Rivera gripped his pen. "When did you last see Todd?"

James shook his head, scanning the desk top. "Oh, I haven't seen him in weeks. Not since the last time he visited our mother. But I spoke to him yesterday. I called him. I just arranged palliative care for our mother. She has terminal cancer. I had some things I needed to tell him. Oh, God." He covered his eyes with his hand. "Now I have to tell her Todd is dead."

"I'm sorry about your mother, James," Rivera said. "Did you and Todd talk about anything else?"

"Yes." James sighed loudly. "Nothing I would mention under normal circumstances, but this isn't normal, so I'll throw it out there. Todd said he was meeting an . . . escort."

Bingo, Victoria thought.

47

"A prostitute?" Rivera asked.

"Yeah." James kept his eyes lowered.

Rivera opened his notepad and made a note. "Is that a habit for him?"

"It wasn't his first . . . appointment. I gave him a hard time about it, but now I suppose I'm glad he lived it up before he died. He had a lot of stress, you know, with the case. It was eating him up. Or—wait, when did you say he was killed? I mean, could she have . . .?"

"He was shot around ten this morning. Someone heard the gunshot. Do you know who he called? Was there a service, or—?"

"No. I don't know. Sorry."

"Did he say where he was meeting her? Would she have come to his house?"

"I don't know. I have no idea how it's done." He let out a sad sort of snort. "My brother and I led very different lives."

"Do you know who Todd may have been seeing—a significant other?" Victoria asked.

"He never mentioned one to me. I mean, if he did, why would he be calling a prostitute?"

"No angry girlfriend, upset about him seeing hookers?" Rivera asked.

"I—like I said, I just don't know." James ran his hand over his head.

"Did he mention receiving any threats? Specific threats?" Victoria asked.

"No. But it's pretty obvious why someone wanted him dead."

"I'm very sorry for your loss." Victoria met James' gaze. "Sorry Todd won't have the chance to live a different life." She got up from the chair. "We plan to catch whoever did this to him. We'll keep in touch."

James Meiser led both agents to his office door and shut it behind them. They walked to the car and got in before speaking again.

"I'll call Sam, so we can establish a time line for Todd Meiser's last few days with his phone and credit card records." Victoria tossed her bag into the back seat. "I think there has to be a girlfriend. But we also need to find out who he arranged to meet last night. Maybe she stayed into the next day."

"A woman does fit with the bloody shoe prints we saw." Rivera started the engine and a second later, his phone rang. "It's the boss."

"What now?" Victoria murmured. "Impatient for our update?"

Rivera pressed the answer button.

"Where are you?" Murphy's voice would have carried through the car even if the phone wasn't on speaker.

"We're just leaving James Meiser's place." Rivera merged the car into traffic.

"I'm about to text you something."

"What is it?"

"The address of a double homicide. It's an elderly couple. Both dead at the scene. No idea who they are yet."

"And you're giving it to us because—?"

"Gunshot wounds. The numbers three and four on their foreheads. And another message."

Chapter Seven

Ned parked his SUV in front of PawTiques, the all-organic pet store. He could have ordered everything Victoria wanted for less online, but Victoria preferred to support local businesses. He attached Izzy's leash and went inside. He walked straight to the shelves with the supplements and grabbed what he needed.

Wearing a tight, V-neck T-shirt, the beautiful young girl at the register leaned over the counter. "Hi, Ned."

"Hmm? Oh, hi Jenny." Ned scanned the bakery shelf. It was filled with dog treats people would want to eat. "I'll take seven of those frosted things."

"Oh! I love that dog. Which one is that?" The girl pressed her palm against her cheek and smiled at Ned.

"Izzy. She's a good dog."

"She's a greyhound, right?" She moistened her lips and ran a hand through her hair.

"A galga. A Spanish greyhound."

"Can I pet her?"

"Uh, sure."

The girl walked around to the front of the counter and crouched next to him. The light, floral aroma of nice soap and fragrant shampoo filled the air. While she stroked Izzy, she looked up, batting her eyes. "Oh! So cute!"

Ned stepped back and nodded. If Jenny was of legal drinking age, she was just barely. "So, how much do I owe?"

After the store he ran with Izzy on the greenway, filled his truck with gas, and stopped at Lowe's to pick up some wiring to patch up a hole he'd seen in a fence on Victoria's property. She hadn't asked him to do it, but he wanted to anyway.

When he returned to Victoria's house, the red hatchback delivering for Farm Fresh Meals stopped at the main entrance in front of him. Ned pulled up next to the car and got out of his SUV.

"Hey, Kristin? Right?"

"Oh, hi, Ned."

"I'm on my way in." He gestured toward the gate. "I'll take that from you."

"Great." She got out of her car and removed a large insulated bag from the back. "Here you go. We put in extra of the root veggies Victoria liked. And the French cobbler. Could you be sure to tell her? I know she doesn't always get a chance to eat what we prepare."

"I'll tell her. No worries about the food. It's all appreciated and none of it ever goes to waste." He patted his stomach and grinned.

"Good." Kristin smiled and kept staring at him like she was in no hurry to leave.

"See ya." Ned got back in his truck and placed the bag of food on the passenger seat. Izzy jumped into the front and stuck her nose into the bag. Ned pushed her back. "Not for you." He waved at Kristin, opened the gate, and drove through.

Entering through the back door, he stopped to size himself up in the hall mirror. He had to bend his knees, since the mirror hadn't been hung for someone six-feet-two. All his time training outside over the summer had turned his brown hair golden.

In the kitchen, he opened his laptop and logged his run. He'd swim tonight and bike early tomorrow, putting his training right on track for the upcoming triathlon. He was ready to refuel in a big way, but the dogs would eat first.

He dug his hands into the giant container of raw lean beef, vegetables, rice, and vitamin supplements, kneading the moist mixture until it was evenly distributed. He scooped measured amounts into labeled bowls and added some premium dog food. Eddie stuck his nose on the counter. "Excited, buddy?" Ned laughed as they danced around him, spinning and leaping in attempts to earn their food quicker.

Working for Victoria wasn't a huge challenge, but he thoroughly enjoyed his job and it left him with more free time than he would have working anywhere else. Two afternoons a week he was able to volunteer as a vet at a not-for-profit clinic for low income people. As long as he stayed with Victoria, he could continue to pay off his graduate school loans faster than he had ever previously imagined *and* help pet owners who otherwise might not be able to afford care.

And then there was Victoria.

He smiled.

The dogs inhaled their food in seconds, barely chewing. By the time he set down the last bowl, he was back to collecting the first and depositing them all back in the dishwasher.

After cleaning up, he walked outside and sat down on the back patio. Absentmindedly rubbing Eddie's ears, he gazed out over the back of the property. The whole set up never ceased to amaze him—the acreage and trails, the agility course, a pool just for the dogs—it was like a canine Disneyland. He had an entire wing for himself—a "nanny suite"—bigger by far than his own condominium. He stayed there when Victoria went out of town. But when she came home, he left.

It was hard to keep his thoughts from turning to Victoria. There were just too many reasons to admire her. She worked hard every day to rid the world of trouble, make it an easier place for others to live in. Who would ever imagine someone with her privileges and background wanting to do that? She once told him that being the recipient of a huge trust fund was simple but incredible luck but being an FBI agent was an earned honor. He agreed and his respect for her went through the roof. He'd tried to ignore his daydreams of running his hands through her hair, kissing her . . . but they were only growing, along with his determination. Not a one of his friends would ever say that he wasn't determined. He had six ironman triathlon finishes to prove it.

His phone rang.

"Hey, baby brother. Just calling to see if you can come over on Tuesday night. My friend Katie is in town visiting. She's smart and adorable."

"Can't. I have plans."

"What sort of plans? Actual going out plans or more of babysitting those dogs?"

"I'm going out to dinner with my boss to talk about our trip to Spain."

"Ah. All my joking aside, don't mess things up. You've got a great thing going there. If you're happy that is."

"Yeah. I know. But would it be so bad if we shared a bottle of wine and ended up—"

"Are you paying attention to the world right now? She could accuse you of sexual harassment, fire you, and try and sue you just for—"

Ned laughed. "She's not like that."

"Look, you can have wine with Katie and me. I've got a case I brought back from vacation that I'm excited to share. How about we switch it to Sunday afternoon instead? Brunch?"

"All right, all right."

"If there's ever going to be something between you and your boss, you need to let her make the first pass. And make sure it's loud and clear. That's all I'm saying. And you'd be wise to listen to me and take my advice whenever you are so lucky as to receive it."

He chuckled. "I know. I'm not going to do anything stupid. But if she ever makes a pass at me . . ."

"She's crazy not to be madly in love with you by now, so maybe she's not quite—"

Ned laughed. "There's nothing wrong with her. She just doesn't get close to many people." He thought about the one time he'd asked Victoria about her mother's death. Her reaction had given him all the information he'd needed for an armchair diagnosis of intimacy issues. "But, hey, I will take your advice."

"Good because I'd never steer you wrong. Love you, Ned. Gotta go."

"Love you, Lori."

What would it take to change Victoria's mind about him? Would she ever come home at the end of the day and be as excited about seeing him as she was about her dogs?

He had to tread carefully. And be patient. Victoria was worth whatever it might take.

Chapter Eight

Victoria settled back against the leather seat, watching the road ahead. "I can't believe there was a murder on the Triple Falls trail. It's a popular hiking destination."

Rivera draped his arm over the top of the steering wheel. "Wonder who got killed."

"Murphy said 'older couple'. I interviewed a witness from one of Butler's warehouses awhile back, can't remember his name now, but he was on the old side. Maybe his wife was with him. What a shame." She tapped her phone. "I still need to call Sam."

Rivera stayed silent while Victoria spoke to one of their intelligence analysts, Sam, her favorite person in the office because he was always polite and pleasant, no matter that everyone's requests came in as emergencies. He was ideally suited to weather the ongoing stress in the office.

"What can I do for you?" Sam asked, as if he was idling his time when in reality, he was multi-tasking for a dozen agents.

She updated him on the murder scene and asked for information on Todd Meiser's phone records and anything to help them identify the prostitute James Meiser mentioned.

"I'm on it. You be safe out there." Even over the phone, his smile traveled through his words.

Knowing Sam would get back to her soon, she ended the call and slid her finger down her phone screen, searching through her mail. "Nothing from forensics yet." She set her phone down against her leg and looked at Rivera. "What do you think the message at this crime scene says?"

"We'll find out soon enough. You always hike alone?"

"Me and my dogs. And my pistol." She patted the holster at her side.

"And you get cell reception in those woods?"

She grinned. "Sometimes." She knew he worried about her. She was lucky they had been assigned to work together increasingly more often lately. Rivera could be gruff. He was a man of few words. Nothing wrong with that. On the contrary, sometimes working with him was almost as good as being alone.

"We're almost there. I just have to make a quick call." She pressed the contact button for Ned. After a few seconds, she said, "Hey Ned, it's me again. So, I'm going to have to work over night. Can you stay?"

"Absolutely."

"Thanks. Something came up. It might last a few nights, but I'll keep you posted on my schedule as soon as I know."

"Okay. Be careful."

"I will. I've got to go. Thanks again."

Rivera tightened his grip on the wheel. "So, whenever you tell Ned to stay at your house, he's automatically available?"

"Yes. Because it's part of his job." Why did Rivera sound condescending? Her unpredictable schedule was the reason she paid Ned a salary that exceeded her own. He was always expected to be on call. "To do my job well—"

"Which you do—"

"I need to know my dogs are well cared for. Most of them were rescued from horrific situations."

"I know."

"So he's essentially expected to be on call 24/7. And if that's so ridiculous, then why have we pretty much signed up to do the same?"

Rivera's face broke into a smile. "Touché."

The agents drove in silence past scenic farms. Victoria stared out her window, taking in the scenery in a way she hadn't on previous trips with her dogs, because she had always been alone and driving. The rolling acres and white fences made her think of her mother, mainly her mother's love for dogs and horses—all animals, really. If only she'd said yes to more hikes with her mother when she'd been alive. With a sigh, she switched mindsets, reviewing every detail of the scene at Todd Meiser's house. And then somehow, she sensed Rivera was looking at her, even as he drove.

"What?" She fiddled with the buttons on the dashboard, turning down the heat and having it blow out only from the bottom vents.

"Nothing."

"Think these crimes are related?" She grabbed her bag and found an elastic band in the inside pocket.

"Yes." He grimaced. "Unless a group of psychos sent out a memo with a special signature for today."

"Let's hope that's not what's going on here." Victoria gathered her hair back and fastened it into a ponytail.

"Meiser's death reminded me of something, but I'm not sure what. Like I had a déjà vu when I first saw him on his floor."

"Another case? Was it the blindfold? The number on his forehead?"

Rivera shrugged. "Don't know."

"Well, we've got a two, a three, and a four so far. I'm wondering if there's a number one out there that we haven't found yet."

Rivera frowned. "I was thinking the same."

Victoria peered out the window at downed trees from last night's storm. The forest had thickened, marked by an occasional trail entrance. "Okay, the parking area is coming up soon. It's not well marked and easy to miss."

Rivera slowed down. Victoria leaned forward. "There!"

Two giant stone pillars marked the entrance to the gravel lot. A news van was parked near two police cruisers and a sheriff's car.

"Oh, jeez," Victoria said, unfastening her seat belt. "They got here before us."

Rivera parked, and the agents opened their car doors. Amanda Jones rushed toward them as if running from a fire.

"What do you think is the chance of them holding on to the information about Todd Meiser, like we requested?" Victoria asked as she shut the car door.

"Are you kidding?" Rivera formed a zero with his thumb and middle finger.

Murphy's car squealed into a nearby spot and stopped with a lurch.

Amanda flipped her long hair carefully over her shoulders, framing her face. She was still catching her breath when she spoke, which added to the drama of the scene her sidekick was recording. "Two homicides in one day? What's the story? Can you tell us anything about the double murder on the Triple Falls Trail? Is there an unknown killer on the loose?"

Rivera stepped to the side and Victoria answered. "We just arrived, and what we know we can't disclose at this time. But as soon as we have information we can share with the public, you'll be the first to know. If you don't mind waiting here in the parking lot, we'll be sure to give you something you can broadcast when we're done here."

"Fair enough. Thank you." Amanda continued to walk alongside them, the video still rolling.

With an angry expression, Murphy edged between the agents and Amanda, essentially bumping Victoria out of his way. Victoria stepped backward and almost stumbled over something on the ground. Rivera's arm shot out to support her. She steadied herself and mouthed "thank you."

Murphy barked at the reporter and videographer. "I'm the SAC on this case. You can't be here. This is an active crime scene. You need to leave." Holding on to his jacket, he raised his arm, pointing to the parking lot exit.

"Agent Heslin said we could wait here until you've finished your investigation. We won't go beyond the area that's been taped off."

Murphy glared in Victoria's direction, then glared at Amanda. He shook his finger toward the main road, causing his jacket to wave up and down beneath it. "Leave. Now."

Victoria offered a discreet apologetic look to the reporter and camera man, who retreated back toward their van. After all, they were only trying to do their jobs. And if there was any danger, the public had a right to know about it as soon as possible so they could take proper precautions. Like not go hiking for a few days until they figured out what had happened here.

There were three other cars in the parking lot, a Honda Odyssey, a Toyota 4-Runner, and a Subaru Outback. Their owners could be in danger, or, one of the cars might belong to the killer, still hiding somewhere in the woods.

"I'll get the plates." It only took a few seconds for Victoria to take pictures of the makes, models, and plates. Rivera waited for her, eyes roaming the area.

The trail ahead had been cordoned off with crime scene tape. A young female deputy guarded the opening.

Putting on his FBI jacket, Murphy spoke to the officer. "How far up the path are they?"

"Not far."

Murphy ducked under the police tape. "Make sure to keep everyone off the trail, especially the media."

The deputy nodded. "I've already had to turn a few people away. They weren't happy,"

"There are trails on the other side of the main road, about a half mile up. Maybe you can direct them there." As soon as Victoria said the words, she wanted to take them back. What if the killer was still out there? She scanned the area, looking for people. "Watch your back, okay?" she said to the deputy as they passed her.

Murphy led the way, grumbling, "my team is losing right now because I forgot to wear my lucky shirt."

"Did you forget last week, too?" Rivera asked, grinning.

"I'm not in the mood," Murphy said, checking his watch. "Three murders in one morning tend to do that to me. I'm supposed to go to my kid's chorus concert tonight. I swear the school moved this thing to the weekend because of my wife's insistence. She wants me there. I've got to leave here before five."

A short walk up the trail, Murphy sauntered up to the Sheriff and put his hand on his shoulder. He introduced himself and his agents to the two other male officers crowding the trail. One of them stepped back, nudged the other, and whispered something. They both looked at Victoria and grinned.

Victoria ignored them and focused on two panting dogs that were tied to a nearby tree. It wasn't warm. They were stressed. They stood alert in their matching leash and collar sets, protecting their owners, who also weren't going anywhere. A surge of anger mixed with compassion temporarily distracted Victoria. She forced down her emotions and turned her attention away from the dogs and to their owners. This job was one of the ways she could make

60

a difference in a world with too many awful people, too many awful circumstances.

The bodies of a man and a woman were sprawled across the dirt path. In their sixties or seventies, both had silver hair, wrinkled bronze skin, and lean bodies. Victoria wouldn't have called them elderly, as one of the first cops on the scene apparently had. The word elderly reminded her of fragile senior citizens with walkers and canes. This couple wore hiking boots, shorts, and lightweight shirts. Their backpacks were still attached, as were their broad-rim hats, secured by strings underneath their chins. Their wide-open eyes and shocked, pained expressions wrenched at Victoria's heart.

Victoria always asked the same questions at a crime scene. What motivated the killer? Why this couple? Why here? Why now? Because answers to the *how* and *why* questions almost always led them to the *who*.

The husky officer stepped forward. "This guy found them and called 911." He gestured to a thin man with a hiker's strong calves leaning against a tree. In a tie-dyed shirt and bandana, he looked like a hippie hold-out from the seventies. A backpack with a sleeping roll and tent attached lay next to him on the ground. He straightened up to speak to the agents. "I was camping overnight. I found them when I was leaving this morning."

Murphy studied the hiker. "Did you see anyone else?"

He shook his head. "The only other people I passed before I found them were a group of women. Three of them. Don't know that they came this way. Two other trails intersect with this one farther up."

The Sheriff's eyes traveled from Murphy to Agent Heslin as he spoke. "Two officers went to find them."

"Can I go now?" asked the hiker. "The Sheriff said I had to wait for you, but now that you're here . . ."

Murphy set his hand on the man's shoulder. "Give Agent Rivera your contact information. We'll be in touch and we might need you to identify the women when we find them, make sure we located the ones you saw."

"Sure." The man gave his information to Rivera. "So, I can go now?"

"One second," Victoria held up a finger. "I just tried to send a message. No reception. How were you able to call 911?"

"I had to walk back to the parking lot and call. They told me to wait for the cops."

"What kind of car did you drive here?"

"A white Toyota 4-Runner."

"Did you hear anything?"

"Like gunshots? Or people screaming? No."

"Okay. Here's my card. Call if you think of anything else." Unless he suddenly remembered he had seen someone running down the trail with a gun, she couldn't imagine he would think of anything else that would be helpful, but it never hurt to make the request and hand out her card, just in case.

Once the hiker left, Murphy walked around the couple, studying the scene from all angles. "From the surrounding pool of blood, they were definitely shot here. The man was shot first, in the heart at close range, possibly trying to shield his wife. He was facing the shooter when he died."

Blood soaked the man's torso. Only his shirt collar indicated his top had once been white. The number three was written on his head in black ink. Below the number, the word CHEATER was scrawled in the same ink.

Behind him, the woman was lying on her side. She had also been shot in the chest. The number four was written on her temple.

"No attempt to hide the bodies." While Victoria studied the scene, she was annoyingly aware of the Sheriff's eyes on her. Wearing gloves, she swatted at the insects honing in on fresh blood, removed the woman's backpack, and examined the contents. It held a collapsible dog bowl, several bottles of water, dog treats, granola bars and trail mix. "It's pretty clear what they were doing out here." Her face was set in stone as she glanced at the dogs, whining to get closer to their masters. She focused hard on them to make sure a tear didn't escape her eyes.

Rivera opened the man's backpack. He found their wallets and car keys, more water bottles and two rain ponchos. "Robert and Anne Cossman. They're from Baltimore." He held up a blue and green hotel key card. "If this is current, they were staying at the Sonesta Hotel and Suites."

"If they're still checked in, I want you to search the room," Murphy said. "Find out what connection they have to the Butlers and Todd Meiser."

Rivera nodded.

Victoria walked slowly toward the dogs, crouching down. "We're going to find out who did this to your parents. And meanwhile—"

"Heslin." Rivera cocked his head and gave her a warning look. "Don't even think about it."

"You sound just like my father. Are you going to take them, then?"

Rivera sighed and shook his head but said, "Sure, why not?"

Victoria straightened with her hands on her hips. "Why not? Because for one, you have terrible allergies. We also work too many hours a day and you don't have anyone to take care of them." She squatted down, allowing them to sniff her. Untying their leashes, she read the tags on their collars. "Come on Leo and Bella. You'll be okay with me for a little while." With their leashes in hand she spoke to the officers. "I live near here. I'll take care of the dogs until we know where they're going, until we find out if the Cossmans have family that wants to take them."

Murphy narrowed his eyes at Heslin. "You've got work to do. You can't be babysitting dogs today. Someone can take them to the pound."

"No, sir. It's not necessary." Victoria's response was quick and firm. There was no question about her determination.

Murphy glanced at his phone. "Forensics is still half an hour out. They're going to want to comb those dogs for evidence. I need to go. You got this?"

Rivera nodded. "Got it."

"Yes." Victoria glanced down at the dogs. Leo tipped his head back to look up at her. She smiled at him.

The sheriff and the officers stood to the side, watching the agents interact.

Looking his agents in the eyes, Murphy's voice was forceful. "Figure out who is doing this and stop them before there's another victim."

Rivera folded his arms. "About our watch on the other Butler witnesses tonight—"

"I'll find someone else." Murphy grumbled. "You've got three murders now, don't let this thing blow out of control. Can't believe this . . . this . . . whatever it is and the Butler case fiasco." Murphy stared down the trail, one hand on the fingers of the others, getting ready to pull off his gloves. Taking a last glance around, his eyes settled on a small dot of white in the corner of Mr. Cossman's mouth. "Wait. What's that?" Murphy stooped to part the dead man's lips. He slid out a small piece of paper and studied it. His scowl deepened. He looked up, stared straight at Victoria, and said, "What the hell?"

"What is it?" Rivera asked, walking over to his boss.

Murphy glared at Rivera. "It says—'Dear Agent Victoria Heslin – Does your partner treat you well?'"

64

Victoria's mouth dropped open. She thought she must have heard wrong, but Murphy's expression told her otherwise. "My name is really on there?"

Murphy narrowed his eyes. "What partner, Heslin?"

"I have no idea. I don't really, I don't have a . . . a partner."

With a deep frown, Murphy pointed at Rivera. "They probably mean you."

Rivera shrugged as a flush of red colored his cheeks.

Still frowning, Murphy slid the note into an evidence bag and held it out for Rivera. "Give this to forensics when they get here." He turned to the Sheriff. "I want my agents to talk to this couple's family first."

"All right." The Sheriff didn't look happy, but he agreed.

Murphy pointed a finger and moved it from Rivera to Victoria. "Find out why someone says this man is a cheater. Find the connection to the Butler case." The SAC left without looking back.

Victoria stared at the corpses, an unsettled feeling growing inside her stomach. She didn't want to be the focus of anyone's attention, especially not a killer's.

Chapter Nine

Forensics arrived shortly after Murphy left. They scoured the scene for fibers, hairs, footprints, anything that might be meaningful to help them hunt down the killer and send him to prison. They finished with the dogs as the rain began—wiping out any last traces of evidence—and handed them over to Victoria. With the two dogs leading the way, she headed back to the parking lot leaving the forensics team and the Sheriff behind.

Rivera started after her but stopped and wheeled around. "Be right back, I'll catch up to you." He took a few steps back to the crime scene. "Sheriff, can I speak to you for a sec?"

The Sheriff walked over. "What?"

Rivera lowered his voice so no one else could hear. "Think you and your men can not drool next time Agent Heslin is present? Let's try to be professional here. I've got new shoes. I hated getting your slop on them."

"Hey, now, we didn't—"

Rivera glared at him. "No, I'm sure I imagined it. And now that we've had this nice little chat, I'm sure I won't imagine it again."

"Yeah, I'll talk to the men." He held out his hand. "I didn't get your first name."

"Agent."

Rivera walked away without shaking hands and caught up to Victoria. Her blonde ponytail swung back and forth from shoulder to shoulder as she walked. Her movements had the athletic grace of a long-distance runner. She hopped over the ditches in stride, climbed over the large rocks and bulging tree roots effortlessly.

The note addressed to Heslin was bugging him, like he'd been caught red-handed doing something he shouldn't have been doing. He'd done nothing wrong—wishful thinking didn't count—yet he had the sudden urge to confess. For all he knew, he wasn't even the partner the note mentioned. He had to drop his paranoia. It might send them down the wrong track of thinking. If Victoria had a partner, it wasn't him.

From ahead on the trail, Victoria interrupted his thoughts, her voice kind and gentle.

"What's that?" He called out. "What did you sa—"

Victoria was leaning over, talking to the dogs.

"Oh." He frowned, continuing down the path, his cheeks suddenly warm.

She straightened again. "We'll be talking to your family soon. And we'll get you some water."

Rivera couldn't help but smile. "What kind of dogs are they?"

"I don't know. Mutts. I think one is part Boston Terrier, one looks part Labrador."

They settled the dogs into the back seat of the FBI vehicle and buckled up. "Glad you don't have to babysit the witnesses tonight?"

Victoria stared out the window. "Sure. I mean, yeah, I'd rather be home than watching someone else sleep."

Rivera sneezed once and then twice more in succession. He opened his window all the way and leaned his head toward the fresh air.

"Told you." Victoria smirked.

His stomach growled. "Want to grab some dinner? We passed a burger place on the way."

"No. I'm not hungry." She exhaled loudly. "Their lives revolved around those people."

"What?" He furrowed his brow. "Whose lives?"

"The dogs. They just lost everything. Their little world was just tossed upside down, and they don't understand what happened."

"Neither do we. Too bad they can't tell us."

"Did you know, they'll never forget the voice or scent of whoever harmed their people. Never." She rifled in her bag and offered Rivera a tissue. Bella, the little black terrier, was still panting. Victoria held out her hand. He edged closer, sniffed her hand, and allowed her to pet him. Leo, the lab mix, was lying on his side holding his head up and watching every move in the front seats. "I know." Victoria said, still focusing on the dogs. "It's very hard to lose someone you love. It sucks. It really does."

Rivera sneezed.

Victoria rubbed the dog's head. "Shh. He doesn't mean it, Leo." She faced forward and attached her seat belt. "Let's go straight to the Sonesta Hotel."

Rivera nodded as Victoria's phone rang.

"It's Sam." Victoria put the call on speaker phone. "Hey, Sam. I was just about to call you."

"Beat ya to it." The noise of shuffling papers came to them over the speakerphone. "I combed Todd Meiser's phone records. I'm pretty sure I found the prostitute's number, called on Friday at three in the afternoon, a ten-second call, probably asking him to call her, and then a return call from that number later in the evening. I left a message. It's a woman's voice, very sexy, suggestive, asks callers to leave a message if they are trying to make an appointment for—well, she doesn't say what for. I'm waiting to hear back from her. It's not a registered phone. No way to trace it."

"Thanks, Sam. Call as soon as you hear from her. Get us an address and we'll go talk to her."

"Will do. Anything else?"

"Unfortunately, yes. We were just at the scene of a double murder. Also shot at close range with numbers written on their foreheads. The husband had the word cheater written on his."

"Same killer as Todd Meiser, then?"

"Certainly seems likely."

Sam whistled.

"Their names are Robert and Anne Cossman from Baltimore. First, can you find us a close relative? Children, maybe?"

"Sure. What's the connection between the Cossmans and Meiser? I mean, besides the MO, the numbers, and the words?"

"Don't know yet. I'd like to know who they've seen and called since they arrived in Virginia. Check their credit card statements, too. Look for anything that he could have cheated on— taxes, a business deal, his spouse…"

"I'll try to help you find something. Talk to you later."

"Thanks, Sam." Victoria pressed end and stared out the window. "We have a series of victims, all killed during the day, with close-range gunshots . . . all with the writing on their foreheads. Does a stone-cold killer for hire do that? Or a wacked-out nut case?" She toyed with the end of her ponytail, eyeing the passing scenery. "What connects them? Could they just be random murders?"

Rivera answered only with a nod. She hadn't asked what the deal was with the note bearing her name, the question now at the forefront of his thoughts. Someone was toying with them, or at least with Victoria, trying to send her a message. But why?

"Meiser's connection to the Butlers is still the most likely motive. We just have to figure out how the Cossmans fit into the whole Butler scenario," he said.

"Yeah, I was thinking the same."

An itchy feeling spread over Rivera's face. He twitched his nose. It was just getting started. His sneeze cut through the sound of his phone ringing. "Rivera." He sniffed.

"Hey. This is Sheriff Montgomery. We located the three women—the ones our hiker saw. Looks like they were unaware of the couple who were killed. The women took a different entrance to the trail."

"Thank you, Sheriff." Sniff. "Keep us posted. We'll do the same. And I'm sure our SAC will arrange for all of us to meet soon."

"Okay. Oh. About your request. I spoke with the men. It won't happen again."

"I appreciate that." Rivera ended the call and dropped his phone in the center console.

"What do you appreciate?" Victoria asked.

"Just him getting back to us."

Victoria picked up her phone from where it rested next to Rivera's and checked her messages. "Sam already sent me information on the Cossmans' son, Frank. He lives nearby and apparently works from home." She rubbed her chin. "Wonder why the parents weren't staying with him."

"Maybe he couldn't have the dogs there."

"Maybe," Victoria said.

"Get the directions. Let's see what he has to say." Rivera sneezed again and swallowed back the fluids swiftly accumulating in his throat.

# # #

Victoria studied the row of modern condominiums while walking up to Frank Cossman's unit. Everything about the shiny new homes said upscale, pricey. She glanced back at the SUV. "We can leave the dogs in there with the windows open for now. It's nice and cool."

"You're the expert."

She rang the doorbell and waited. A man opened the door partway and stuck his head through, like he was just popping out to tell them to go away, they had the wrong address. He had thick hair and looked neat and sharp in a light gray suit. His eyes moved from Rivera to Heslin and their solemn expressions.

"Frank Cossman?" Rivera met his gaze.

The man nodded.

"I'm Agent Rivera and this is Agent Heslin. We're with the FBI."

Continuing his wary glances between them, Cossman opened the door fully.

"Can we come in and sit down for a moment?" Her question left no doubt that this was serious business, but there was a warmth to her words.

Frank led them into a sparsely decorated, modern living room. He and Victoria sat down. Much the same way she had with the dogs, Victoria kept her voice kind and compassionate when she broke the news of his parents' death.

"What? I just . . ." The color drained from his face. "Are you sure it's my parents?"

Rivera leaned his weight against the doorframe. "They had their wallets with them, their license photos match up. But we will need you, or someone else in your family to make a positive ID."

His voice cracked. "They were here to see me, but also to go hiking. They were always hiking. It was their favorite pastime. Always brought the dogs."

71

"We have their dogs with us now," Rivera said.

"Huh? Oh." He gazed past the agents toward the front door, then down at his shoes. "Are they going to a pound?"

"No." Victoria took a quick look around the condo and out through the back window. No sign of a yard. "Is there someone in your family who could take them?"

Frank sighed. "I'll um—I'll see if my aunt will."

"All right." Victoria shifted her weight and crossed her legs. "They'll be at my house until she can get them. I have a separate enclosure for them with access to the outside. They'll be properly cared for."

"To say the least," Rivera murmured.

Frank fidgeted with his hands in his lap. "So, you'll hold on to them for a few days?"

"Sure." Victoria's shoulders shifted forward as she studied the victims' son. It upset her that Frank Cossman hadn't seemed to know the dogs' names, at least not right away, and wasn't rushing to get them.

Frank asked a few more questions. They couldn't tell him much about an active case, which worked out well because aside from the circumstances of the Cossmans' death, the agents had little to share.

Rivera leaned forward. "Do you have any ideas on who might want to hurt your parents?"

"No one. They were the least likely people . . ."

Rivera clasped his hands. "Somebody thought otherwise and made their point with a few bullets. You sure? Any recent arguments they mentioned? Any neighborly disputes?"

Frank shook his head. "No. Nothing like that I'm aware of."

"Did he play tennis, bridge, golf? Any activity where someone might have gotten bent out of shape about him cheating?"

"No. And if he did, he wouldn't cheat, and he wouldn't even be playing with people who would take it that seriously. He's not like that."

Victoria didn't correct Frank's use of the present tense when talking about his father. "Did they have debts?"

"No. I'm pretty sure their house has been paid off for years. They buy their cars with cash. They live a simple life. Gardening and hiking, doing yoga. What kind of debts do you mean?"

She thought of all the illegal activities the Butlers oversaw—trafficking of drugs, people, money laundering . . . she wasn't about to mention them all. "Gambling?"

"Definitely not."

"Would you know if they are in any way familiar with Raymond Butler or his family?"

"Who?"

"He's about to be on trial for—"

"Oh. That Butler. No." Frank crossed his arms and rocked forward. "My parents might know who he was from the news. They're news junkies, but that's it. My father is a retired dentist, he wouldn't—they wouldn't—why are you asking?"

"We're exploring the possibility that your parents' deaths were related to the upcoming trial."

"Not possible."

"Your father had the word 'cheater' written on his forehead," Rivera said. "Sounds personal."

"Do you know what that might be about?" Victoria touched her necklace.

"I have no idea what it could be about or who could have written it."

"Were you aware of any infidelities in their marriage?" Rivera asked.

73

"Absolutely not. Absolutely no way." Frank lifted his eyes toward the ceiling and his face contorted with a wave of anguish.

"Do they visit here often?"

"I don't know." Frank's gaze moved back to the agents. "I just moved here not too long ago from DC, but I'm pretty sure they've come to the area to hike before. They wanted to see my new place, my mother brought a few things, like house warming gifts. It's not big enough for them, I mean, they insisted on staying in a hotel."

"Can you give us a list of their closest friends, people they did business with, so we can start talking to them?"

"You mean, right now?"

"Yes, whatever you can come up with right now. If you could also list their habits and routines, that would help. I'll give you my email and as you come up with more, you can send them to me." Victoria slid a card from her bag.

"Why? They weren't involved with anything, they don't even live here, this must be some random mistake, like mistaken identity, or just being in the wrong place at the wrong time. . . I don't know." His voice grew quieter and cracked as he spoke. "No one would have a good reason to murder my parents." His voice quivered. "I'm sure of that."

"It's our job to find out what happened." Victoria handed Frank her card.

"Was—was anything stolen?"

"Not that we're aware of. You can let us know if anything is missing when you confirm their identities." Rivera stood up.

"Yeah. Sure. Okay." Frank stood and wiped his palms on his pant legs. "I'll get you the names. I've got an address book. This is . . . I can't believe this."

"We're very sorry," Victoria said, as Frank left the room.

The agents exchanged glances. Rivera shrugged and folded his arms. Victoria sensed they had accomplished all they could with Frank Cossman.

Frank came back with names and numbers on a piece of paper. Rivera took the paper. "Last thing—where were you this afternoon?"

"Me? You can't possibly—" Frank lifted his eyes toward the ceiling. "I was here, I've been on the phone with clients all day. I can give you a list of names and times."

"Please do. We're heading to the hotel where your parents were staying. You'll think of other things. Send them to us. Agent Heslin's email is on the card."

"Of course I will."

"Please call your aunt. She can contact me about Leo and Bella," Victoria said. "We're very sorry for your loss."

Frank led them to the door. "Thank you, I mean, thanks for coming out here."

The agents stepped outside. At the car, Victoria whispered, "I know you believed him. But we're still going to find out if he or any of their children had a reason to want them dead."

"Yep." Rivera typed the address for the Sonesta Suites into his phone, took out a few pieces of his spearmint gum, and started the car.

#

At the hotel, Victoria took the Cossmans' dogs for a quick walk then put them back in the SUV. They hung their heads out the window, watching her as she walked away. She spotted Rivera standing in front of the cash register at the Sonesta Suites Hotel kiosk. He stuck his wallet into his back pocket and peeled the plastic off the top of a Benadryl bottle.

Victoria couldn't imagine anything much worse than being allergic to dogs. But Rivera wouldn't complain. He never did. The

75

only time she caught a glimpse past his emotional armor was at a sports bar. Near the end of the Xavier game, Rivera let loose with some uncharacteristic outbursts of encouragement for his alma mater.

She went over to him, placing her hand on his upper arm. "Sorry about the allergies."

Rivera shrugged, holding up a plastic card. "Got a room key."

"Let's check it out then."

They walked down the corridor over worn turquoise carpeting. The agents put on gloves and Rivera slid the plastic card into the slot at room 383. A green dot lit up and he opened the door.

Inside, Victoria took in the room—two closed suitcases, pairs of shoes lined up side by side, dog bowls and dog beds. Nothing on the surface indicated the people staying in the room had just been brutally murdered. Inside one of the small suitcases, under a neatly folded sweatshirt, Rivera found a laptop. He slid it into an evidence bag for the IT department.

Victoria scanned the small space again, looking for anything. "Should we have techs come in?"

Rivera shook his head. "Doesn't look like anything happened here."

"I'll take this." She pulled a large, yellow bag down from the top shelf of the closet. She unfolded the top, peered inside, and moved the contents around to make sure it really contained dog food. "This is excellent."

"I figured you had a year's supply at your house."

"If they switch food suddenly, they're likely to be sick. Now I can mix some of theirs with some of mine."

Rivera rolled his eyes, but with the hint of a smile. "I'm starving," he said as they left the room. "Do you want to grab dinner now then call the Cossman contacts?"

"I'd like to get back to the office, get my car and get home. Let's split up the research." Victoria sighed. She'd be thinking about the murders long into the night, focusing on every little detail. The day had started out so well, a long walk in the woods with her dogs after the cleansing rain, and ended so terribly, with three murders and a note for her from the killer. She was determined to find out who had ruined the day for so many people.

Rivera nodded. "I'll be up late. Call me if you find anything."

Chapter Ten

The garage door rose in silence, revealing Ned's black Ford Explorer inside.

Victoria pressed her fist against her lips. "I forgot to call him."

She parked her car and glanced at the dogs. "You stay here. I'll be right back. I need to introduce you to the pack one at a time. Just don't show any fear and things will go well. They're all very accustomed to newcomers."

Entering the large mudroom, she inhaled the fresh scent of lemon and vinegar. The floors were gleaming thanks to the visit from her cleaning crew.

Her pack crowded the room to greet her. Izzy wiggled in and out between her legs. Eddie smiled, his gums pulling back to reveal his teeth. His tail curled up into a circle behind him. Myrtle jumped up and down. Charmer sniffed in cute, quick little snorts.

"I'm home. Yes. I know you smell new dogs. We have visitors. Calm down and you'll get to meet them."

The house phone rang. Victoria headed to answer it. Ned walked around the corner shirtless, wringing water from his dripping hair with a towel. He saw Victoria and stopped short. Their eyes met, and both were silent.

Victoria smiled, shifting her gaze away from Ned's chest and to the phone. Something tingled inside her stomach.

Ned pointed at the phone. "I'm guessing that isn't you calling to say you'll be back soon."

"I'm sorry, Ned." She shook her head, her cheeks still a little hot. "Sort of a last-minute change of plans and I forgot to call you."

"No problem. Hold on. Just let me finish getting dressed. I just went for a run and—be right back."

Victoria opened the fridge and poured herself a glass of water.

Ned returned wearing a T-shirt, skin still glistening from his shower. "I can . . . I mean, I can stay if it helps, or I can go and come back tomorrow . . ." His eyes moved from Victoria to the dogs, a slight shrug of his shoulders.

"Um . . . I guess it's whatever is most convenient for you. I'm going to be up really late working on some new cases . . . really, whatever is best for you."

Ned crouched down to rub Myrtle's side and scratch Cooper's neck, keeping his eyes on them. "Sounds like you're beat, and you've still got work to do . . ."

It might be nice to be in his arms. "Yeah, it was quite a day." She started to bend down to take off her shoes, but remembered she had a reason to keep them on.

"I saw you on the news today. You and another agent."

"Really?" She frowned, thinking about what might have been revealed to the public.

"Coming from a crime scene in front of a small house. Then again later near the Triple Falls Trails, another murder scene." He let out a low whistle.

Victoria chewed on her bottom lip. If Channel 14 had aired footage of her after the first crime scene, that might partly explain the note left for her at the second. Although the content of the note was still a complete mystery.

Ned straightened up and smiled. "I should probably go home and water my plants."

"Oh, you have plants?"

"No." He laughed. "I'll just come back tomorrow after you leave for work."

She nodded. "Ned . . . Thanks. For this. For everything. I—"

"You think your new case will be wrapped up before the trip?"

"Yes, absolutely. I mean—hopefully—but remember, if for some reason I can't leave, you'll still go to Spain without me?"

"I will." He laughed. "I promised, didn't I?"

"Good. Just making sure. Actually, before you go, can you just help me with something?"

He smiled again. "Of course. What is it?"

She tilted her head toward the garage and offered a sheepish smile. "We've got some temporary guests."

A hint of confusion crossed his face, but only for a fleeting second. His eyes lit up and he smiled. "Ahhh, sure . . . let's see what type of guests you've got out there."

They both started toward the garage at the same time. His arm grazed hers, startling her with a tingling sensation. She stopped, putting more space between them, still thinking about the feeling. For right now, that was enough. She didn't want to lead him on. He was too important to her.

"Sorry." He stepped aside and extended his arm. "Lead the way, boss lady. Can't wait to see what you brought home."

She walked ahead of him, and in spite of the day she'd had, couldn't help but smiling as his warm laughter echoed through the mudroom.

Victoria opened the back of her SUV. "They're from the crime scene."

"Really?" Ned stood still, letting the dogs sniff him. "Look, you've had a long day. Let me take care of these guys and you go settle in."

"Thanks." Victoria exhaled loudly. 'That would be nice. I can't wait to change. My clothes were wet half the day."

"Go ahead. I've got this."

She stood under the shower spray, letting the heat soothe her shoulders and cascade over her low back. She didn't know what she was feeling or what she wanted from Ned. She didn't want to lead him on and make him think there could be something more than there was. She liked him. She really did. Everything about him. He was handsome, smart, fit, loved her dogs—what more did she need? But was it stupid to try and see if there was more? Because she sure didn't want to risk losing what he was already providing—peace of mind, trust, reliability. None of them small things to be taken for granted.

After the shower, Victoria put on a silky robe and left her bedroom suite to see how everyone was getting on. In the family room, Ned was kneeling next to Leo and Bella. "How are the little ones doing?"

Ned laughed. "They're only little compared to your pack. And they're doing great." That's when he looked her way. His eyes opened a little wider, he covered his mouth with his hand, and quickly turned his attention back to the dogs. It was his turn to blush.

Victoria pulled her robe tighter over her camisole and sleep shorts. "Good to hear. I knew they would be okay."

"Yeah, they're going to be fine here." Ned stood up. "So, guess I'll be going."

"Thanks."

"Sure thing."

He walked from the room and the door to the garage closed quietly behind him.

Victoria took his place, crouching down with the new dogs and murmuring to them. "I shouldn't have done that, come out

81

here in my robe, should I? He's a gentleman and I'm sending mixed signals, aren't I?"

Leo licked her chin.

Chapter Eleven

Kelly Smith zipped up her coat and shifted her feet from side to side. Her fingers wrapped around the door handle as she scanned the dim and quiet parking lot and settled her gaze on her husband, who was walking toward the car. "We're going to be late."

Jason pressed the unlock button on the key fob. Something inside the Jeep honked and the locks flipped up. "No, we're not. There's at least twenty minutes of previews."

Kelly opened the passenger door and slid into the seat. "I love the previews. They're sometimes more entertaining than the movie. We have to hurry."

"I want to stop at a store and get some candy on the way. It's too expensive at the theater."

"No." She gave Jason her cutest pleading face. "We don't have time."

Jason started the car. "I'm pretty sure there's a CVS on the way. I'll be quick. In and out."

Kelly turned on the heater and rubbed her hands together. "No, sweetie, you're never just in and out. That's why we missed the nine-thirty show."

Jason grinned. "I'll get you red licorice."

"Fine. And something with caffeine. Like if they have a cold Starbucks latte in a bottle. I don't know if I'm going to make it through the whole movie. It's so late."

"Not my fault." Jason grinned. "I'm just trying to satisfy my bride."

Kelly licked her lips, smiling.

Putting the car in gear, Jason placed his hand over his wife's. As they pulled out of the parking lot he glanced in the rearview mirror. A gray Honda with one headlight followed close behind. The Smiths made a right turn and then at the next stop light, a left.

"Hmm, that the same car?" mumbled Jason.

"Hmm, what?"

"That car back there. I saw that same car when I dropped you off to get your nails done. That lady was behind me. I got out and told her she only had one working headlight. Guess she didn't get it fixed."

"That was nice of you to tell her."

"Lot of good it did." Jason snorted. "I got drenched doing it. And now she's following us."

"No good deed goes. . . unnoticed." Kelly tossed her long hair over her shoulder.

"It's no bad deed goes unpunished."

"You don't do bad deeds, so all you need to know is my saying. If it wasn't a saying before, then it is now, because I just made it up."

"Well, okay then. Notice away."

Kelly laughed and leaned toward her husband to peek in the rearview mirror. The car was still behind them, looking unbalanced without two glowing circles in the front.

"Strange how that car pulled out of the parking lot exactly when we did."

"Just a coincidence," Jason said.

Kelly pushed a button for the radio and twirled the knob until she found something she wanted to hear. "There it is!" Kelly pointed to the CVS as they were about to pass it.

Jason hit the brakes and jerked the wheel to the left. Praying he wasn't about to cause an accident, he glanced up in time to see the Honda make the same quick turn. Frowning, he parked the car directly in front of the store.

Kelly's eyes met his. "I'll wait here. Be quick."

"I won't let you down." Jason leaned in to give her a quick kiss on the cheek before jogging into the store. The automatic doors slid open, but Jason stopped to peer back at Kelly inside the Jeep. The Honda had parked right next to their car. Jason crossed his arms. The woman behind the wheel stared straight at him. He stared back. He hadn't paid much attention to her in the pouring rain yesterday, but he was pretty sure he recognized her as the same person. He only needed a minute or two inside the store, but he didn't want the candy badly enough to leave Kelly out there with a potential stalker.

Another car caught his attention. A police cruiser drove into the shopping center and parked right behind the Honda, blocking its exit. A policeman got out of the cruiser, his eyes on the Honda. He walked to the driver's side and gestured for the woman to roll down the window. The woman's expression immediately changed in a way that struck Jason as unusual. Not annoyance or resignation, but pure terror. Eyes wide, stricken, a deer in the headlights, like how he must have looked that time in high school when he was pulled over. His car held a keg, drunk friends, open bottles and nowhere to hide any of it.

The officer said something to the woman. He walked around to the front of her car and pointed at the broken headlight. Kelly was also watching from inside the Jeep.

Glad the cop had arrived when he did, Jason shook off the uncomfortable feeling—probably just being paranoid—and headed into the store. After Jason paid, the officer passed him heading to the register, carrying a bottle of aspirin.

Outside, the one-headlight Honda and its driver were gone.

Chapter Twelve

Rocking back and forth against the cloth seat, hardly noticing the cars passing on either side, Beth chewed away on her lower lip. When that uniformed officer appeared out of nowhere and stepped right up to her car, panic overwhelmed her. She could barely think, barely move. She was lucky her heart hadn't stopped then and there. She'd sat paralyzed, aware of the gun on her lap like it was a smoldering coal. Her first thought—someone from her list, someone she hadn't yet killed, had finally taken his or her butt down to the police station and provided a detailed description of her and Danny.

Her stomach roiled thinking about what could have happened if the stupid cop had been more thorough—if he'd lowered his gaze from her face and seen her gun, if he'd asked for a license and registration instead of issuing a polite warning to fix her headlight. What would she have done if he ran her plates? She didn't know exactly what he would have found. She seriously doubted Danny had bought the car the way most people did, with actual money handed over to a rightful owner.

That was a narrow escape. I'm done following them. That cop was a sure sign it's time to quit for the night and hightail it back to the hotel. Stupid headlight. Danny was supposed to take care of that sort of thing, but he almost never did. Lately, she had to do absolutely everything while he was away on his business trips—where he spent money but had yet to make any. And when he was home, he sat around drinking beer after beer and complaining.

And the Smiths were proving to be a royal pain.

After glancing behind her for what seemed like the hundredth time, she snapped on the radio and scanned through the stations, in search of news on a channel with an even number.

She settled back against the seat and was starting to relax a bit, her shoulders no longer tense and tight. The news came on. She cranked up the volume on the radio. They were reporting the day's most mentionable events—three homicides. All of them happened to be perpetrated by her. It was almost surreal, hearing the serious, reverent tone of the announcer, knowing she alone had made it happen.

"Todd Meiser, a key witness in the Raymond Butler prosecution—"

Who the hell was Raymond Butler? What did he have to do with anything? Fuming, racking her brain for where she'd heard that name before, she missed the rest of the report about Meiser. The news anchor prattled on about the old people she killed at Triple Falls and asked for anyone with information related to their deaths to contact the FBI.

She tipped her head back and laughed. The cops and FBI didn't seem to have any idea who had killed any of them. A few of the news reports she'd heard had referred to her as a male—bunch of sexists. No one, aside from Danny, seemed to have a clue that she was the one responsible.

But why didn't the news report say anything about the note for Agent Heslin? Didn't the authorities know it was left by the killer? Wasn't that interesting and newsworthy? Had Agent Heslin even seen it? Frowning, Beth twirled the ends of her hair. She'd have to do better. She sighed and bit into her lower lip, chewing the side that wasn't yet tender and raw. At a stoplight she checked her reflection in the rearview mirror and swiped at the hint of blood on her lip. She opened her mouth wide and slid her jaw from side to side to loosen it.

Chin up, Beth! Three murders so far—not counting the first, the one she wouldn't think about, didn't quite remember, and didn't want to. Not too shabby. She'd accomplished quite a bit for one day. "Why did I doubt myself?" But she knew exactly why and whose fault it was.

She wasn't receiving credit for what she'd done, but if getting credit for the murders meant going to jail, she could live without it. The important thing was that Danny now knew what she was capable of doing. She had shown him. And herself.

Grinning, she remembered how she felt running down the trail after killing that couple. Her heart pounded, her skin tingled, her muscles were fueled with a strength she hadn't even known she possessed. She felt wild and . . . alive. For years she had stolen information online, hunched over her computer, always looking over her shoulder. A slight adrenaline rush had always accompanied the niggling fear, but nothing like what she experienced today. Today had been different. More exhilarating. More real.

She relived the scene in her imagination, picturing her escape down the hiking trail without a soul around to stop her, her blonde hair flowing in the wind. Everything she saw and heard had been amplified, heightened—the twigs snapping at her sides, birds chirping in the sky, yet distant and separate. She was the only thing that mattered. In her mind, she had on dark pants and a fitted white shirt, the same ensemble worn by Agent Heslin, instead of the jeans and sweater she actually wore. "I did it," she whispered.

The giant yellow arches of a McDonalds came into view on the busy road ahead. The dashboard clock told her it was close to eleven. Her empty stomach cramped. She hadn't eaten much all day. She doubted Heslin ever ate at McDonalds. But Beth didn't have the luxury of time to figure out where Heslin *would* eat, so she steered into the drive-thru lane and ordered a salad, French fries, and a diet Coke.

She ate the hot, salty fries driving back to her hotel and they were gone by the time she reached her room. *Oh, no. Damn.* She stopped outside the door, her key hovering above the slot. Would Danny be angry because she hadn't brought him any food? A little too late to be thinking of that now. She still had her salad and would share it with him, but he wouldn't be interested. And she couldn't very well eat it in front of him. Not if he was hungry and in one of his moods.

"Danny?" She balanced her drink against her chest and held the door partway open. A sliver of weak light filtered in through the slit in the drapes.

Silence.

The muscles in her shoulders and chest tightened as she stepped inside the dark room, flicked on the light switch, and tried to look everywhere at once. The room was empty and still, appearing as she left it, except the bed was expertly made. No empty cans or bottles littered the tables or counters. No signs of take-out containers or empty pizza boxes.

She crept to the bathroom and peeked inside the open door. The used towels had been replaced with folded ones. New packaged soaps had been positioned around the sink. A white curtain hid the interior of the shower. *Better safe than sorry.* Almost holding her breath, she gripped the edge of the shower curtain, braced herself, and yanked it aside like she was tearing off a Band-Aid.

The shower was empty except for brown mildew stains in the tile grout.

Beth left the bathroom, both puzzled and relieved. Where was he? She had the car, so wherever he went had to be on foot. Maybe he'd hooked up with a younger woman he met randomly in the hotel. Wouldn't be the first time. An aching pit began forming in her stomach and a heavy cloud of hopelessness descended over her like a shroud. She pressed her lips together and squared her shoulders, willing herself not to care, to stop thinking about it. *Let him. Just let him. You don't need him. Two, four, six, eight, ten, twelve, fourteen . . .* The counting made her feel needy and pathetic, but rarely could she stop once it started. She walked back to the front door, turned the lock, and flipped the bolt.

Sinking into the couch, she pulled off her shoes and threw them across the room. She grabbed the remote and pressed down hard on the buttons, flicking through channels until she found some local news.

"Heavy rain in the forecast yet again for tomorrow. Stay alert for flash flooding. If you see standing water, do not attempt to cross it."

Two, four, six, eight, ten, twelve, fourteen . . .

She tapped her fingers on the table, unable to finish listening to the meteorologist. He was trying hard to make the rain sound like the end of days. With more force than necessary, she mashed her finger against the remote and changed to another news program, a sportscaster wrapping up his piece.

. . . twenty-two, twenty-four, twenty-six, twenty-eight, thirty . . .

She put her feet on the table, set her salad in her lap, and started eating. After a few bites, the picture on the screen switched to a woman with lush red hair, a plunging V-neck sweater, and an intense look in her eyes.

"Breaking news today—Is Virginia facing a serial killer's spree?"

All counting ceased. Beth dropped her plastic fork, swung her feet off the table, and bolted to an upright position. *Serial Killer.* Was it her? Is that what they were calling her now? An image of Todd Meiser's dumpy yard and home filled the large screen in front of her. Yes! A flush of pride warmed her skin. A surge of power radiated through her body. Maybe this was how Danny felt and why he got off on hurting her.

But then the news reporter brought up Raymond Butler. Again! They were all suggesting a connection. "I don't even know who the hell Raymond Butler is, so there's no damn connection! He has nothing to do with this. I did it! I did it! All by myself! Me!"

Without taking her eyes from the television, she pushed aside the remains of her salad.

The image on the television changed. There they were again. Agents Heslin and Rivera in the parking lot near the Triple Falls Trail with the same reporter Beth had seen on her phone earlier in the day.

She scooted to the edge of the couch and leaned closer to the screen.

Agent Heslin's smooth blonde hair had been pulled back into a ponytail. As she approached the reporter, a military-type guy claiming to be the SAC, whatever that meant, edged her right out of the way, stepping in front of her. Heslin teetered a bit, looking down as if she had stepped on something she didn't expect to be there. In an instant, Rivera was at her side, his hand on her elbow. It wasn't a big deal, not like she would have fallen off a cliff or anything, but he was there to protect her nonetheless, as if he were her knight in shining armor. Beth narrowed her eyes and caught the split-second flash of anger on Rivera's face as he glanced at the overbearing guy. When Rivera turned back to Heslin, his expression softened just a bit, despite the determined set of his jaw.

"Hmmm." Beth's mouth spread into a smug smile, like she knew his secret. "There's no mistaking it. He's in love with her."

The news story on the television changed to angry, egotistical politicians in suits arguing about a budget, but the snapshot of the agents standing side by side remained clear at the forefront of Beth's mind. She rolled it over and around, savoring the image like a mouthful of expensive wine. "Rivera." She said his name aloud, letting it roll off her tongue.

Did Heslin love Rivera back? She should. He was handsome enough. Took care of his body. And it looked like he cared for her so much, like he would never hurt her. But the female agent didn't appear to be paying attention to him the way he did to her. They didn't act like Jason and Kelly Smith, going out of their way to touch and make googly eyes at each other. Of course, how could they? They were at work. They had to look professional. Perhaps their after-work behavior told a different story.

Beth dragged her laptop across the table until it was in front of her. What else was there to learn about the lovely Victoria Heslin? Typing in Victoria's name produced several links about the death of her mother, Abigail Heslin. Eyes gleaming, Beth scanned from line to line, soaking up the information.

After three days in captivity, heiress Abigail Heslin succumbs to a heart condition.

Captivity? Beth hit the back arrow, selected another article, and kept reading. The story said tragedy struck one of America's wealthiest families. Billionaire heiress Abigail Heslin was kidnapped for ransom. After three days of captivity, under the stress of her captors and without the medicine for her heart condition, she suffered a heart attack and died within hours of the FBI tracking her down.

The story must have been huge when it happened ten years ago. Victoria Heslin would have been around nineteen or twenty years old at the time. She must have been so worried, but maybe she trusted the FBI would do their jobs and find her in time. How interesting that Victoria ended up working for the very same organization that failed to save her mother. Interesting indeed.

Within a few minutes, Beth had access to the county tax records database and Agent Heslin's home address. Shortly after, she had control of the agent's security system. She was no longer tired. With a determined smile, she stuffed her feet back into her shoes, snatched her car keys off the table, and rushed out the door.

Chapter Thirteen

After the new dogs were settled and Ned left, Victoria got the outdoor fireplace going, turned on a heating lamp and sat on the patio with a soft blanket over her legs and a mug of hot tea. The dogs lay down one by one around her and she gazed out at her property, remembering the first time she'd seen it, many years ago. Fortunately, as much as she avoided social gatherings, she had agreed, for once, to accompany her father to an afternoon party in late spring. Some sort of fundraiser, she'd forgotten what or who it was for.

On that day, elegant women in sundresses sipped flutes of champagne offered on silver trays. A quartet played soft live music and dozens of canopied tables had been spread across the lawn. The house was exceptionally decorated, but all Victoria really noticed were the acres and acres of flat yard and the adjacent trails. The estate was exactly what she wanted. When it came on the market three years ago, she immediately bid above the asking price, unwilling to lose the opportunity, and marking the first time she'd used any of the trust from her grandfather on something other than donations. Her father grumbled that it was more house than she needed, and he was right. But it wasn't the house she wanted, it was the yard. The perfect yard for animals. She'd reminded her father that there were fewer investments better than a fabulous piece of property. The back yard wasn't quite as pristine as when she moved in, seven dogs, not to mention the frequent foster, running, peeing, and digging could do that in no time, but it could be fixed. Yards were meant to be used, not just admired.

It really was perfect. Her mother—who'd mostly owned greyhounds, but also took in a long parade of rescues—would have wholeheartedly approved.

The serenity of the large landscaped yard, aided by the rippling murmur of a fountain, created a peaceful oasis where she could escape from the world. Being alone—with her dogs—was always what she needed to recharge her energy. The day's horrific crime scenes had dominated her every thought since she stepped into Todd Meiser's kitchen. Now, she wanted to clear her mind before she revisited the details, hoping to see each scene with a fresh perspective and perhaps think of something she might have missed.

She finished the last sip of her tea, set down her mug, and uncrossed her legs. Enough relaxing. She and Rivera had three murders to solve. At the beginning of a case, the questions always outweighed the answers. But that would change as they put together everything they learned combined with information from detectives, forensics, and the ME's office.

There's no way the numbers on the victims' heads were a coincidence, so what did they mean? Soon enough they would have the forensic report on the bullets and know for sure if the crimes were connected. In the meantime, what were they missing? What connected Meiser and the Cossmans? Why did the perp write the numbers? What purpose did they serve? A message to us? A need fulfilled for the perp?

Frank Cossman had come through with a list of names and numbers, his parents' closest friends and neighbors. With a tablet and stylus, she began digging for the truth.

After a few hours, and nothing helpful to show from it, she set aside her note pad. Taking a deep breath, she held it, and let it out slowly. The temperature had dropped from chilly to cold. A hazy sky blocked the stars. Wind rustled the branches and leaves.

She glanced at the time on her phone. It wasn't too late to call Helen to discuss the case. It'd be worth it, even if meant wading through a probe of her personal life or lack thereof. Helen Bernard was one of the few people Victoria completely trusted.

She wrapped the blanket around her shoulders. As her call connected, the dogs leapt up, staring alert toward the backyard.

"Stop. Leave the raccoons alone. Sit down."

"Victoria?" Helen said.

"Hi. You're still up?"

Eddie let out a long, low growl. Victoria placed her hand on top of his head.

"Of course. I'm about to pour myself a glass of wine. What's going on there?"

Victoria's dogs flew off the patio and raced across the yard. Only Leo and Bella remained on the steps, staring out after the others. Not all dogs were wired to chase. "Can you talk for a few minutes?"

Helen would know exactly what that meant. But that didn't mean she'd let Victoria get right to it.

"Are you still all alone in that big house?" Helen had always been direct.

"I'm not alone. I have my dogs." As she spoke, they were flying gleefully across her back yard.

"Take it from me, remember I was one of the bureau's best profilers—"

"I know." The dogs stopped, sniffed the ground, and turned around in a pack.

"It's good to love what you do, but not to the exclusion of everything else."

Victoria pulled the blanket tighter around her shoulders. "Like I said, I've got—"

"What does having a dozen dogs tell you?"

"I don't have a dozen dogs—"

"That you have a gaping hole in your heart that needs to be filled. Don't pretend a dog—or however many you have—can fill it. On your death bed, you won't say, 'I wish I'd have logged another twenty hours on the MacDougal case and rescued five more dogs.'"

"Actually, I might. And it's seven now."

"Good Lord! Stop making my point. Seven can't do what five couldn't, because it's not really about the dogs."

Victoria laughed. "Maybe we can discuss my 'gaping hole' another time, since I'm really not convinced it exists." The dogs returned, panting, looking pleased with their chase. Victoria petted each of them. "Actually, believe it or not, I said I would go to dinner with someone."

"Is it the agent you've been working with? He's easy on the eyes."

"Rivera? No. I like working with him. But the dinner is with the guy who takes care of my dogs."

"Ned? That's his name, right?"

"Good memory."

"I'm not that old. My memory is still exceptional. If you wanted a date, there's no shortage of interested and eligible bachelors out there. You can venture beyond your own house."

"I know but would they be interested in going out with me the FBI agent, or me the heiress?"

"Or you—the young beautiful blonde? You won't really know until you give someone a chance, will you? Even if it doesn't work out, the finding out process can be fun."

"I'm happy. I like my life."

"Can't argue with that, I suppose. But please don't cancel that dinner if you can help it."

"I'll try."

"I mean it. I know how introverts work. No cancelling. Now, I've got my wine. Poured an extra big glass. Tell me, what's going on there."

Victoria's smile disappeared. "So here's why I called. I've got three murders and we know they're somehow connected, but we don't know how yet."

"Start from the beginning. And then we're coming back to the dog thing. The man thing, too."

Going through the facts aloud forced Victoria to sort through what they knew and what they needed to know, in an objective and logical manner. Sharing it with Helen allowed for a mentor's insights.

"It's way too early to know how this ends. Don't be impatient. Sometimes we never know. You have your facts laid out. With each additional piece of the puzzle you get now, you try to see what you need to complete the picture. You'll see what fits."

"That's the problem." Victoria sighed. "Nothing fits."

"Then you either don't have enough puzzle pieces, and you need to be patient, or you aren't looking at it the right way. Maybe it's not a cow puzzle, maybe it's a puzzle of horses but in the very corner there's one cow. See?"

"Gosh, that's a big puzzle, then."

"Which is why we can't solve it tonight. Get some rest. Magnum PI reruns are calling me."

"Why would you watch schlocky detective shows when—"

"Magnum was a detective? I just like the short shorts on Tom Selleck. Later."

Victoria had to laugh. She wasn't any closer to a motive that made sense for the Cossmans and included Todd Meiser, but the facts and the questions were more obvious. When she said goodnight to Helen, she was yawning and ready to go to sleep. Waking up with a clear head was the best thing she could do to get results.

"Time for bed." She led Leo and Bella behind a small gate in an enclosure built to separate fosters or injured dogs from her pack. They had a room all to themselves and their own dog door leading to a separate outside area, but they could still see and hear her and the rest of the dogs. "You're in here. Just until I know my dogs are okay with you, and you're okay with them." She rubbed each of them behind the ears and then sat and watched them sniff the new area. "At least you have each other."

She yawned again as her dogs trailed behind her into the bathroom, watched her brush her teeth, and followed her back to the bedroom.

"Good night everyone. Sleep tight." Victoria flipped off the light switch and sank into her bed. Below her pillow lay her personal gun. The thought of something happening to her, something that would leave her dogs without their owner, was enough to keep it nearby. If it could happen to her mother, it could happen to her. She wasn't about to be anyone's victim. Around her, the dogs grunted and sighed until the room fell silent.

Chapter Fourteen

Beth hurried out of the hotel with her hands stuffed inside her pockets. She shouldn't be allowing herself this distraction. Not while she still had witnesses to eliminate. What if visiting Heslin somehow prevented her from finishing the job that would keep her from going to prison? But she couldn't seem to alter her current plan, even though it defied common sense. It was as if Heslin and Rivera were calling to her, as if they were in desperate need of her help and she couldn't ignore them.

"Where are you going?" Danny's growling voice carried across the lobby.

She whirled around. Crossing her arms, she answered, "Not really your business. Notice I'm not asking you where you've been."

"Uh. Can I help you?" the woman working the front desk asked, her face a mask of concern.

Beth glanced around. The hotel employee was still staring at her. Beth's eyes shot daggers back.

"I'm sorry." A forced-looking smile took shape on the woman's face. "I thought you were speaking to me."

"I wasn't. I was talking to my husband." Beth marched out to her car, half hoping Danny would go away so he didn't ruin everything for her. This thing she was about to do, it was her thing. But at the same time, she didn't really want to be alone.

"Why are you wearing your hair like that? You've never pulled it back like that before." Danny's tone communicated the scowl she would surely see on his face if she fixed her eyes on him.

Frowning, Beth ran her hand over her head and down the length of her ponytail. "Thanks for noticing."

He scoffed. "It makes your forehead look huge. You look like the Addams Family girl. You know, the hideous one."

Sometimes it was like he could read her thoughts. She did her best to ignore him, keeping her mind occupied with her own plan. They said little else on the long drive that took them from city lights and billboards to lengthy, dark stretches of trees and hedges. When the distance between each driveway was greatest, she slowed the car to a stop and idled in front of a giant iron gate. They had arrived at Victoria Heslin's residence. The agent's home wasn't visible from the road, but it was back there somewhere, at the end of a long, fancy-paved driveway. Small spotlights lining the road beyond the gate illuminated tufts of tall, unusual grass, bushes shaped with precision, and neatly-trimmed trees—the kind of stuff that requires regular landscaping. The darkness beyond was different than elsewhere. Not depressing, not hiding unknown horrors like back at the Sonesta Hotel, but alluring, almost a tease concealing whatever constituted the unlit surroundings.

"Wow," Danny said.

"Don't let it fool you. The wealthy, with their landscapers and cleaning crews, have plenty of their own problems. They're only better hidden."

"How would you know, Beth?" He sneered.

"Because I read and watch the news, idiot." She eased up on the brake and let the car coast past the entrance, about the length of a city block.

"What are we doing here?" Danny hissed. "This isn't part of the plan."

"It will only take a few minutes. There's something I have to do." She parked off to the side of the road on a wide patch of lush, green grass.

"You going to try to get in there?"

She nodded without looking at him. "I'm not just going to *try*. I'm going in."

Danny laughed. "Terrible idea, Beth. This place represents insane money. Has to have high tech security and video monitors."

Her pride got the better of her and she smiled, even though she hadn't intended to share even a speck of information with him. "I've already scrambled the signals and shut off the alarms." Truthfully, there hadn't been any alarms activated. Surprising, for a property like that at night, and also puzzling. Closing her eyes and taking a deep breath, she hoped she wasn't mistaken.

Danny grunted. "Better be something worth stealing in there. You get caught, I never heard of you. Give me the keys."

She ignored his comments, but she couldn't help pondering his words. Was this worth the trouble of what could happen if she got caught?

"You think you're anything like that agent? She's a confident trust fund chick. She'd never do things just because someone told her she had to. She's nothin' like you, Beth."

Bristling at his words, Beth scrambled out of the car and called back, "Shut up." As usual, he just couldn't stop trying to get under her skin. But this time, his intent backfired. He'd just given her more reason to go ahead with her plan. *Her* plan. Not his. She knew he wouldn't follow. He wouldn't get his hands dirty. He saved all of that for her. Always had.

"Get back here," Danny screamed after her. "Don't get your stupid ass caught over your girl crush. You aren't done with what you have to do!"

Beth stopped, but not because of Danny. Hell, no. She just needed to think. And she had to pee thanks to the huge diet Coke she drank earlier. She dropped her jeans and squatted down on the side of the dark road. "Oh, damn." Her underwear hadn't been completely clear of her stream. Once her pants were back in place—now with an irritating wet spot against her lower back, a frustrating reminder that she hadn't been able to handle the simplest of tasks—she studied the fence, walking alongside it. The bushes on the other side formed a thick barrier at least six feet tall.

Agents probably did stunts like this all the time, climbing over obstacles, pulling themselves up ropes. She could handle it. But as far as she could see in the dark, there really was no break or opening in the bushes. *This here's as good a place as any.* She stretched her sweater sleeves down and around her hands to protect them from the tiny spears mounted on the top of every post. Huffing and puffing, with the spears digging through her sweater and into her skin, she hauled herself over the fence.

Amidst the snapping and cracking of branches, she dropped the rest of the way, plunging into the bushes. She landed hard on the other side, falling on her hip. Stinging flashes of pain shot from the scrapes on her arms and ankles, and her hip ached. A branch snagged her hair, tugging strands from her ponytail. She squeezed her eyes shut and forced herself to push through the scrapes and claws of bushes until she was free.

With an aching, angry sigh, she paused to pick the leaves and twigs from her body. When she finished putting her ponytail back together, she was ready. Finally, the lights from the house were visible in the distance.

Like going to the fricking Biltmore mansion. She'd been to the estate in Asheville when she was younger and had never forgotten the place. Its size and the wealth it represented were awe inspiring, but there was also something ominous and creepy about such an obscenely gigantic home, its cold stone walls and floors, the claustrophobic bare-bones servant quarters in the attics and basements. They visited in the fall around Halloween, just like now, when the skies grew dark early. As they made their way to the parking lot, she glanced over her shoulder. In the shadows between the trees, it was the ultimate haunted house.

Pull yourself together. This isn't a haunted house. It's Agent Heslin's home. And if you want to speak with her, you need to get your butt up there.

Cursing her damp underwear and her dirt-smeared knees and elbows to take her mind off her doubts, Beth took a trembling step toward the house. Soft earth squished under her weight as each footstep sank into the ground.

Two, four, six, eight, ten, twelve, fourteen, sixteen, eighteen, twenty. . .

Chapter Fifteen

Izzy let out a deep woof. Victoria rolled over and opened one eye. Izzy was always the first to alert Victoria to anything out of the ordinary—like the occasional visitor. She flew off the bed and ran toward the doorway, her brown brindle coat blending seamlessly into the dark bedroom.

"Shhh. Be quiet. I need to sleep."

Within seconds, all the dogs were on their feet and barking. What had woken them? With a touch of sleep still clouding her thoughts, Victoria imagined Ned had stayed the night in the guest wing and was just getting something in the kitchen. But just as quickly, she remembered he had gone home long ago. Had she set the alarms? No. She rarely set them during the day or night, afraid the dogs would set them off, and last night was no exception.

The barking escalated. Victoria wasn't hearing the excited yelps from earlier when the dogs chased something through the yard. These gruff barks were intended to send a firm message—this is our house. Which meant someone was there who didn't belong. She whipped her gun out from under her pillow and stood up, the hardwood floor cool beneath her bare feet. Her skin crawled with tiny goosebumps as she listened. In the sliver of light coming from the bathroom, the dogs' shadows stretched and twisted against the walls like hunched, contorting demons. Eddie slipped through the partly closed door and disappeared. From behind their enclosure, Leo and Bella watched, ears flattened, tails tucked underneath their bellies.

She wedged her cell phone under her arm, turned on the light, and crept out of her room toward the center of the house. The sheer size of her home intensified her concern—so many rooms and corridors where someone could lurk and hide. In a whoosh of movement, Izzy and Eddie ran past her and rushed outside. The dog door—large enough for a person to climb through—slapped shut behind them and clicked into place. That was good. If someone was on her property, they weren't inside. Yet.

"Exterior lights on." Victoria's voice was steadier than her nerves.

Light flooded the patio and yard. Angled against the wall, Victoria scanned the area. Izzy and Eddie trotted back inside, huffing, and shaking their heads, their fur damp. "Good dogs, good dogs," she whispered. She hoped they sensed her tension, she wanted to confirm their instincts—it wasn't okay for someone to be out there in the middle of the night. *If* that was the case. She hoped there was another explanation.

Facing the back door, Eddie growled.

It's probably nothing. I'll just check the monitors and go back to bed. A niggling sensation reminded her that just because it was most likely nothing didn't mean it was always nothing. It was definitely something when her mother was abducted in the middle of the night while the rest of the family and dogs were at their lake house.

Years ago, alone, in an equally big house, had her mother heard something, then tried to convince herself she was being silly, that perhaps whatever she'd heard wasn't anything more troubling than an animal invading the garden? Did she pass up the opportunity to call 911, thinking there was some innocuous explanation right up until the terror-filled instant she realized she was wrong? Had she thought it was probably nothing right up until the instant when strange men grabbed her, tied her up, and hauled her away from the home she would never see again? Victoria would never know the answers to those questions, but she knew she did not want to repeat mistakes from her family's past.

106

With a shudder, she cocked her gun, crept through the kitchen, and opened the door to the control room. Each screen inside the room would show a video feed from cameras spread around her house and property.

When she entered the room, in spite of all her training, an icy current ran up her spine.

Eerie gray static danced menacingly across the otherwise blank screens. Her heart pounded. Never had that happened before.

Closing and locking the control room door behind her, she called the security company.

Someone answered immediately. "Wentworth Security."

"This is Victoria Heslin. My code is GALGA081895SR2."

"Confirmed, Ms. Heslin. How can we help you?"

"I believe I have an intruder, maybe not in the house, but outside. I didn't have the security system activated before I went to bed, so no alarms went off, but my video feeds are down. Can you check on them?"

"Yes, Ms. Heslin. Do you think you or anyone else in the house is in danger? Do you want me to call 911? We can have one of our security personnel out there in . . . ten minutes, or do you want me to contact the Sheriff's office and have a patrol car come by?"

Victoria studied the gray screens, pushing away the thought that they were mocking her. Something was very wrong. But the dogs were no longer barking. She stared at her gun, curling her toes on the tiled floor. After years of living in a constant state of worry because of what happened to her mother, Victoria signed up for self-defense classes, and then studied martial arts. She hadn't wanted to live her entire life in fear. When she joined the FBI, even though her awareness of criminal behaviors multiplied, her paranoia disappeared as her training and experience progressed. By the time she graduated Quantico, her sense of empowerment was complete. She was now entrusted with protecting the lives of others, and more than capable of doing so. She could take care of herself.

"Ms. Heslin, are you still there? Should I call 911 for you?"

"No. No, thank you. No need to send anyone here. I'm the only one in the house and I'm armed. I just want to know what is going on with my surveillance cameras."

"Do you need a technician dispatched this evening, or would you like to make a service call for tomorrow?"

"Let me look around. I'll call back to place a service call."

"Okay. Thank you." She took a deep breath and ended the call.

She opened the door in a shooting stance, her gaze darting around, ready to pull the trigger if necessary. No need to announce her presence as a federal agent. This was her home.

The dogs lifted their heads from where they were sprawled across the floor on their sides. Izzy jumped up first and the rest of them scrambled to their feet and surrounded Victoria, each completely focused on their master. Whatever they heard earlier was no longer a perceived threat. Whatever, or whoever they heard was gone.

Ordering herself to calm down, Victoria sat at her desk with her weapon close by and checked her messages, aware of every slightest noise. Exhausted, but wound up like a tightly coiled spring, she eventually returned to bed and replaced the gun under her pillow. Tomorrow would require all her focus. She needed to sleep, especially because there might be some sleepless nights ahead as the investigations moved forward. But details and images from her long day kept flashing through her mind: brain matter, blood spatter, gaping bullet holes, numbers scrawled in black ink across ashen skin, a note left for her, and the bouncing gray static on her security video screens.

A clap of thunder echoed through the walls. Izzy jumped onto the bed, circled, then lay down, draping her head over Victoria's ankle. Victoria pulled the soft sheet and comforter up to her chin and concentrated on the dog's soft, rhythmic exhalations.

As a thunderstorm rocked the night, Victoria slept again while her darkest fears took shape in nightmares.

# # #

Shaking with fear, her heart pounding like crazy, Beth ran through the darkness. She landed wrong and her ankle twisted to one side. She yelped as a jolt of pain shot up her leg. Limping as fast as she could, she kept moving across the wide expanse of yard between her and the fence.

At any second, she expected to get slammed to the ground from behind, pulled backwards, and torn apart.

Just as suddenly as it started, the barking stopped. Nothing jumped on her back or tore at her skin. But would they come back? *I'll act crazy, stomp, and wave my arms around to freak them out. Or did that only work with bears?*

She shivered, thinking about what might have happened, what still might happen. A small winged creature darted past overhead, flapping too close for comfort. She shielded her face, bracing for an attack straight out of a horror movie. Since the moment she set foot on Heslin's back porch, it was as if someone flipped a switch to let loose a deranged circus from hell. The sudden barking and growling—like a kennel full of crazed dogs lived inside the house. And not little yappy dogs like her sister's. Dogs with deep, guttural voices—a bunch of giant drooling beasts like German Shepherds, Rottweilers, and Doberman Pinschers, snarling and snapping their razor-sharp teeth, ready and willing to tear out someone's throat. That someone could have been her if she hadn't taken off running for her life. Maybe the dogs were the reason Heslin hadn't activated her security alarms—no need for them.

Ankle throbbing, she continued with a wincing gallop movement toward the thick bushes. She ducked her head and covered it with her arms, forcing her way through the bushes to the fence. Tiny spears dug into her hands as she lugged herself over and collapsed on the other side in an exhausted heap. Her chest heaved with ragged gasps of breath. Not her finest moment.

The wet earth soaked through her jeans and top. She finally stood, brushing off debris and fixing her hair so Danny wouldn't know what she'd been through. Sweat trickled down her sides, further chilling her in the cold air.

Where was the damn moon when she needed it most? Unsure if she was heading in the right direction, she painfully hobbled toward the front gate, focusing on calming her heart and lungs so it wasn't like she was still running an obstacle course. As her fear dissipated, her anger grew. Things had not gone as she expected. Not even close. She'd had to flee like a scared and helpless animal, a terrified little rabbit, like prey rather than the predator.

She turned on her phone flashlight and aimed the small circle of light on the ground in front of her feet. When the large iron gate loomed ahead, she unfolded a note from her pocket and wrapped it around the fence where it was sure to be seen.

The note would have to do for now. Next time, she'd be better prepared.

Chapter Sixteen

A persistent whine broke through Victoria's slumber in the otherwise silent room. She rolled from her back to her side, jostling Izzy off her legs. The sad sound continued. She sat up and rubbed her eyes, the comforter falling in soft folds around her waist. The first specks of morning light entered the room. Her alarm hadn't gone off yet. The dogs rarely stirred until she got out of bed. Who was whining? And why was she so tired? As she woke fully, her memories returned—Leo and Bella, the disturbance after midnight, the malfunctioning security cameras.

"Listen up, Leo and Bella, I like my dogs to be quiet until the alarm goes off. So if you're still here tomorrow, gotta remember that. Please." She tossed the covers aside, stood up, and left the bedroom, followed by her dogs.

Walking through the main floor, her eyes darted to every corner. A quick check inside the control room proved the video monitor feeds and security system were working. The security company had left her an apology-laden message saying the technology had experienced a mysterious but temporary glitch and then restored itself. Victoria wasn't comfortable with the "mysterious glitch" explanation. Quite a coincidence for a night when she thought she might have had an intruder. She intended to find out exactly what happened. It might be time for a new security company. She returned to her bedroom to brush her teeth and pee. Her smooth skin always paled when she didn't get enough sleep, and dark circles had formed under her eyes, but it was nothing a little tinted moisturizer couldn't hide. She changed into running clothes and clipped her phone onto her jacket. As she passed the safe in the mudroom, headed outside, she debated grabbing her gun and holster, but decided against it.

Fog descended from a gray sky heavy with thick clouds, another soaking downpour almost a certainty. The scent of recently cut grass and damp earth had been intensified by yesterday's rain. The yard was littered with leaves and twigs blown from the foliage. Stepping off her back patio, she spotted footprints in the mud. Hairs raised on the back of her neck. A size seven shoe was her estimate. Gazing out through the mist at the tall bushes that framed her yard like a wall, she imagined someone hiding behind them, waiting. But her dogs, with their extraordinary hearing and scent detection, were calm and quiet, so no one was there. She crouched down and took pictures of the shoe prints with her phone.

She followed the footprints around the side of her house and toward the front of the property. Broken branches and trampled bushes indicated where the night time visitor had climbed the tall fence. Victoria straightened, rubbed her chin, and thought. She wasn't being paranoid if the threat was real. But how concerned should she be? She walked the perimeter of her home. No one had attempted to enter. Someone would be foolish to try and break into her home alone—yet she only saw one set of prints. The intruder might have been nothing more than a teenager on a dare. Egged on by her friends, hadn't she once been dared to scale the neighbor's brick wall and swim a lap in their pool when she was younger? Her soaked hair and clothes had provided the proof of her daredevil behavior. That might be all it was, except . . . there was the concerning issue of the security feeds.

Unwilling to climb through the bushes and jump the fence, Victoria jogged to the entrance to see if she could pick up the trail on the other side. Steps away from the gate, she spotted something small and white standing out against the black iron.

Careful not to ruin any fingerprints, she unfurled a wet slip of paper from around the bars and opened it like it was an ancient, fragile manuscript. Diluted purple splotches of ink smudged the paper. She squinted to decipher all the letters.

112

Without trust, you have nothing. Do you trust Rivera, and can he trust you?

Chapter Seventeen

Driving to the office, Victoria pressed the phone to her ear as she pulled onto the interstate. She'd barely said hello before she yawned.

Rivera chuckled. "Late night?"

"Sorry. I sent you the summary notes I took after making calls and reviewing the research we got from local detectives."

"I looked everything over. Sent back my thoughts. Not much for us to go on."

"Nope. Not yet."

For a few miles, they brainstormed ideas about the murders, discussing the profile of whoever was responsible.

Victoria yawned again, although this time it might have been a nervous reaction rather than from her lack of sleep. She took a deep breath. "I had an unexpected visitor last night."

"A visitor?"

She told him what she'd found, including the note.

"Wait. You let me drone on and on about our case homework and then decided to drop that little bomb on me? What the hell?"

"Guess I was still processing the information." She turned down the heat because the warmth was making her sleepy.

"Any idea what the note means?"

"Nope. I was hoping you might."

He huffed. "Do you have it to give to the techs?"

"Yes. It was wet, not sure about prints, but they can at least compare the writing and the paper with the other one. I'll bring it to the lab as soon as I get there. You know, I think this focus on me could be the killer's weakness. It might be how we put an end to this."

Rivera grunted.

"Listen . . . don't tell Murphy. Let me tell him."

"Sure. But tell him right away." Rivera ended the call.

Victoria scanned her ID card and entered the FBI building just in time for Murphy's update meeting. Rivera was already seated at the table in the windowless conference room. His fingers tapped the table like he was playing the base notes of a piano piece. He studied Victoria as she took the adjacent seat, leaning toward him. "I dropped off the note. They'll analyze it to death for us— including the handwriting—but with the lighter staff on Sunday, results will be delayed."

Rivera nodded. He followed Victoria's gaze to the wall. Pictures from yesterday's crime scenes were displayed on a white board: a gruesome close-up of Todd Meiser's bloody face was taped above a wide view of the Cossmans lying across the hiking trail. Normally there might have been lines, some solid, some dotted, drawn between the images to illustrate the connections. There were none.

Murphy entered. "All right, I'm here." He slapped Rivera on the shoulder as he passed behind him. Before taking a seat, he dropped his notepad on the table and plunked his insulated thermos down beside it. "Let's get to it. Here's what I know. We now have two major crimes in the course of twenty-four hours and a media frenzy brewing. The media sure does love themselves a serial killer." He clutched his thermos. "Meiser's death might come with an explanation, one that ushers a boatload of blowback for us— should have been under protection, blah, blah, blah—you all know I wanted them protected. The Cossmans' deaths—well, until we have an explanation, their deaths came straight out of nowhere. More frightening for the public. More blowback for us. So let's put their fears to rest . . . what do you have? Thoughts? Leads?"

Victoria and Rivera exchanged brief glances. She knew what he was reminding her to do, but she managed to ignore the frown on his face. "How was your son's chorus concert?"

"Fine." Murphy grunted.

"Good. Glad you were able to make it. Well, it'll be easier to figure out the who, after we know the why. So we're focusing on what connected the Cossmans to the Butler trial. We're also looking for any reason someone might want them dead."

Murphy took a swig from his thermos and wiped his hand over his chin. "Obviously."

"So far, we're not seeing that connection. No one Rivera or I spoke with could give us a reason someone might want the Cossmans dead, nor could we connect them to the Butlers, or Meiser. They don't appear to have posed any threats or crossed anyone."

Repetitive thoughts raced through Victoria's head. *What did the victims have in common? What have we missed? And why the notes for me?*

Murphy stared at Rivera. "Anything to add to that bunch of nothing?"

Rivera coughed, giving Victoria a side long glance.

Murphy wasn't looking at her. In a plea for Rivera to give her just a few more minutes, she held one finger up just above the table.

Rivera noticed and gave the slightest shake of his head before answering Murphy's questions. "Sam gave us their credit card receipts from the past two days, since they arrived in town. Nothing we found puts Meiser and the Cossmans anywhere near each other."

116

Victoria pointed to the white board. "So, if we're staying open-minded here—the crimes show almost no passion, no excessive violence—the victims weren't tortured, their deaths appear to have been instant. Yet the murders don't appear well planned or connected in any way aside from the numbers on their heads."

"If that information was leaked, someone else could have copied it," Rivera said. "We asked to keep a lid on those details, but the neighbor who found Meiser saw it, so did the officers and the techs. At the Cossman crime scene we had police, the sheriff, the hiker, techs. . . any of them or all of them could have mentioned it to someone."

"And the note left for you at the Cossman murder scene—" Murphy narrowed his eyes at Victoria. "That suggests some pre-planning. It also suggests the killer is messing with us or has some sort of fixation on you."

"Well . . ." Victoria grasped her necklace. "There is something else. Someone left a note on my property last night. I think—"

Murphy plunked his forearms on the table and leaned toward her. "What do you mean, a note? What did it say?"

Victoria told him.

"Seriously, Heslin? That should have been the first thing you told me." He scowled at Rivera. "Did you know about this?"

Victoria answered, not wanting Rivera to be in trouble for keeping quiet about it like she'd asked him to do. "We don't know that it's related to the other crime scenes."

Murphy sighed heavily and sat up straight in his chair. "Let me know if forensics matches it to the others. If so—well, we'll cross that bridge when we come to it."

Victoria let out the breath she'd been holding and smiled inside, relieved she was still on the case. She wanted nothing more than to catch whoever killed Meiser and the Cossmans.

Murphy's phone lit up on the table. He ignored it and took another gulp from his thermos. "What about the Cossmans' hotel? Did you or the cops find anything there?"

"Nothing with the staff," Victoria said. "They all had alibis."

"The police have spoken to every person who stayed at the hotel in the past week. They made up an excuse about lost and found items, they didn't want to cause a panic, but wanted to make sure they were all alive and well. We have three guests we still haven't spoken with. Jim Johnson—might be a fake name. Paid with cash." Rivera glanced at his notes and smirked. "Jason Bourne also paid in cash. And one guest was using a stolen credit card."

Murphy plunked his elbows on the table, rested his chin in his hands. "The one using the stolen card. Tell me about him. Or her."

Rivera flipped a page in his notebook. "He was in room 332. When I called Thomas Wilson, the person whose credit card was used for the stay, I got an elderly man in San Francisco. Mr. Wilson hasn't left the Bay Area in years. Whoever was staying in room 332 had opened a new credit card in Thomas Wilson's name. He had the room reserved for three days, but one of the cleaning attendants reported that the bed hadn't been slept in after the first night, and his belongings were gone.

"So we don't know the criminal's real name or what happened to him?"

"Correct." Rivera tapped his fingers over his notepad.

"At least we haven't found his body yet. Prints?"

Rivera shook his head. "The woman who cleaned the room found empty beer cans, but she threw them out and they're long gone. We dusted the door handles, the remotes, and the phone. But it's a hotel room, there are too many. Didn't want to drag the lab down this alley when we don't have anything to connect him to the murders, and as far as we know, he left before Meiser was killed."

Murphy grunted. "See if the card was used anywhere after he left."

"We did." Rivera flipped his notepad closed. "It wasn't."

"Keep the account open and put a trace on it so we know if it gets used again." Murphy grabbed his belongings and stood up. "Well, get back to it. Let's hope we get some leads today, from somewhere."

Victoria left the meeting room and walked straight to her office. Cloudy morning light filtered in from a small window above her head. She opened her laptop and checked on her house. All the video feeds were working. On one screen, Izzy wandered through the kitchen, staring up at the countertops and sniffing here and there. One of her favorite things to do was to leap on top of them and search for errant crumbs. No doubt she'd try it soon enough. Ned might even find her there when he arrived in a few hours. The other cameras showed the rest of the dogs were fast asleep.

Victoria had to find out what happened to cause the temporary glitch in her video cameras, but for now, the murder cases came first, until a glance at her phone showed her father had left a message. If he needed something from her, she'd better find out what it was, or he'd be calling back soon. Her father was a wonderful man, but he had no practice with being ignored. She pressed the play button and raised her phone to her ear.

"Tori, darling. Hope you are well today. My attorney called. A sizable amount of money left your trust. Two hundred thousand dollars. You know I trust you, but Fenton just wants to make sure you aren't in any . . . trouble. Just call me. Love you."

Victoria deleted the message and set down her phone. Make sure she wasn't in trouble? What on earth did Fenton imagine she did with the money? She rolled her eyes. Fenton was supposed to be her attorney as well. He should call her directly if he had concerns. Although, she didn't want to explain every dollar she spent, nor should she have to. She had good reason to keep her

119

transactions secret and anonymous. She didn't want the publicity, and with her career, she couldn't have it. Federal agents were supposed to live quiet, private lives. The public didn't need to know she existed.

Rivera popped his head in the opening of her door. "You okay, Tori?"

She turned her chair to face him and offered a slight smile. "Absolutely."

He handed her a coffee.

She peered into the paper cup. "Do I want to drink this?"

"It's fresh. I just made it."

"Thanks." She took the cup and wrapped both hands around it, letting the warmth seep through her skin. "I know I must look a little rough around the edges. Not much sleep last night. But I'm fine."

"If you're worried about—"

"Good, you're both here." Murphy burst into Victoria's office, hitching up his pants. Victoria quickly scooted her chair out of reach to avoid a slap on her back or shoulder. Murphy didn't discriminate, every shoulder apparently beckoned to him. At least it was shoulders and not rear ends, or he'd be facing more charges of harassments than he could count.

Murphy directed his gaze at the top of her head. "Heslin, do you color your hair to make it blonde like that?"

"Uh, no. I've never colored my hair. This is the hair I was born with. Why?"

"I just called down to forensics. Their report isn't ready, but they gave me something. There were long blonde hairs on that silk scarf from Meiser's house. Techs thought they could be yours and wanted a sample."

"I don't see how—"

"Relax. They're not yours. And I told them you weren't that sloppy. The hairs they found were brown hair dyed blonde."

Victoria met Rivera's gaze. "We need to identify the prostitute Meiser was with and see what color hair she had."

"Or if Meiser had a lover who found out he was with a prostitute." Murphy wagged a finger. "He could have taken the girlfriend to a real nice dinner for the same amount of money he paid the hooker."

Rivera wrapped both hands around his mug. "You think the hypothetical girlfriend got that mad?"

"When it comes to a woman scorned, there are no limits." Murphy slapped Rivera on the shoulder before walking out.

Victoria called after him. "So, you're willing to consider that Meiser's death might not be related to the Butler trial?"

Murphy yelled back from the hallway. "Of course. I'm willing to consider his Grandma did it, but it's not likely."

Victoria swiveled her chair back to face the center of her desk. "Between the small footprints and the long blonde hairs, there's a woman involved. But there's no good reason for a scorned girlfriend to then become a serial killer."

The agents' phones beeped at the same time. Victoria read the message. "Okay. Ballistics just confirmed the bullets matched. The same gun killed Meiser and the Cossmans. So that's good. Finally a connection besides the numbers. At least we know for sure they're connected."

"Same hit man, different client?"

Victoria shrugged. "I really don't see any evidence that either was a professional hit. Even though I know it's the best and only motive we've got so far with Meiser." She took a sip of her coffee and flinched. It was a far cry from a spiced pumpkin latte, but she took another sip because she didn't want to make Rivera feel bad. She swallowed the second bitter gulp and stared at her notes.

A day later, and the same two questions remained. How were the crimes connected? Why would anyone want to kill the Cossmans?

Chapter Eighteen

After tapping around on the top of the bedside table, Beth sat up and found her phone. She jammed her finger on the button to stop her alarm. Running her hand through her matted hair, she stared blankly at the wall. Her eyes drooped closed. She clutched a pillow, plopped back against the mattress, and rolled onto her stomach. She should get up, but she didn't want to. *Need more sleep.* Her body ached. The bed was comfortable, the pillows decent. *Just a few more minutes . . .*

"Get out of bed, lazy ass," grunted Danny. "You've got to get the Smiths before they're out of here."

Danny was right. Jason and Kelly got lucky yesterday when the cop showed up. But today would be their last day flitting around town being all sweet to each other like it was their honeymoon. It had to be. *Because I'm not going to jail. Please, God, don't let them have called the police already.* She rarely prayed, only when she was in dire danger of being caught for something. Now was as good a time as any.

She pushed herself out of bed and trudged into the bathroom. She rubbed her eyes and frowned at her puffy face, her flattened hair, and the dirt caked under her fingernails. She stripped and turned on the shower. The water helped soothe her soreness. Jumping through the bushes and over Heslin's fence had not been one of her better ideas.

Alone in the room while getting dressed—*just like Danny to go down to breakfast without me*—she turned on the television. In no time at all, she'd found a news update about what she did. Her

123

face lit up as she turned up the volume. The brawny guy, he must be the boss of the other agents, gave a statement about Todd Meiser's death and what it meant for the Butler case. The Butlers again! Those freeloaders sure were getting a lot of attention for what Beth had done.

During the commercial, she rifled through the clothes in her suitcase and pulled out wrinkled black pants and a white blouse, the most business-looking outfit she owned. She purchased them just in case she needed to pretend to be someone sort of professional for one of Danny's business schemes. The pants were a bit tight around her thighs and the shirt poked her underarms, but it made her feel official. Confident. Powerful. Like someone deserving of respect. When packing, she'd envisioned completing the outfit with her black, floral scarf—no longer an option thanks to Meiser—and going somewhere kind of nice. She and Danny were on vacation, after all.

Just over a week ago, he had plopped down on their couch, opened a beer and said, "Next week is our three-year anniversary."

"It is?" She knew their anniversary date, but she had a hard time believing *he* had remembered.

"We should celebrate. Let's get away for a few days."

"Really? Okay. Sure," she'd agreed. "Where should we go?"

"I already picked a place out. It's in Virginia. I used to go there when I was a kid. There's a waterfall with a mind-blowing view."

"Waterfall?" Beth had asked, still surprised he'd suggested a vacation. "Remember I showed you that article about that woman who slipped from the edge of a waterfall and fell to her death? Was that the same place?"

Danny took a gulp of beer. "Nah, that was somewhere in North Carolina. You remember that, huh?"

"Yes." The story was too morbid to forget. Beth wasn't a fan of heights, and she shuddered at the thought of tumbling to her death and smashing to bits on the rocks below. But it wasn't often that Danny suggested they do anything together, aside from watching television. She wasn't about to put down his idea even if it involved traipsing along the edge of a waterfall.

"Anyway, we're going to hike up to the falls when we get there. It's going to feel like we're on top of the world. And . . . I've got a surprise for you." He grinned.

"You do? What is it?"

"Can't tell ya. But you'll just have to trust me."

Beth smiled. Everything about his out-of-the-blue suggestion was unusual. Danny hadn't been romantic since they got married. He hadn't paid much attention to her at all lately, other than to show his irritation over one thing or another. She might have been a little more suspicious if she hadn't been so hopeful. "What about the new business you've been working on?" *Our million dollar sure-thing.* "Can you leave it for a few days?"

Over the past few months, Danny had been leaving town for a few days at a time. His new business venture was supposed to make them a lot of money. One million dollars was the figure he used. She'd asked, but he hadn't shared any details. Beth had yet to see anything come of his travels. Just a bunch of hotel and meal expenses, but he seemed passionate about whatever it was, she had to give him that.

"Oh, yeah. It can wait a few days for me." He downed the rest of his beer. "I'm closer than I've ever been. It's just a short matter of time before it happens. Then it will be like hitting the jackpot. Guaranteed." Grinning, he tossed the can toward the trash and missed.

Now, here they were, in Virginia on their supposed vacation. A nice dinner was likely to happen. That's what people did on anniversary trips, although they probably used credit cards with their actual names on them. Lately, Danny never wanted to go out anywhere with her. Which was strange because when he came back from his recent business trips, she'd found receipts for some upscale restaurants. Not like super fancy, can't-get-a-reservation types of places, but still a big step up from Bubba's Take-out Barbecue. Well, tonight would be different. She'd go without him. She'd find a nice sit-down restaurant with waitstaff and cloth napkins and candles on tablecloths, the type of place where Rivera might take Heslin. She'd enjoy a good meal by herself.

After she killed the Smiths.

Studying her reflection in the mirror, she removed the studs and rings from her ears, setting them at the back of the sink until only one earring remained in each earlobe. She was ready.

She drove back to the Sonesta Hotel, her ground-zero, stakeout spot. She didn't see the Smith's Jeep. She parked facing the hotel entrance to catch them coming in, or to catch someone else from her list coming out. An hour went by. Boredom always made her crave a salty or sugary snack, but she had no food. She rotated her index finger from side to side, chewing on her cuticles. To pass the time, she called Danny to give him an update. He was probably laying around the room watching television and sleeping. What she really wanted was for him to bring her something to eat, which was impossible because she had their car. The truth—she was lonely and wouldn't mind just hearing his voice. The call went to his voicemail.

"This mailbox is full and cannot accept additional messages." She'd always been annoyed by the bossy, robotic woman who came with the phone service.

Beth sighed and returned to watching through the windshield. Where were the Smiths? According to the hotel's computer— pathetic—almost anyone could hack into that system—they were still checked in. But what if they had left without checking out? What if they'd taken off without stopping at the Sonesta's front desk like she and Danny had done?

Clasping her hands repeatedly, she watched the digital clock, counting the seconds until the minute changed. *Two, four, six, eight, ten, twelve, fourteen, sixteen . . .*

126

Out came—what was his name—room 125—he was on her list. Horrigan? Yes—Steve Horrigan. He had no social media presence that she could find. She knew almost nothing about him. For all she knew, he was one of those guys who was living in a different decade technology wise.

She couldn't just wait around for the Smiths any longer. Cursing them for eluding her too many times, but mostly because of their stupid happy faces and marital bliss—which she doubted was even real—she followed Horrigan's black Ford pick-up out of the parking lot. The Smiths should stop acting so sappy, stop the irritating public displays of affection, and take a clue from couples like Rivera and Heslin. Their love was evident in subtle glances, but they didn't go out of their way to throw it in anyone's face.

Tailing Horrigan to the edge of the city, annoying hunger pains pinged across her stomach like mini lightning bolts. When she passed a Bojangles, she considered forgetting about Horrigan and stopping for food. She managed to steel her resolve by thinking about the gross food they must serve in prison. She had a job to do if she didn't want to find out more about prison slop first hand. From a street lined by woods, Horrigan pulled his truck onto a dirt road. So did Beth. Her car bounced in and out of ruts and mud puddles but she barely slowed down. He would see her following. She didn't care. Her stomach growled. She needed to get it done.

At the end of the road, he parked in a cleared area large enough to hold a few cars. He got out and grabbed a tackle box and fishing pole from the back. He smiled and waved as he passed her window. Beth looked down at her legs, pretending not to see him. Better to let him march deeper into the woods.

She waited until he disappeared on a narrow path. When she got out of her car, the wind cut through her thin, silky blouse. She wrapped her arms around her body to ward off the chill. Wishing for a coat and something warm to eat—a hot chicken biscuit would be perfect—she hurried after him. The path ended in an open area near a river. She heard a cough, looked left, and saw Horrigan.

He set his tackle box down. "Can I help you?" He sounded amused, without a hint of fear.

A strong wind blew against her. She tucked her chin. "Why would I need your help?"

"You followed me here. And it don't look like you came ready to fish." One side of his mouth lifted into a smirk.

Okay, so she wasn't the best follower, not like when she was stalking people online. Then she was great. She stepped closer, one hand inside her purse turning her gun around so she could pick it up and be ready to shoot. The gun refused to move. The damn muzzle was stuck on something. Had to be the hole in the inner lining, the one that occasionally ate her lipsticks and spare change, the reason she and Danny couldn't find one of the car keys for months. Scowling, she kept her eyes on Horrigan but had to put both hands inside her purse to get the gun loose. "I think you know why I'm here, Steve. You saw me! You know and I know that it's just a matter of time before you decide to tell someone."

Horrigan leered. "What are you doing?"

The gun finally jerked free inside her bag. She kept it hidden.

"Okay. Whatever, lady. I think you've been drinking. But I'd like to know what you think I saw." With his hands on his hips, he took a few steps in her direction. "Why don't you go ahead and tell me what's going on and why you're here."

A strong gust of wind howled past, fueling her anger. Her pulse thumped like a drum in her ears and throat. How dare he mock her and act like he had the upper hand! The old Beth might have let him intimidate her, hunched her shoulders and hurried away, but the old Beth was gone, replaced by a stronger version who didn't have to take his or anyone's crap.

"This is what's going on, Steve." She yanked the gun out of her purse and curled her fingers around the grip.

His eyes bulged. He held up a hand and backed away. "Whoa, hold on there. Just lower that thing. No need for—"

"You going to try and outrun my bullets, or just stand there and tell me you really don't know what I did?"

"I don't know—honest to God—you have me mixed up with—"

"Like hell I do." She pulled the trigger three times. He jerked as each bullet met his body. Beth's arms shook with each shot, but she held tight to the gun.

With a vacant, shocked stare, Horrigan swayed in slow motion at the edge of the woods. Blood soaked his hands, squirting through his fingers as he clawed at his chest. His legs collapsed, and he slumped to the ground on his back, gurgling and groaning.

Beth dropped the gun. Steering clear of his streaming blood, she grabbed his feet. After a few dragging steps, his dirty boots slid off in her hands, and she toppled backward onto her bottom. "Damn it." She scrambled up and wiped her hands on her pant legs, threw the boots into the woods and resumed pulling on smelly, damp, threadbare socks. *Gross.* She managed to drag his body a few yards into the trees and bushes, stopping twice to catch her breath. He was no longer groaning when she took his keys and rifled through pockets for his wallet. She grabbed his tackle box and fishing pole and threw them into the woods after him.

Her arms were limp, wiped out from shooting and dragging Horrigan's heavy body. She straightened her clothes, damp with sweat, and scowled at the dark, dirt smears on her shirt and pants and the muddy area covering her butt.

Grabbing her gun off the ground, she hurried back to the cars, *hope no one heard the gunshots,* and threw everything from her car and glove compartment into Horrigan's truck. It was time for a switch. With the rag and a bottled water from his floor, she wiped down every surface inside her own car, focusing on the steering wheel, the door handles, and the gear shift. She didn't have a record, they wouldn't find her fingerprints in the system, but Danny . . . he'd been convicted of several petty crimes. If they found his prints, he'd lead the authorities right to her. As she hurried through the work, her new mantra played in circles in her head: "I'm not going to jail, I'm not going to jail, I'm not going to jail . . ."

She backed the truck out, yanking the wheel left to face forward. Another pick-up rounded the corner, spewing dust in its wake. *Really? Now? You've got to be kidding me.* Her heart rate spiked as the vehicle drove straight toward her, filling up the one lane road. Her new mantra evolved into a frantic counting spell. With one hand, she put the vehicle in reverse, gripping the gun with the other, certain the approaching driver was there because he heard the gunshot.

The truck pulled up beside her, the driver's side only a few feet away. Her fingers tightened around the gun in her lap. *Two, four, six, eight, ten, twelve . . .* A middle-aged guy wearing a blue plaid flannel shirt and a ball cap lowered his window and stared at her.

She rolled her window down too, lifting the gun a few inches. Her heart thumped harder.

He leaned forward with a big smile on his face. "Fishin'?"

"Yep. I was." She did her best to act natural, but her smile felt tight and forced, like it might crack. She closed her lips, so she wasn't baring her teeth like a rabid animal.

The guy shut his engine off.

Crap! He was staying. She had to get out of there. But at least he wasn't there for her.

"Any luck?" he asked.

This time her smile was the real thing, full of pride and satisfaction. "I caught exactly what I wanted to catch today."

"Good for you. Hoping for the same."

"Ha!" She revved the engine and sped away. It wasn't luck, eliminating him.

That's when it hit her. *No! Oh, no! No! No!*

Her breath caught, and her heart skipped a beat. Everything felt wrong from the pit forming in her stomach to the dizziness spiraling around her head. In her haste, she'd forgotten to write the number five on Horrigan's forehead. Numbers were important, even the odd ones. Numbers brought order. Numbers were necessary. And, to make it worse, she hadn't left messages for anyone.

Chapter Nineteen

Chris Roberts slowly reeled in his line, pulling slightly left, up, and left again, to get it unhooked from the twig it had snagged on. "Come on, Betsy. Come on, girl. There we go," he whispered to himself. Once the line was free, he eased his way downstream, whistling, and cast from his new spot. He'd been standing next to the river for an hour, without getting a nibble.

The thirty-something blonde lady must have taken her luck with her when she left. She was a funny one. She had an edge about her, a nervous look, not what he expected to see on the face of anyone who had just spent time hanging out by the river. Strange that she was out there. She wasn't dressed for the outdoors. He could only see her head, shoulders, and a bit of her torso. Her silky white top hadn't fared well while she was fishing. Kind of looked like she'd had an unhappy spill in the sand, or a roll around in the bushes. Another poor office worker trying to snatch a break from a dismal cubicle and get some fresh air, like he used to do. He grinned. Or maybe she drove all the way here only to discover that nature is actually dirty, before scurrying back to the safety of her office's four gray walls. He shook his head. Nah. Just before she left, her nervous look had been replaced with one of triumph. She'd be back for more.

He rolled his neck from side to side and reeled in his empty line again. Across the calm water, a small dark spot scurried about. A beaver. It climbed out of the water on the other side of the bank. Roberts smiled, content. There was no place he'd rather be, except maybe doing the same thing in Colorado, or Montana. It was the quiet hum of nature that appealed to him. The lull of the clear water streaming gently past, the whitecaps that arced over the boulders and rocks, the lack of artificial noise.

He set down his fishing gear and opened his thermos of herbal green tea. It was better hot, and in this weather, it would be tepid in no time. Winter was extending its icy grip into the fall season.

Back in the clearing, he had parked near another car. He would have heard it leave if the engine had started, so it was still there. Where was its owner? Might be nice to have someone to talk to for a bit.

He finished his tea and, with his hands inside his fleece lined pockets, stared across the river, taking a deep breath of the fresh, chilly air. He stepped back toward the cover of the woods to relieve himself. He gazed in through the trees, admiring the colorful fall foliage, until something caught his attention. The handle of a fishing pole stuck up through the brush. He chuckled. Odd—but not entirely unusual; wouldn't be the first time a day with no fish got under a sportsman's skin and—like an irritated golfer who missed a three-foot putt—he threw his equipment into the woods. The pole was a sturdy one. Was it salvageable? He ambled into the woods, toward the discarded piece of equipment. When he was close enough to grasp the pole, he caught a glimpse of something else.

Red liquid glistened across the bushes, dotting the leaves as if they were diseased. And then . . . he had to blink to make sure what he saw was real. He dropped the pole, and backed away in quick, stumbling steps. His hands flew to his chest. "Oh no. Holy mother…." A thin sweat broke out over his skin.

The dead man's eyes had stared up at the gray sky, his expression frozen in horror. Roberts could barely think or breathe. Had the man moved? He didn't think so but—*Oh, God!*—he wasn't sure. *You have to check!* Roberts crept forward again, gripping the sides of his head. The man's shirt was soaked in blood, a pool of it covered the ground beside him. *Oh, he's dead! He's definitely dead!* Roberts' eyes darted around. His pulse thumped, rushing blood past his ears, louder than the river. He yanked his phone out of his shirt pocket. It slid out of his sweaty, shaky hands, flipped through the air, and landed in the blood.

"No!" He squeezed his eyes shut. Bile rose in his throat. He had to lean forward, resting his hands on his knees, and wait for the nausea to subside. The dead man's face was etched in his brain, the gruesome expression and lifeless eyes staring at him from inside his mind.

He wanted to race back to the car and lock the doors. But he had to call for help. Tears sprang from his eyes as he grabbed his iPhone from the puddle of blood seeping from the dead man. Holding the phone away from himself, he ran back to his bag, where he had a rag. He cringed and gagged as he wiped the deep red liquid off his screen. A sudden noise came from the woods. He jerked around, heart racing. A squirrel scurried up a nearby tree trunk. Damn. If he hadn't just peed, he surely would have wet himself. Muscles tight and tense, he scanned the area again. The quiet isolation of the river bank had become a source of terror.

Praying for God's help, he pounded 911 into his phone. His fingers slipped on the numbers. He had to hit the back button and start over again. *Come on, come on, come on!*

"911. What is your emergency?"

"I just found a dead man. He's near the river. Near the clearing when you turn off . . . off . . . I can't even remember . . . *where am I?* . . . Fordham Street!"

"Your name, please."

"I'm Chris Roberts." His lips trembled. "I was fishing. That's when I saw him. Jeez. He's been shot. At least I think he's been shot." Roberts gathered his gear in one arm, dropped his empty thermos and almost tripped hurrying to pick it up. He flung his bag over his shoulder. With his new pole dragging across the ground behind him, he hurried toward the clearing where he'd left his car.

134

"Mr. Roberts, I'm sending someone to your location. You should hear the sirens in a few minutes. Is there anyone else in the vicinity?"

Roberts peered over his shoulder, scanning the river bank and the woods. He'd reached the clearing. "I don't think so, but . . . there's another car here."

Chapter Twenty

Beth wiped grease off her hands with a napkin as she swallowed the last bit of her hot dog. Slumping down in the gas station parking lot, she pulled out her cell phone and called Danny. One less witness to worry about, and only three left. She wanted to share that news. Her call went to his voicemail. Again.

Asshole better clear out his messages one of these days. She made a mental note to tell him when she saw him later. She'd been harboring so much anger towards Danny lately. She had a vague, almost surreal but ever-present feeling that they'd had a huge fight recently, but she couldn't even remember what it was about. His business venture? Or. . . she just didn't know.

She put the truck in drive and headed back to the Sonesta Hotel. She liked being high up above the ground, it made her feel in control, like the boss of the road. Too bad the interior smelled like cigarette smoke. But here's what else smelled like cigarette smoke—prison. So it was a good reminder of what she was determined to avoid.

As she was pulling in to the hotel lot, a middle-aged man with dark skin and a paunchy stomach walked toward his car. Arnold Gomez. Thanks to the "special reunion" pictures he posted on his Instagram page yesterday, she knew where he was going. He was running late, thank goodness. He should have left a while ago if he was going to meet his nephew when he said he would.

She rummaged in her purse for a scrap of paper and a pen. Wrinkles formed across her forehead as she leaned forward and scribbled her next message. This time she would be prepared. With a smile, she tucked the paper in her pocket, drove across the parking lot, and fell in behind Gomez's Hyundai. Turn after turn, she followed him closely, but not too closely.

Beth glanced at her speedometer. He was doing at least 48 in a 35-mph zone. She frowned. Wouldn't that be just her luck if a cop pulled her over and searched the vehicle. She had no idea what Horrigan had stashed under the seats. He could be a drug runner for all she knew, although he seemed too boring of a guy for that. Still, to play it safe, she let up on the accelerator even though it meant increasing the distance between her and Gomez.

None of the people passing in cars paid her any attention. They weren't staring out their windows or switching lanes to avoid her. She was just a random person in a Ford F-150. They didn't have an inkling of what she had done or what she was about to do. No one expected something bad to happen during the day. Even Danny seemed nicer when the sun was out, before his first drink woke up his mean streak and each additional drink intensified it.

Gomez left the main road and drove onto a side street. Small homes gave way to apartment complexes. At a sign offering two months free rent, free cable and Wi-Fi, Gomez slowed down and entered the Hampshire Apartment Complex. Beth gripped the wheel tighter, her arms growing rigid. Her heart raced. *Just a few more minutes.*

Ignoring the "Drive Slow – Children" signs, Gomez wove through the apartments to the back and parked in front of building D. Beth parked nearby. She tucked Danny's gun in her purse and stepped down from the truck. Gomez was still in his car. Looking around, she saw no one else. Too good to be true? Nah. Even if someone came out, who would try to stop her? They might call the police, but she would be long gone by then. And if they were lucky enough to catch her license plate, it would lead to Steve Horrigan. They'd be looking everywhere for him, thinking he was the killer, at least until he started to smell and someone eventually discovered him.

A terrible sensation descended over her. Something she couldn't pinpoint but knew was bad, like a nightmarish déjà vu. She closed her eyes and leaned against the side of the truck, hoping it would pass.

A car door softly clicked shut. The car beeped as it locked.

No time. Pull it together. She opened her eyes. Gomez was walking away. *Do something.*

"Freeze!" Slightly dizzy, she managed to stand with her legs apart, both hands on the gun, her voice level but loud, pretending she knew exactly what she was doing from experience. And she really did have some by now. But the strange, unsettling feeling made it hard for her to focus.

Gomez spun around and placed his hand on his chest. "Me?"

"Yeah, you." Her voice cracked. *What is wrong with you, Beth?*

"Uhh, why?"

"You know who I am." She stepped forward, a little unsteady.

"No." He shook his head. "I don't know you."

"Don't lie to me. It's too late for that."

"I think you've made a mistake, lady." Gomez glanced toward the apartment building and took a step backwards.

"I haven't made a mistake. I'm Agent Heslin. FBI."

He cocked his head to the side and shrugged. "What do you want?"

"I want you to do what I say, so no one gets hurt." Her knees beginning to quake like they had in the hotel room yesterday. If she was going to shoot him and not miss, she had to get a lot closer. "Just get on your knees." She echoed her words in her mind, wanting to sound confident and in charge. Impressive. Powerful. "There's something important happening here. FBI business."

"Why do I have to get on my knees?"

"Don't ask me questions. Just do it." Her hands were trembling. She gripped the gun tighter, like it might fly out of her hands any second. She moved close enough to see his dark eyes darting about. A muscle in his neck quivered and tensed as he lowered himself to one knee.

Beth held her chin up, moving closer step by step, eyes fixed on the scar running across the man's cheek. Just like Danny's scar. And somewhere in those few seconds after he kneeled, Beth no longer saw Gomez's dark skin and shaved head. She saw Danny. And for once, he was doing what she asked him to do.

He sprang up and ran toward her. Beth blinked, not believing her eyes. Her mind flashed to the time she accidentally knocked over Danny's full, opened bottle of whisky and he came after her with a hockey stick.

A rush of panic flooded through Beth's veins. As quick as she could, she pulled the trigger. Once. Twice. The kick from the shot rattled her teeth and jerked her back. Danny staggered to the side then stumbled backwards, a shocked expression overwhelming his features. A knife fell from his hand and clattered to the pavement beside him. He crumbled over with a groan.

Beth ground her teeth. The heat of her anger spread across her face. *How dare he? Where was the respect for a federal agent?* He'd tried to trick her, acting all cooperative while planning to stab her as soon as he had the chance. Just like Danny. Pretend to be all nice so Beth wasn't expecting the blow that might send her tumbling down the stairs, backwards over the chair, or wherever she happened to be when his rage blew up. But this time, she had shown him. She stepped right up to Gomez and pulled the trigger a final time. The gun only emitted an empty click.

Damn! She glared at the gun. *Now I have to figure out how to reload it.*

Her breaths came short and fast. Her whole body shook as she hid the gun inside her purse, but the unsettling feeling from earlier had disappeared. At her feet, Gomez stopped convulsing and lay still.

She rummaged in her purse for the Sharpie. *Where is it! Gotta clean out this bag!* Finding it, she scrawled the number six on the center of his forehead. Below it, she wrote, *You'll be sorry.* "I'm more than a punching bag and sex toy." She tucked the scrap paper with her note into his mouth. With a smug, satisfied smile, she hurried back toward her car.

"Uncle Arnold!"

The voice broke Beth's reverie. She stopped, rooted to the spot. *He saw me!* Now, the nephew needed to go, too. But her gun was empty.

The young man ran toward his uncle's body. He stopped suddenly, picked up the knife from the ground, and scanned the area with his chin lifted and his eyes blazing.

Beth backed away, still watching. The nephew walked forward again, sank to the ground, his hands covering his mouth, one knee in the spreading puddle of blood. With a sudden jerk of his head, he rose to his feet, looking left, right, and over his shoulder, the knife still in his hand.

Beth froze as the nephew's eyes met her own.

Danny's words echoed through her mind. *Who do you think you are, Beth? You can't do anything.* Her posture changed. No longer channeling the confident demeanor of Agent Heslin, she slumped her shoulders and waved her hands around in frantic, panicked motions. *No one would ever suspect me.*

"He's been shot!" she screamed. "I didn't see who did it. I'm—uh—I'm going to get my phone and call 911!" She ran the rest of the way to Horrigan's truck as if she was hurrying to call for help. Instead, she drove off, tires screeching around the corner.

Chapter Twenty-One

Kelly walked through her living room, wheeling her suitcase behind her. She sniffed, turning her nose up. The whole place smelled a little musty. There was no food in the fridge, of course, and the dehumidifier would need to be emptied before that green stuff started growing inside it. She had to run a dark load of clothes right away so her favorite yoga pants would be clean for tomorrow. But it was good to be back.

She lowered the volume on the TV. Jason had already disappeared into the bedroom. For him, it just wasn't home without all the televisions going at once. Picking up a pen, she started making a list.

Eggs, butter, bananas . . .

Behind her, the TV mentioned a shooting. She glanced at the screen. Her pen dropped. Her stomach flipped. "Jason!"

Jason rushed into the living room. "What's wrong? Are you okay?"

Kelly fumbled with the remote, pausing the news and then rewinding it. "Look!" She pointed at the paused screen, her eyes wide.

Jason followed her gaze. "What?"

Kelly pressed play, waving her hands in front of her, her eyes fixed on the television. "That dead guy was in the room next to us!" Kelly's hands flew to her face and the remote hit her in the nose. She lowered her hands, wringing them in front of her chest. "In our hotel."

"Are you sure?"

"Yes! I remember his face, and that outfit. It doesn't really match. He was wearing it at breakfast yesterday. He sat one table over from us. He said hello to me because I saw him when he first checked in, when you went to park the car and I went up to the room by myself. He was in the hallway then. Same pants, different shirt. He was in the room right next to us."

On the television, the news anchor stepped to the side, revealing a man lying on his back on the ground. "Law enforcement needs your help identifying this man. He was found by the Rocky Bend River off Fordham Street this afternoon, with no identification."

A digital black bar covered parts of the man's torso and his entire face, hiding something Kelly could only imagine was terrible. He wore a dark green sweatshirt, flung wide open, a blue shirt patterned with pink fish and gray fishing poles, and camouflage cargo pants.

The camera went to a close shot of the newscaster with the crime scene image behind him. "The unidentified man has heavily tattooed arms."

"If you recognize him, please call the number below. Anyone in the area who heard gunshots between the hours of eight and ten in the morning are asked to notify authorities."

A tip line number scrolled across the bottom of the screen.

"Whoa. I don't remember him." Jason frowned at the screen and twisted his hands together. "And now he's dead?"

"Not just dead. Murdered!"

"Can't believe they showed a dead guy on the news. I didn't think they were supposed to do that."

"They said he was shot. Well, they said something about hearing gunshots. They don't know who he is. What should we do?"

Jason rubbed his hand over his chin. "We call that number. Tell them what you said, so they can figure out who he is."

Kelly paused the television again, flapped her hands against her sides and paced in a circle. "You do it. Hurry. I'm too nervous right now. I'll tell you what to say."

Jason called the number, taking deep breaths. "Hi. This is Jason Smith. I'm calling because I have some information about a murder we just saw on television." He put his hand over the phone and spoke to his wife. "They're transferring me."

A few seconds later he spoke again. "The man who got killed, he was in the room next to us at the Sonesta Hotel in Virginia."

Kelly held onto his elbow, bouncing on her toes, shaking his arm. "Do you remember our room number?"

"Okay. I can hold."

Kelly jostled his arm again. "I can't remember our room number. Do you know it? We have to tell them what room we were in. He was to the right. But if you were facing our door, he was to the left."

"Facing it from the hallway or from inside the room?"

"From the hallway. From the hallway."

"Okay. Calm down." He put his arm around her. "I'm on hold. They're going to connect me to someone. I can't remember the number either right now. I mean, I knew it, but . . . somewhere in the middle of the second floor. They can always look it up."

Kelly grabbed a throw pillow from the couch and paced around the room.

"I'm still on hold. Wait, they're transferring me to a detective."

"Put it on speaker so I can hear what they say." She hugged the pillow to her chest.

Jason gave his contact information and told the police what they knew.

"Thanks for calling in on the hotline. Let us know if you or your wife think of anything else."

"Oh. Okay. We will."

Kelly bounced on her toes some more, shaking Jason's elbow again.

"Uh, can you hold on for a second?" Jason asked the detective.

"We should tell them about that lady following us." Kelly nodded, her whole body bobbing up and down.

Jason moved his mouth away from the phone and whispered to his wife. "That's not relevant, Kel. And we don't really know that she was following us."

"They said they wanted to know about anything suspicious," Kelly whispered back, her eyes as wide as possible. "She was suspicious. Weird and suspicious. Maybe she followed that guy too. And now he's dead. She had a gray car—"

"A Honda—"

"A gray Honda with a big dent in the front and the headlight wasn't working. Tell her, Jason. Please."

"No." Jason covered the bottom of his phone with his hand. "That lady has nothing to do with this. And we've done enough."

"Then let me tell them."

"So *now* you're not too nervous?" He shook his head.

She held out her hand, her big brown eyes pleading.

Jason sighed and handed his cell to his wife.

144

Chapter Twenty-Two

Rivera was turned backwards, backing a black SUV out of the FBI garage when his phone lit up with a call.

Victoria lifted the vibrating device from the center console. "It's Detective Sullivan. I'll put him on speaker. If it's not about the case, take it off real quick before I hear something I might not want to hear."

Rivera laughed and cranked the steering wheel to his left. "Sully won't say anything you can't handle."

"You're forgetting the time he called me a snob."

"He didn't call you a snob. He asked if you were one. Valid question, considering."

"After we saw him at Meiser's house, I meant to ask you how he's doing now, you know, with the drinking . . ." She let her words trail off to accept the call, pressed the speaker phone button, and handed the phone to Rivera.

"Sully. What's up? Victoria Heslin is with me and you're on speaker. We're on our way to forensics."

The detective spoke in a hushed voice. "Another victim of the Numbers Killer. At the Hampshire Apartments complex."

"The Numbers Killer?" Rivera asked.

"That's what the media are calling him."

Rivera blew out a big puff of air. "So much for keeping the info about the numbers internal. When did it happen?"

"Few hours ago. We've already done our jobs here. I noticed no one from the FBI showed up. Not sure why no one has called you yet—sorry."

"Shouldn't he have called us?" Victoria whispered to Rivera, frowning.

Rivera whispered back, "he's calling us now," then spoke to the detective. "Sure thing. Appreciate this. Wait—was there another message written on the victim?"

"Hold on. Someone asking me a question here." Sully must have covered his phone because muffled conversation continued on his end of the line.

"I'm looking up the address." Victoria typed into her phone.

Sully returned. "You there?"

"We're here. Are they sure it's our same guy?" Rivera asked as Victoria said— "You need to make a U-turn here."

"Sure as can be without forensics and ballistics. He had the number six written on his head, same as the others. Looks like number five got skipped, or we haven't found the body yet."

"Was there another message on him?" Rivera cranked the steering wheel around a median to head in the other direction.

"Yeah. On his head. 'You'll be sorry.' And they found another note. Another note with your name on it, Victoria."

Victoria gripped her thighs, bracing herself for the information. "I'm just really popular this week, aren't I? Well, what did it say?"

"It said, 'Agent Heslin, watch your back.'"

Rivera's nostrils flared.

A cold chill traveled down Victoria's spine. Her thoughts flew to her late night, uninvited visitor, the footprints in her yard and patio. She didn't want to let the killer unsettle her like this, but goosebumps formed on her skin just the same. She crossed her arms and rubbed her shoulders. "Well, I—I guess the killer doesn't know me very well. I always watch my back. Thanks for calling us, Detective. We're on our way."

"Later." Sully disconnected the call.

Rivera gripped the wheel. "That note is a direct threat," he said through gritted teeth. "I don't think you should go anywhere alone until we've caught this guy."

Victoria tapped the gun in her holster. "I've got this thing here with me at all times. And another around my ankle. But, you know what, just in case, I should ask Sam to see if anyone from one of my past cases was recently released from prison."

"No need." Rivera slowed the car to a stop for a red light.

"Why not?"

"Because I've already checked."

"Oh." She was quiet for a moment. "When did you do that?"

"After we found the first note."

"And?"

"We didn't come up with anyone."

"Hmm." Victoria rubbed her hands together then placed them under her legs.

"Murphy's probably going to take you off the case now."

She had been thinking the same. She stared out the window, away from Rivera. "Well, until then, I'm still here. So let's hurry up and get to the Hampshire Apartments. Now that the killer is sending me personal threats, I want to catch him more than ever."

Rivera gazed past the police tape to study the apartment complex—rows of identical buildings, mustard-orange on the bottom, whiteish with mildew stains on top. A few porches overflowed with trash—mattresses, boxes, rusty bikes. Others were much nicer—a colorful bistro table and chairs, one with large potted and hanging plants, some Halloween decorations. "Any surveillance cameras around?" He stared over Sully's shoulder, still scanning the buildings.

"There are cameras, but they don't work."

"Great."

Blood stained the pavement in the parking lot. Crime scene techs had left evidence markers and tape behind, but the corpse was en route to the medical examiner's office.

"The guy's nephew is over there. Name is Hernan Gomez." Sully gestured to the young man sitting on the curb. "He had a gun on him, no permit, but it hadn't been fired. We took it. Also had a knife."

"Okay. We'll talk to him. Might as well."

Rivera and Victoria walked over to Hernan Gomez. Wearing a ball cap, the young man's face blazed with anger. He didn't look any older than twenty and might have still been a teenager.

"I know you'll have answered some of these questions already, but please bear with me," Rivera said. "He was your uncle?"

"Yeah." Hernan kicked at the ground with his shoe, scuffing it back and forth.

"Did you see anyone else around when you found him?"

The young man wiped at something under his eye. "Like I already told the cops, no one except some lady. She left to call 911. She told me she didn't see who did it."

Rivera made a note on his notepad. "Did she come back?"

"Nope." Hernan pulled on the rim of his cap and avoided Rivera's eyes.

"What did she look like?"

Hernan shrugged. "I dunno." He pointed to Victoria. "Sorta like her."

"Good, that helps. Was she taller, shorter, heavier?"

"Heavier, maybe. And she wasn't as pretty."

"Okay. What about hair? This color, same as Agent Heslin?"

"Yeah."

Rivera and Victoria exchanged a quick glance.

Hernan shrugged. "I don't really remember much. I was, you know, blown away about my uncle."

"That's okay," Rivera said. "That's a good description right there. We're going to have you work with a sketch artist on a computer, see if you can remember more."

Hernan nodded. "Because you think the woman mighta killed him?"

"We need to talk to her. Hear what she might have seen. She might be scared, too. Did you see her leave?"

"Yeah. She drove off in a black pick-up. Back part was open. Like no cover on it."

"That's great. Glad you noticed that." Rivera wrote on his pad. "So, you live here with your uncle?"

"He was here visiting me. We were going to lunch."

"Were you with him when he was shot?"

"No, I was upstairs in my apartment waiting for him to get here."

"Can you show us your place?" Victoria asked. The police hadn't gone inside. She wanted to get in there before any evidence could be hidden or destroyed.

"Yeah. Over here." Hernan mumbled as he trudged toward his home.

Rivera stayed where he was. "I better call the boss."

"Find us when you're done." Victoria caught up to Hernan and walked alongside him. "What sort of man was your uncle?"

Hernan shrugged again. "I don't know what he was into. Not getting shot type of sh—stuff. Nice, real nice, but—you know— boring. Worked in a warehouse somewhere. Moving boxes and stuff. He was the manager."

"Do you know where he worked?" Victoria asked.

"Nah. Sorry. He told me, but I forget the name of the place."

"That's okay, we'll find out." She stopped outside Hernan's door and looked around.

Hernan unlocked his apartment door and held it open. "Why'd he have that writing on his head?" Hernan frowned deeply. "That was freaky."

"We're not sure yet." Victoria stepped inside. Apparently, Hernan didn't watch the news. "Just wait over there, please." She gestured toward the corner where she could keep an eye on him as she explored the small space. The entire apartment could fit into her kitchen. Xbox games and controllers were scattered around the main room and on the table top. In the kitchen, a trash can needed to be emptied, a stack of dishes filled the sink, and a cereal box sat open on the counter. In the bedroom, clothes were strewn across a single twin bed.

"If your uncle was staying here, where did he sleep?"

"He wasn't staying here. We were just hanging out during the day. Getting to know each other. He's my dad's brother and I don't know my Dad. So he just found out I existed. I just met him for the first time a few days ago."

That explained how little he knew about the man. Victoria opened the closet and peered inside. "So he was staying somewhere else?"

"I don't know where he was staying. I think he said he knew a guy who lives around here."

"But he didn't say who?"

Hernan shrugged and sank down into his ratty couch. He dropped his head into his hands. "I didn't ask him. Oh, man. This is unbelievable. My uncle was a good guy. I know he was. Not like my—You got to catch this—"

"We'll find whoever did this. You can count on that. This is my card. Call me, please, if you think of anything that might be helpful, or if you remember who he was staying with."

Hernan took the card and nodded.

"Is there someone you can call to come hang out with, so you won't be alone?"

Hernan shrugged.

"You're holding up really well, and we appreciate the help. Can I call someone to be with you? Your mom, a friend?"

"I'm fine. I'll deal with it."

"Okay. Maybe you can visit a friend then."

"Yeah. Okay. Okay. I'll do that."

Sensing the annoyance in Hernan's voice, Victoria said goodbye. She left as Rivera was striding up the path to Hernan's apartment. Rivera stopped suddenly and stared off in the distance toward the woods lining the back of the complex.

"Hear that?" Rivera took a few quick steps toward the trees, then took off running.

Following Rivera's lead, Victoria pulled her gun from her holster and dashed into the woods after him. When she caught up, he was putting his gun away.

"It was just a deer." He shook his head, breathing hard. "Sorry."

"No, problem. A sprint works better than caffeine." She tucked her weapon back where it belonged.

"I just thought, if she's leaving you messages- it's likely she's sticking around to see your reaction to them."

"I know." Victoria walked next to Rivera, taking deep breaths, her heart still pounding.

"Learn anything from the nephew?"

"Not much. He barely knows his uncle. Gomez was divorced. No kids. And he wasn't staying here. Hernan isn't even sure where he was staying or where he lives, so we'll have to find out. I'm sure the detectives already have. You?"

"I left a message for Murphy. He was supposed to make a public announcement on the case at five. Then called Sam, asked him to search for connections between all the victims. If we're lucky, Gomez is the missing link connecting all of them."

"Hope so."

Rivera took a last look back at the woods. "And . . . I just got off the phone with the 911 shift manager. There were three calls to 911 about this shooting. All from males. None from a woman."

"You were busy. I think it's safe to say our killer is a woman with blonde hair. And Hernan didn't find her at all suspicious. But did she want him to see her, or did she get caught?"

Rivera ran his hand over his hair. "Either way, it's a short matter of time before we catch her."

"Let's try for catching her before another body comes in."

Chapter Twenty-Three

With a tennis tournament playing on his television in the background, Jason Smith tore open an envelope and threw its contents into the growing pile of junk mail. Kelly sat in a recliner nearby, reading. Jason's phone rang. She looked up from her novel. "Who is it?"

Jason lifted the device. "Unknown. I'm not answering." He set it back down.

Kelly leapt from her chair and grabbed his phone off his desk. "Hello," she said breathlessly.

"This is Federal Agent Victoria Heslin. It's urgent that I speak with Jason and Kelly Smith."

# # #

At the local police station, the Smiths sat in a small room with a table and four hard chairs, across from a tattooed woman with two nose piercings and jet-black hair. A big, burly officer in civilian clothing, with a close-cut beard and side burns, sat with them.

"Why are we here, again?" Jason asked.

The officer cleared his throat. "The information you provided led us to identify Steve Horrigan, the man you saw on TV earlier. The car you described with the dent in the right front, the one your wife thought was following you, it might match the one found at the crime scene this morning. The plates were stolen, the car isn't registered. And, we have three victims who were checked into the Sonesta, your hotel, when they died."

Kelly turned to Jason. "See that, baby, good thing we told them about that lady. Glad we didn't stay another day in that hotel."

The tattooed woman tapped a pencil on the table. "Tell us what you remember about the woman driving the car, and I'll do my best to create her image."

Jason clasped his hands in front of him. "She was probably around thirty years old, maybe a little older. She had blonde hair. Not thick like Kelly's, but not stringy either, just average hair. She wore it down, parted in the middle."

Kelly toyed with the ends of her hair. "And it was pulled back in a ponytail when I saw her. She was parked in a car next to me. Before she drove off, she stared at me—really stared, like she hated me or something. It freaked me out. I knew something was seriously wrong with that woman."

"We'll make a version with each hair style." The artist showed them different features on her laptop, asked questions, and used short quick strokes of a stylus to shape the woman's head, her hair, her cheeks, and her eyes.

The Smiths studied the image.

Jason frowned. "Can you make her eyes a little more . . . lidded? And maybe a little more . . . dull?"

"Okay." A hint of a grin crossed the artist's face.

Jason studied his wife—her glossy, smooth hair and glowing complexion, her lush pink lips—and offered her a smile meant to reflect his appreciation. He turned back to the sketch artist. "She had sort of an overall disheveled look to her."

The artist nodded, adding lines and shading. When she was finished, she'd created a portrait of a sad woman with a distrustful look in her eyes, like she'd had a tough life. She didn't look like a killer, but more like a victim. "What do you think?"

"That's pretty good." Jason nodded. "Seems about right best I can remember."

Kelly agreed.

The artist tilted her head, studying the picture. "Any other distinctive features, birthmarks, scars?"

Jason shrugged and shook his head.

"Okay." The officer stood up. "Just sit tight awhile longer. Some FBI agents need to speak with you. They're on their way."

"We spoke to them earlier." Kelly crossed her arms in front of her chest and rubbed her shoulders.

"Right." The officer walked toward the door.

Jason took off his jacket and wrapped it around his wife. "Cold?"

Kelly nodded.

"Can I get you anything while you wait?" the officer asked from the doorway.

The Smiths asked for water bottles and settled in, holding hands, exchanging anxious glances and nervous smiles until the officer returned. He waved them toward the door. "Okay. They're ready for you."

The agents were waiting for the Smiths in a room with more comfortable seating and a window. The change in rooms felt like an upgrade. "Hi. I'm Victoria Heslin, with the Federal Bureau of Investigation." The female agent shook hands with Kelly, then Jason. "We're grateful you called the tip hotline today. Your sketch was very helpful. We just compared it to another image from someone else at a recent crime scene. The sketches are similar. You've been a big help to our investigation so far. Especially since you noticed the car she drove."

"It was my wife who wanted to mention the woman following us." Jason's eyes beamed as he glanced at his wife. He had teased her that this wasn't how he wanted to spend the evening—at the police station—but she had done good. At the prompting of the agents, he repeated the information they had shared with Heslin earlier in the day.

"This is important. Did you ever see that woman inside the Sonesta Hotel?"

"No. We didn't," Jason said.

"I'm positive I didn't," Kelly added.

"What made you notice her following you?" Victoria asked Jason.

"So, first she was behind us when I dropped Kelly off at the mall near our hotel, to get her nails done. Her headlight was out so I told her."

Victoria's face lit up. Rivera was already out of his chair and tapping his phone, most likely calling the police impound lot, asking someone to turn on the Honda's headlights and check the left one.

Jason shifted his gaze from Rivera back to Heslin. "Then she was behind us again when we were going to the movies last night. We left the hotel and stopped at a store to get snacks. She followed us right from one parking lot to the next."

"Did you find that strange?" Heslin asked.

"Oh yeah. But then a cop pulled up and I let it go. He must have said something to her about her headlight, I saw him pointing to it. And when I came out of the store, she was gone."

"She left as soon as the cop talked to her," Kelly said. "So creepy. Why was she following us? What did she want?"

Victoria shook her head. In light of what happened to three other hotel guests, she could make an educated guess about what

156

might have happened if a cop hadn't come along, but she had no proof yet.

Kelly picked at her nails. "I really don't think I'm going to sleep well again until you find her."

"We will," Victoria shifted in her seat and crossed her legs.

Kelly clasped her hands tightly together. "That hotel was awful. I can't believe we ended up there. It looked nothing like it did online."

"We'd like to show you some pictures. Please tell us if you came across any of these other people while you were at your hotel or at any other time." Victoria set out a picture of Todd Meiser, from before he died.

Kelly and Jason both said no.

"What about this married couple?" She set down a picture of the Cossmans.

"Oh no." Kelly clamped her hand over her mouth. "I did see them! They had cute dogs with them. Is that...oh my God! That's the couple who were murdered when they were on that hiking trail!"

"Where did you see them?" Victoria slid the stylus from the side of her tablet.

Kelly perched on the edge of her seat, knees bouncing. "I saw the husband taking the dogs out one night. Our first night, because it was when I went to fill the ice bucket. And I saw them both at breakfast one morning."

"Did you speak with them?"

"No."

"Did you see them interacting with anyone else?"

"No."

Rivera showed them a picture of Arnold Gomez, just in case he had made an appearance at the hotel for some reason. Neither had seen him.

"Why is this happening to people that stayed at the Sonesta with us? Why are they dead?" Kelly twisted her fingers together in front of her chest.

With a grim expression, Jason reached for his wife's hand and squeezed it.

Victoria swallowed hard. "We aren't sure yet."

Chapter Twenty-Four

The agents drove back to their office checking leads, requesting data, and sharing information. Since it was Sunday, traffic was light. The drive was taking a lot less time than usual.

Rivera lowered his phone from his ear. "Okay. Listen to this." His voice might have sounded calm and controlled to anyone else, but from the hitch in his breath, Victoria knew he was excited about something. "The Honda they found near Horrigan's body matches the Honda the Smiths said followed them from the hotel. Broken left headlight. That puts this blonde woman at the Sonesta Hotel, at least in the parking lot, and at two of our crime scenes. And her hairs put her at Todd Meiser's crime scene and in the Honda, not conclusively, the DNA tests will take a while, but at least the hairs are a visible match under the microscopes."

Victoria clapped her hands. "So who owns the Honda?"

"The vehicle and the plates were stolen, and its been wiped clean of prints."

"Of course. Otherwise it would have been too easy."

"That's not all." Rivera tapped the steering wheel. "Remember little Gomez said the blonde woman left the parking lot in a black pick-up? Well, guess who owned a black pick-up?"

"I'm betting on Steve Horrigan."

"Exactly. We've got an alert out on the truck. The description will be on every electronic billboard within a few hundred miles of here. Every patrol officer in the mid-Atlantic will be looking for it."

"So we know what our killer looks like, sort of. But who is she? Why is she doing this? And why did she choose these people who don't seem to have anything in common?"

Rivera's expression turned grim. "And why is she sending messages to you?"

"I have no idea." Victoria looked out the window, lifting her eyes toward the sky. Having seen little of the sun in the past few days, it was hard to tell if it was dusk, or if the clouds were thickening and darkening in preparation for another rainfall. Or maybe both. It had been another long day. Ned would have fed the dogs their dinner hours ago.

"I've got to send Ned a message and let him know I'm coming home." She had to do a better job of keeping him updated on her schedule, or it really wasn't fair to him. He had his own life. But what if she didn't text ahead to let him know he could leave? What if she showed up and maybe he stayed and maybe they just hung out together for a while? Wouldn't that be just what she needed to clear her mind, relax, forget about her work for a few hours so she could see everything again with an objective, clear mind in the morning?

"What are you thinking?" Rivera asked.

"Nothing. Just . . . looking forward to going home tonight."

Who was she kidding? A few hours with a nice guy talking about something other than murder probably was exactly what she needed, what she *should* do. It was how normal people spent their after-work time—right? But was it fair to Ned? It would be impossible not to think about the cases and the crime scenes, not to text Rivera when a new idea or question occurred to her. That wasn't fair to Ned. She wouldn't be very good company at all.

She typed a text—*I should be home in an hour. Thanks for everything*—and pressed send.

#

Victoria pulled into her garage. Ned's SUV was still there. That was unusual.

She entered the house through the garage. The dogs jumped up and went crazy greeting her, even Leo and Bella. She put her bureau-issued gun and holster in the safe. An incredible aroma emanated from the kitchen.

She walked into the kitchen. Ned was standing over the sink. "You're still here." *Oops-that sounded rude.* She smiled warmly to cover up her faux pas. She really was happy to find him still there. "Something smells amazing."

"That's dinner and there's a plate waiting for you if you're hungry. I waited for you to get home because I just have to show you something." He smiled ear to ear.

"What is it?"

"It's a surprise." He walked into one of the family rooms. The dogs had all lain down, a sure sign Ned had given them plenty of exercise during the day.

"Izzy, come," Ned called.

Izzy leapt from her bed and trotted to Ned, her body wagging side to side.

"Okay, ready for this?" Ned's enthusiasm could not have been more obvious. He was bursting to show her the new trick he'd taught Izzy. His smile was contagious. Just what she needed to push the murders out of her mind, if only for a short time.

#

Ned left a few hours after Victoria arrived home. They'd hung around, laughed, and emptied several bags of organic dog treats teaching the dogs new tricks together. The evening had been light-hearted and fun.

Just a few minutes after he pulled out of her garage, she had a phone call from him.

"Hey. I'm still here, at the end of your driveway. There's someone waiting in a black sedan outside the front gate. Says he's an FBI agent."

"Oh, sorry. I should have mentioned that. He's a colleague. He's keeping an eye on me."

"Why do you need someone to keep an eye on you?"

She closed her eyes and rubbed her temples. "It's just work stuff. Go home and get some sleep. I'll call you tomorrow about some ideas I have for the trip."

"You sure? Because—"

She smiled. "I'm sure."

He sighed. "Okay."

"Hey. Thanks for tonight. It was fun. Just what I needed."

"Yeah? Well we can do it again sometime. My boss lets me have a pretty flexible evening schedule."

Victoria laughed. "Great to know. We might just have to do that. Have a good night."

Chapter Twenty-Five

Victoria took her seat at the conference table with Rivera, three other agents, local detectives, including Sullivan, and government officials. Most were absorbed with their own phones. The Chief of Police made small talk with the mayor, waiting for the meeting to begin. Victoria poured herself a glass of water from the pitcher on the table.

Pictures of Arnold Gomez and Steve Horrigan had been added to the montage of images lining the white board. Listed in chronological order were the messages left on the victims and the notes addressed to Victoria.

Todd Meiser - #2 - *Liar*

Robert Cossman - #3 – *Cheater*- Sonesta Hotel.

Anne Cossman - #4 - No message found – Sonesta Hotel.

Note to Agent V. Heslin with Cossmans: *Does your partner treat you well?*

Note on Agent V. Heslin's property: *Without trust, you have nothing. Do you trust Rivera?*

Steve Horrigan – no message, no number. Suspect's car left behind. Sonesta Hotel.

Arnold Gomez – #6 -*You'll be sorry.*

Note for Agent V. Heslin with Gomez - *Watch your back, Agent Heslin.*

The names Jim Johnson, Thomas Wilson, and Jason Bourne, the only guests at the Sonesta Hotel who had not been located, interviewed, and alibied, were circled with question marks around them.

Murphy entered the conference room, unsmiling. With a curt nod he acknowledged a few of the people seated around the table, slapping the Chief of Police on the shoulder as he passed. He set his Bulldogs thermos down. "Let's get started." He fixed his eyes on Victoria. "Heslin, go ahead."

Victoria pushed her chair back, stood up, and turned on her tablet. Full of neat bullet-point lists, underlined phrases, starred and capitalized items. Rather than reading from the notes, she kept her gaze focused on the faces around her. "We haven't identified our perp yet, although we have a description. Here's what we know. We have five murders—four males and one female—that we know were caused by the same gun. We think the numbers represent the order in which the victims were killed, and the ME's findings support that."

The mayor raised her hand as she spoke. "I thought the man they found by the river didn't have a number on him."

"Correct." Victoria folded her arms. "But ballistics match, and the Honda left behind at his crime scene matches one witnesses saw the suspect driving."

"I see." The mayor settled back in her seat, looking uncomfortable.

Victoria gestured toward the white board. "The victims don't seem to have been targeted by race, age, or gender, unless Anne Cossman was simply in the wrong place at the wrong time, which is possible. But most likely, these aren't hate crimes in the typical sense." She made eye contact with the Chief of Police. "We've spent the morning combing through your team's interviews with the victims' employers and family members. We compared your reports to our own, as I'm sure the detectives are doing as well." She nodded at Sully. "We've found no commonalities. The victims don't appear to share friends, family, activities, attorneys . . . nothing."

"So why them?" the mayor asked.

"The connection must exist from the killer's point of view." Victoria clasped her hands in front of her body. "These people have done something to her."

"Her?" The mayor's mouth hung open.

"Yes, ma'am. We believe the killer is female," Victoria said. "The victims have done something to wrong the killer, at least from her perspective. It could be anything. All of them are from out of town, except Todd Meiser. All but Meiser and Gomez stayed at the Sonesta hotel."

"Where was Gomez staying?" the mayor asked.

"We're not sure yet." Sully shifted in his seat and cleared his throat, staring at the white board as he answered.

"So have we looked into everyone else staying at the hotel?" the mayor asked.

Sully answered. "We have three guests still unaccounted for. Two left after one-night stays. Might not have even stayed overnight. Both paid cash. We're thinking they met a woman or . . . a paid date. It happens in that hotel. The third is Jim Johnson. The minute that Mr. Johnson comes back for his stuff, we'll know about it. We're trying to track down all three of them." The detective swirled his coffee absentmindedly with a stirrer. "You know, maybe the victims all drove too slow or cut our killer off changing lanes."

Sully's suggestion was an attempt to diffuse the tension in the room, but anything was possible. Victoria pointed to the whiteboard. "The killings took place in daylight, three of them in open, public areas. They're sloppy, not well planned, with prints, hairs, fibers and other evidence left behind."

A colleague of Sully's interlocked his fingers, resting his hands on the table. "The killer also left behind a scarf."

Heslin nodded. "However, there's no match for any of the fingerprints in our systems. We believe the perp just recently became unhinged somehow."

The Chief of Police made a fist and tapped it on the table. "Unhinged. Sloppy. New at killing. You've got the hotel connection. And yet, you—I mean, we—still haven't caught the person."

Rivera cocked his head. "It's only been three days."

"Only three days?" The chief's voice rose. "Have you been reading the papers? Or watching TV? It's wall-to-wall coverage. We need this case closed yesterday."

Victoria took a sip of water from her glass, giving herself another second to think. "Based on the footprints, the hairs left behind, and our descriptions of a suspect seen at two of the crime scenes, we're looking for a woman in her early to late thirties, with straight brown hair dyed blonde, about five foot four. She's been seen wearing her hair down and also in a ponytail. She may not have a job, since the crimes have occurred at different times throughout the day."

"Did anyone see her at that hotel?" the mayor asked.

Murphy set his thermos down with a thump. "No."

"So we've got a female serial killer in our city?" The mayor fiddled with the top button of her blouse as she spoke.

"Yes." Victoria nodded. "A spree killer, actually. More than one murder in a short period of time, different locations, no cooling-off period between them. It's possible she's not acting alone, but she's our only suspect at this time."

"Isn't that unusual? Doesn't that make it easier to find her?" The mayor let go of her button.

"Yeah," Murphy said. "It cuts our potential suspects in half, so we only have 150 million possibilities—in the USA."

Victoria addressed the mayor. "Men are more likely to be serial or spree killers because they're more socialized to express their aggression outward, more likely to hunt down victims. And it's rarer for women to kill using guns. But none of that makes our jobs easier. We really don't have statistically significant samples of female spree and serial killers to study. And on average, female killers manage to evade arrest for much longer than men."

Sully twirled the stirring stick between his fingers like a tiny baton. "What type of spree killer do *you* think we're looking at?"

"The short timeframe for these kills argues for a mission-oriented killer, someone with a purpose for elimination, like revenge. But, as I said, the murders are highly disorganized, So, it's possible we have a visionary killer."

"Can you elaborate?" the mayor asked, again clasping her top button.

"Visionary killers select their victims in a way that tends to appear random to investigators. They're usually suffering from psychosis, having delusions or hallucinations that compel them to kill. The victims they choose are directly related to their psychosis."

"Like David Berkowitz," Rivera said. "The 'Son of Sam.' He claimed Satan, or a demon told him to commit murders."

"I thought it was his dog." Sully laughed.

"Yeah. And like our killer, he also left letters for the police." Rivera crossed his arms, placing his hands on his biceps. "Some visionary killers believe or come to believe they are someone else entirely."

Victoria made eye contact with her colleagues around the conference table. "Female spree killers still attack for the same reasons as men, though—anger, revenge, the need for control, mental illness. Based on the messages she's left, it's likely she's been wronged by a man, a boyfriend or husband. She appears to be leaving messages related to that experience."

"Are we even considering that the Butlers had anything to do with all these killings anymore?" an agent asked.

"We're still considering everything." Murphy set his arms on the table. "Until we can rule it out with absolute certainty."

"Well, then . . ." The Chief of Police shifted his gaze to the notes on the wall, then settled it on Victoria. "As far as I can tell, in addition to the hotel, what connects these victims—and their murders—is you, Heslin."

"Excuse me?" The pitch of Victoria's voice rose. Beside her, Rivera sat up straighter.

"It was you who convinced Todd Meiser to testify," the Chief said. "Then we've got the couple killed hiking with their dogs, and I understand that hiking with your dogs is one of your big hobbies. And all the notes were left for you. Someone is obsessed with you."

Victoria crossed her arms and shifted her weight. "The first note was left when the Cossmans were murdered. It's possible the killer saw Rivera and me being interviewed on television after Todd Meiser was murdered. Channel 14 was on the scene when we left."

The chief rolled his eyes "Where I come from, when we hear hoofbeats, we think horses, not zebras. You are in this up to your eyeballs. Let's not overlook the obvious just because it's uncomfortable for you."

She turned red. "I've never met... I've never met the Cossmans, Steve Horrigan, or Arnold Gomez. And it's not me that our suspect seems to have taken an interest in."

The Chief maintained his hard stare. "Could have fooled me."

"She appears to be focused on . . . an imagined relationship between Rivera and me. Perhaps she . . . has some displaced anger towards us." Victoria inhaled deeply, took her time exhaling. "At this point, I'm certain we need to focus on what connects these victims in the killer's mind."

The Chief leaned forward. "Still, is there anything you want to share with us? Anything that might shed light on the messages written on the victims? Liar. Cheater. You'll be Sorry. Is it possible those messages were intended for you?"

Victoria opened her mouth to speak, closed it again. She clasped her hands behind her back to keep from curling her hands into fists. Sully coughed and averted his eyes.

The Chief's gaze roamed from Victoria to Rivera. "Is there something going on with you two? Because if there's something we don't know, and it allows this perp to keep killing, accumulating victims . . ."

Another detective jumped in. "If the FBI is going to be taking the lead on these cases, don't be making things worse for us. We're the ones who have to take the heat for these deaths."

Rivera glowered at the detective. "Don't forget—we live here. This is happening in our backyard, too."

Murphy cut in. "Enough. We're not going down this territorial battle path. The FBI was called from the beginning because of Meiser's connection to the Butler case. Now that we have a serial killer on our hands, we would have been called in anyway. This is our case, no doubt about it, but I like to think that we're all working together in the best interest of the public, to catch this killer."

Rivera set his hands on the table. They were still and steady, as usual, steady as a rock, but the muscles around his eyes tightened. His voice sounded carefully controlled. "To address concerns anyone may have, there is nothing unprofessional going on between Heslin and me. There never has been. Everything points to those messages being intended to represent the killer's thoughts on the victims."

"Sorry to say this, Rivera—" Sully looked away from his friend, grimacing. He gestured toward the white board. "But the notes and the one-word messages are directly tied, and the notes are directed at Agent Heslin."

"The killer is unstable." Victoria dropped her hands to her sides, the heat of anger rising to her cheeks. She couldn't believe the turn the meeting had taken. She focused on Detective Sullivan, taking in the hint of red capillaries around his irises and again wondering if he was just overworked or if he'd been drinking. She placed her hands on her hips. "There may be no rational explanation for what The Numbers Killer leaves behind. Insane or not, people do some horrible things without any reason at all."

The Chief of Police narrowed his eyes, offering a slight nod.

"So what can we do?" the mayor asked. "How can you put out extra people to protect the public if we don't know who is at risk?"

Her question met silence.

Victoria cleared her throat and everyone looked at her. Hands on her hips, she lifted her chin, and squared her shoulders. "Finding victim number one might be the key to all this."

Chapter Twenty-Six

After the meeting, it was a relief to be alone. Sitting at her desk, Victoria shook off the feeling that she'd been accused of something. Resentment wouldn't help and would only distract her from the case. There was work to be done. Detectives were still at the Sonesta Hotel trying to figure out how the staff or guests might figure into the murders. Sam and other intelligence analysts were still searching into connections between the victims. The police were handling the calls coming in through the tip lines, and Victoria and Rivera were following up with the few that seemed legit and warranted further investigation. There hadn't been anything else useful since they talked to Jason and Kelly Smith. Victoria also had a pile of paperwork waiting, forms she had to complete from her last case. And she was expected to testify in court during the Butler trial, although she was still waiting on the exact date and time.

Before she'd accomplished much, Rivera stopped outside her door. "Come with me to the ME's office?" He twirled a set of keys in his hand.

"Because you don't want to be alone with Rebecca?" Victoria laughed. "Please don't tell me you haven't noticed she has a thing for you."

Rivera grunted. "I've noticed."

"She reminds me of a young Oprah. She's been divorced at least two years now. Not sure why you don't ask her out."

"So, are you coming or not?"

"Sure. Just giving you a hard time. I was thinking the same anyway." Victoria closed her laptop and stood up. "Let's see what Rebecca has to say about the last two victims. I'll meet you in the parking garage. What car number?"

"Number three. But I'll wait for you."

She stopped. "Rivera, you know I can take care of myself. I don't need a personal escort."

"Maybe I don't want to walk out there alone. You think of that?"

She laughed. "Fine. Give me a minute."

# # #

An accident on the highway had traffic at a standstill. Victoria pulled a protein bar from a pocket in her backpack. "In case of emergency." She held it up. "Want half?"

"No, thanks. But I've got to eat something. You mind stopping somewhere?"

"No. I'm hungry, too." She dropped the bar back into her bag. "When you get to the next exit, there's a little Mexican place on South Boulevard. I know the owners. We used to do spin classes together."

"Sounds great." His stomach growled. "Told you."

"You shouldn't skip breakfast." Victoria laughed. "We're almost there."

Inside The Cantina, the Monday lunch crowd was sparse and they had their pick of the red vinyl booths. Both agents ordered tacos and Rivera ordered a Coke. The waiter delivered waters and a basket of chips with salsa. Rivera dug in to them without hesitating while Victoria turned on her tablet and opened her notes. She had to lean toward Rivera to be heard over the music. "What do we still need to follow up on in our search for a connection?"

Rivera dipped two chips into the bowl of salsa and spoke between bites. "Our background checks covered their previous locations, work histories, insurance agents, gym memberships. There's nothing. It's like you said—she's getting revenge for something they did to her."

"Wish we had a crystal ball right now. Okay. We need to dig deeper on this. And let's go back to the Sonesta Hotel after the ME's office."

"You think the detectives are holding back on us?"

"No, it's not that, it's just, we need to go back."

Rivera grabbed another handful of chips. "What would make *you* angry enough to go after people like that?"

"Hmm. Well, if I was crazy and disturbed enough to have a hit list, anyone who tortures animals would be at the top of it."

"Ahh. That was too easy. I should have guessed it."

"How about you?"

He drained most of his water and set it down. "Pedophiles? Yeah, that's it. Perverts that victimize children."

"So if you saw someone assaulting a child, you would go after them?"

"Absolutely."

"So what did our killer see them do?"

Rivera shook his head. "Or maybe we're looking at it in reverse. Maybe the question is—what did they see *her* do?"

Victoria shook her head and dropped it into her hands. "I don't have any idea."

Rivera stood up. "Be right back. Can I get you anything?"

"No, I'm fine." She tapped the top of her almost full glass of water. "Thanks."

Rivera returned at the same time the food arrived. He stood next to the booth while the waiter placed their platters on the table. He took his seat once the waiter left. "No work-talk while we eat. Let's see if we can do it."

Victoria smiled and powered off her tablet. "So, are you and Renee still good friends?"

"We're friends. We don't talk much. She's seeing someone."

Victoria lifted her taco for a first bite. "Is it serious?"

Rivera shrugged and dug into his own food.

Victoria took his limited response as a lack of interest in the topic. She dabbed at her lip with her napkin. "I like this song."

Pretending his fork was a microphone, Rivera closed his eyes. He began to sing a Dave Matthews ballad.

Victoria's mouth dropped. "Wow! You're really good."

He opened his eyes and stopped singing. "Damn straight I am."

She laughed. "Keep going. I like it."

"If you insist." He finished out the refrain in a smooth, low voice, adding a twang. "How about you sing a few verses?"

"You do not want to hear me sing. I promise." She laughed.

"Come on. Can't be that bad." He took a gulp of his soda.

"Nope." She smiled from ear to ear. "But . . . how about this . . . I'll save my singing for when you're really down and need cheering up, because I promise you will laugh your ass off."

Rivera extended his hand across the table and Victoria shook it. "It's a deal." He grinned and finished the last of his drink. "I know you don't go out much when you're not working, but maybe we should do this for real sometime. Go out to eat, but not under the auspices of work and catching a crazed killer."

Victoria smiled. "That might be fun."

174

Rivera cleared his throat and touched his ear. "Hey, uh, there's something I should tell you."

"Yeah?" Whatever was coming, she had a feeling it was going to be interesting. "What's that look for?"

"What look?" Rivera cocked his head.

"Like you just . . . I don't know. Like maybe for once you're not entirely sure of what you're going to say."

Rivera smiled. His gaze never wavered.

"Have I got something on my chin?" She raised her napkin, hovering it near her mouth.

Rivera chuckled. "Your chin is fine."

"What is it then?" Unsure if she should be frowning or laughing, Victoria settled for an uneasy half-smile.

"I just . . ." He crossed his forearms on the table and leaned in. "The reason we've been working together a lot is because . . ."

"Because?"

"I might have been requesting it."

A smile slowly built on her lips. Her stomach fluttered, although she didn't know what would follow his confession. "You have?" She uncrossed her legs and shifted her weight, tucking a wisp of hair behind her ear. "Well . . . that's interesting. I can't wait for you to tell me why. Or do I want to know?" She placed her hand against her cheek. "I mean, I know I'm a lot more pleasant than Agent Poloski . . . and I never have to leave to pick up my kids or watch their recitals like—Oh, dear—Oh, crap." She shook her head.

"What?"

"Talking about picking up kids—you know, my dogs are sort of like my kids and I forgot to call Ned again. Hold on. This will only take a second." She took out her phone and tapped her contacts. She held up one finger, waiting for the call to connect.

"Victoria?"

"Ned, hey."

"Ah!" Ned exclaimed. His laughter was joined by a young woman's voice.

"Oh, dear! Oops!" The woman laughed again in the background.

Victoria's muscles tensed. She twisted her napkin. "Did I catch you at a bad time?" The pitch of her voice had risen.

"I was pouring wine when you called. Apparently, I can't multi-task as well as I thought. Just spilled it." He chuckled, and so did whoever was with him, a light flirty sound.

"But, it's only . . . it's just afternoon." With a flash of anger, Victoria stared intensely at her empty plate.

"Yep. So, what do you need, boss?"

She shoved a stray section of hair away from her face. "Oh, um, I just wanted to make sure you could come back to feed them dinner and hang out there for a while."

"Sure. Are you going out of town? Did you want me to stay over?"

"No. Actually, you don't need to go back. Don't worry about it, I didn't realize you had plans . . . I mean . . . the dogs will be fine. They've got their dog door. They'll be fine." She frowned and pressed the red button to end the call.

Rivera lowered his head to meet Victoria's eyes. "He can't babysit the dogs tonight?"

"What? No, uh. I guess he's on a date. In the middle of the day. I mean, he didn't say it was a date, but it sounded like one." She rotated her palm toward the ceiling. "I don't know why I'm so surprised. But . . ." She looked away, grabbed a few chips, and chewed them absentmindedly. "It's no big deal. The dogs will be fine."

176

"Can't argue with that. If I'm not mistaken, dogs all over the world manage on their own for hours at a time."

"I know, it's just—never mind. Anyway." She sighed and looked past Rivera, over his shoulder. "What were we talking about before I made that call?"

Rivera settled back against the booth. "You know. Work stuff."

"Right."

"Ready to get out of here?" He looked around the restaurant.

"Yeah. Okay."

Rivera spotted their server and signaled to get his attention.

#

Inside the medical examiner's office, gospel music played through the speakers. Dr. Rebecca Boswell, a licensed pathologist, was pushing a gurney with a zipped body bag. A large presence, Rebecca wore hot pink scrubs and black sneakers. Her sleek hair was pulled back in tiny braids.

"Hello," Rivera called.

Rebecca stopped, stared at Rivera, and smiled. "Agents, welcome." She crossed the room and turned down the music. "I was wondering when I was going to see you."

"Hi, Rebecca. We were on our way here yesterday when we got the call about Gomez." Victoria set her hands on the side of a steel gurney as she spoke.

"Someone has been keeping us all busier than usual, haven't they?" Rebecca shook her head.

"What can you tell us?" Rivera asked.

"Nothing you don't already know." She nudged the bridge of her glasses using the heel of her hand. "Same COD for the victims, shot from up close with a small-caliber weapon. The last one, Gomez, took three rounds to the torso. Nothing unusual about how

177

they died, considering." She shrugged. "I've got Gomez's wallet in the back room still, if you want to examine it. It wasn't on him. It was in his car and somehow it ended up here."

"Not exactly protocol, but as long as it's not lost," Victoria said. "We'll go take a look."

"Follow me." Rebecca led them into an office and grabbed a key from a drawer. "Gloves in a box on the wall over there. Plastic sheeting next to it." She unlocked a safe and stood back.

Rivera set a sheet of plastic on a table. Wearing gloves, Victoria scooped up the evidence bag and removed the wallet from inside it. She unfolded the nicked leather sides. She gasped, and her mouth dropped open. Tucked into one of the credit card slots was a blue key card for the Sonesta Hotel. "You've got to be kidding me," she whispered. "I cannot believe we're just finding this out now."

"Wow." Rivera slid the wallet and card back into the evidence bag.

Victoria glared at the wallet. Her mind raced with frustration, mostly targeted at Detective Sullivan. "I told you—How could—"

"There might be an explanation," Rivera said.

"Whatever it is, better late than never." Rebecca peered over their shoulders. "Significant?"

"Definitely," Rivera said. "I think we've identified missing Sonesta customer Jim Johnson. And now we know why Johnson hasn't returned to the hotel. Gomez must have used a fake name."

With a sigh, Victoria pulled off her gloves and tossed them in the trash. "So far, we've got Todd Meiser on the one hand, and on the other—Sonesta Hotel customers being eliminated. That hotel connects all the victims, except for Meiser."

"We need to get back there now." Rivera tucked the evidence bag with the wallet into his coat pocket.

Victoria nodded. "I'll call Sam on the way. I want to see everything he's got on the hotel staff."

"We've already seen it." Rivera started walking toward the door.

"Did we?" Victoria followed him, walking next to Rebecca. "We, as in the FBI? Because I can't believe this happened."

"Local PD interviewed them all and did background checks, but our agents did, too. I saw the report. Useless. Let's talk to the staff again." Rivera stopped in the doorway. "Thanks, Rebecca. You've been a huge help."

"Anytime. Come back and stay longer next time." She smiled at both agents, but her gaze lingered on Rivera.

"I'm calling Sam." Victoria called as they left the ME's building. "Sam, it's Victoria and Rivera. You're on speaker phone."

"Excellent timing, my favorite agents."

"We know you say that to everyone, Sam," Rivera said.

"I was about to call you."

"What's going on?" Rivera asked, pulling the car keys from his pocket.

"I found the companion Meiser met with. That's what she calls herself. Her name is Olivia Papaleia. She didn't know he was dead, by the way. Finally called me back when she heard. She seems young, cooperative, and afraid. I didn't question her, but she started talking anyway. Said she was in classes all day when he was killed, and she has plenty of witnesses. Said she's never been to his house. She met him at a hotel, where—"

Every muscle in Victoria's body tensed with excitement. "Which hotel, Sam?"

"The Vista View Hotel."

179

Victoria's shoulders slumped. "It's like we were so close to winning the lottery and then the last ball popped up with the wrong number."

"Sorry. And she has no priors. Doesn't even have so much as a parking ticket to her name. And that's her real name, I checked it out."

"Good to know, but from what these crimes tell us, whoever is doing this, it's like she recently snapped," Victoria said. "Five kills in a matter of days. She's either getting revenge or she just recently went nuts. The fact that she has no prior record may not matter."

"Give us her address. We'll try to speak with her right now," Rivera said, opening his car door.

"She has alibis you can check, so you'll know soon enough if you like her for any of these murders. Here's her address."

#

With the escort's address programmed in their GPS, Rivera took the next exit to get them headed in the right direction. "It's only a thirty-minute drive, and sort of on the way to the Sonesta Hotel. It will just be a detour."

"What could have happened to get these people killed?" Victoria said. "Why don't we know?"

"Maybe Olivia can tell us." Rivera opened his container of gum with one hand and shook a few into his mouth. "Do you want to call for backup?"

Victoria read the signs and billboards lining the road: Jesus Saves, Fresh Farm Produce Exit 28, Savvy Furniture Mart, Open 365 Days a Year. She shook her head. "There's two of us. Sounds like she couldn't have done it. Let's just call in to Murphy, let him know where we're going. We'll be fine."

Rivera grunted his agreement. "We'll put our Kevlar on before we go in."

Chapter Twenty-Seven

Wearing FBI vests, the agents stood outside the door of the address Sam provided. Their hands hovered by their hips, just above their weapons as they vigilantly watched the doors and paths around them.

"Ready?" Rivera asked.

Victoria nodded and pressed the doorbell. A woman opened the door. The agents quickly scanned her body. She wore a long, fitted sweater, leggings, and dark-rimmed glasses. There was nowhere to hide an easily accessible weapon on her body that would not be detected.

"Olivia Papaleia?" Victoria asked.

"Yes. That's me."

Olivia was of Middle-Eastern descent with olive skin and shining black hair that formed a single French braid between her shoulders. No trace of blonde. She was nothing like Victoria expected.

The agents identified themselves. With a tight-lipped smile, Olivia made a sweeping gesture to welcome them inside. "Please come in." She closed the door and padded away, leading them to a neatly decorated room. On a glass coffee table sat a laptop, a spiral notebook, and a text book—*Modern Political Theories*. The flickering light of a candle cast a small dancing shadow on the back wall. Victoria caught the light aroma of oranges and cloves, reminding her of Christmas.

"Have a seat." Olivia indicated two chairs, part of a comfortable arrangement of furniture, and plopped down on a couch with plush pillows and a faux fur throw. She folded her legs to her side.

How had this confident woman made Sam think she was afraid? The fact that she'd fooled him gave Victoria reason to be wary.

Rivera scooted forward on the edge of his chair. "We're here because you might have been the last person to see Todd Meiser alive. You were with him beginning on Thursday night at the Vista View Hotel, correct?"

"Yes. He wanted company, and that's what I provide." She batted her eyes at Rivera. "Just company. It's all quite legal. He needed a calming presence. I know he was killed in his home. I was never there."

Rivera's expression remained placid, even Victoria couldn't read his thoughts. "When did you part ways?"

"I was with him for less than two hours. I came back here after. My roommate can vouch for that. She's at work right now, but I'll give you her number."

Rivera jotted down the contact information for Olivia's roommate on his pad. "Did you know Todd well?"

"No. Not really."

"Had you ever met him before?"

Olivia looked down at her bare feet, trailed a pink fingernail across her ankle and under a delicate gold anklet.

"We're trying to find a killer," Victoria said. "We're not here to bust anyone for . . . anything else."

She lifted her chin, dipping her head back. "I'm just concerned, worried really, that I might know something I shouldn't know." She sighed. "But I don't think so. So—yes, I've met him before. A few times. Same place."

"The Vista View Hotel."

Olivia set her elbow on the arm of the couch and rested her chin in her hand. "Yes. The one next to the rail road tracks."

Victoria's and Rivera's eyes met. Victoria's body stiffened. "Isn't the Vista View near the shopping mall? I don't think there are any railroad tracks around it." Her voice took on a new, quiet intensity. "Olivia, is there a chance that you met Todd Meiser at the Sonesta Hotel, not the Vista View?"

"Oh. Yes." Olivia grimaced and tugged on the silver earring dangling from her ear. "Sorry. I do mean the Sonesta. The one with the big blue sign. It's not very nice."

For Victoria, the energy in the room completely changed. She wanted to jump up and pump her fist in the air. It was a challenge to maintain her composure. "Did Todd tell you the name he used to check in?"

Olivia allowed herself a slight smile that didn't last long. "He used the name Jason Bourne."

Victoria nodded, but inside she was beaming. One more unknown hotel guest was now accounted for. "At the Sonesta Hotel, did you see anyone speaking to him, or watching him? Anything that seemed unusual or made you uncomfortable?"

"Well, yes, actually, there was something. Todd arrived before me. He planned to meet me at the back entrance and let me in. I was almost at the back door when a woman ran out. She looked angry, although she might have been afraid, it seemed more like anger. And I think she was crying. A man followed right after her. He yelled, 'Come back here. You don't understand.' Something to that effect. Todd saw them too. Before the door closed, and even after, we could hear them fighting behind the hotel."

"Do you know what they were fighting about? Could you hear them?"

"I could hear that they were upset, but I couldn't tell you what it was about."

"And you didn't call the police?"

Olivia shrugged. "No. It didn't seem necessary. People argue. Their argument just made its way into the parking lot. Besides, I had business to attend to. I had an exam to study for after. At first, I thought about going to see if she needed help. But she was yelling just as loud as he was. It was awful, but it seemed like a domestic affair. Not anyone else's business. And it didn't last long."

"How long?"

"Oh . . . I remember. A train went by. The train runs so close to that hotel, it literally shakes the walls and blasts its horn the whole time. I don't know how anyone sleeps there at night. The sound of the train and its horn drowned out the fight. After the train passed, I don't remember hearing anyone."

"And you didn't see the couple again?"

"I did not."

"Can you describe them?"

"Oh . . . gosh." Olivia rolled her eyes up to the ceiling then back down, settling her gaze on Rivera. "He was an average guy, a little scruffy, not someone who takes great care of himself. He had dark hair, I think. And she was sort of pale, washed out."

"What color hair did she have?" Victoria asked.

"Hmm . . . blonde?"

Victoria pushed Olivia's candle toward the opposite end of the table and set out copies of their sketches. "Does this woman look familiar?"

Olivia set her feet on the ground and scooted forward. "In this picture with her hair down, that could be the same woman I saw. She might have looked like that. But I'm not sure. She rushed by me."

"Anything else you can think of?"

She shook her head. "Sorry."

Victoria set out photos of the victims. "Did you see any of these other people?"

Olivia took her time studying the photos. "I'm sorry. I've never seen them before."

"Okay. Do you know if Todd had a girlfriend, particularly one with medium-length or long blonde hair?"

She smiled. "That's not something I would ask him."

Victoria and Rivera exchanged glances in a subtle, practiced way to see if either had more questions to ask. Rivera stood up and Victoria followed.

"So, I'm all good. You're going to call my roommate?"

"Yes. Thank you for your time." Victoria handed Olivia her business card.

Olivia placed the card on the coffee table and stood up with them. "Todd was nice to me. I hope you find out who killed him. I hope you catch the person who killed all these people."

So do we, thought Victoria, walking toward the front door.

"Rivera," Olivia called, her voice soft.

Both agents stopped and turned around.

Olivia dropped her head in a coquettish pose so only her eyes looked up at him from under her long, dark lashes. "That train isn't the only thing that can shake the walls."

He smiled. "I bet it isn't." Then he turned and walked out the door.

Once outside, Victoria laughed. "Guess she isn't concerned that you're with the FBI."

"Guess not." A red tint crept over his face.

"Looks like she's putting herself through college. Whatever she's doing must pay more than working retail."

185

"That's what they tell themselves, isn't it?"

Victoria nudged Rivera's arm. "It appears to be her choice. I like her. And I like that she appreciates you. And if her alibis all check out, it doesn't look like she is involved in any of our cases."

Rivera rubbed the back of his neck. "Now we know that all the victims were staying at the same hotel. The Sonesta is the key to all of this. We got off track because Meiser happened to be a witness in the Butler trial. From the very beginning of all this, you've been saying his death didn't look like a hit."

"Thank you for pointing that out, I'll take the credit." She smiled. "Let's go back there now, to the hotel. I'm surprised Sam didn't find issues with any of the staff. No criminal records and each of them has an alibi for at least some of the murders."

"Maybe they're all in on it together."

"Hmm. No grievances against the hotel owners. No pending lawsuits. But there has to be something."

On the way to their car, Victoria opened her bag and felt her keys in an inner pocket. "We're not far from the office. If you don't mind stopping there, I'll get my own car. The hotel is sort of on the way to my place. Then you can just take this car home after. I mean, if we have a chance to go home tonight."

Rivera nodded as he opened his door. "I don't think you should go home alone."

"I know. Agent Lampros was at my house last night. I feel terrible that he had to stay up because of me. I brought him muffins and coffee when I left the house. I hope someone else gets stuck with the job tonight." Victoria sat and fastened her seat belt. "Oh. I almost forgot. Again. I need to make a quick call." For the first time, she was anxious about calling Ned. Since she'd interrupted his date, she was worried about what she might hear. She pressed a few buttons on her phone and waited. "Hi. I need you to come by tonight and stay a few hours."

"Sure thing. Oh. Are we still on for dinner tomorrow?"

The dinner was only to discuss their trip. That's all it ever was. So why did it seem like everything had changed? "I'm sorry. Can we reschedule the dinner?"

"You have to eat something tomorrow night. I can meet you wherever."

Victoria sighed. "There's just a lot going on. I doubt I'm going to be able to go, or that I'm going to be very good company if I can make it."

"The news says it's five murders now."

"Yes. The whole city is working on catching the perpetrator, it's not just me." Victoria set her free hand on the door frame, gripping the edge. "Although, my team is supposed to be leading the efforts. I'll keep you posted. I mean, you'll know when I'm free because I won't be begging you to come to my house."

"It's what you pay me for."

"Right. But thank you. How are the new little ones doing?"

"They're doing fine. One of them is a little wary of the big boys, but they're holding their own. No worries. Is someone coming to get them soon?"

"I haven't heard anything yet. To be honest, I forgot. We'll give them a few days and then I guess I'll follow up with the family to see what their plan is. Thanks, Ned. I'm very grateful. I'll talk to you later."

"Good luck and . . . be careful."

"I will."

Rivera wove through the rush hour traffic. "You had a dinner date with your dog walker?"

Victoria slid against the door as Rivera hung a right without slowing the car. "Hey, slow down. Nothings on fire." She laughed. "I'm not really sure it was a date. And *had* is the operative word."

"You have stuff in common with this guy? Besides dogs?"

Victoria shrugged. "I guess that's what I might have found out. It wasn't a real date or anything. We had business to discuss. But it probably wasn't a good idea."

"Really. Huh." Rivera turned on the radio and zipped in front of a slower moving car. He grabbed for his gum, dumped a few pieces into his hand, then slapped them into his mouth. "So, taking care of your dogs—is that Ned's only job?"

"It is now. It's a lot of work. Especially when I'm out of town. You've heard of concierge doctors? Well, he's like that, except I'm his only client. And it's not me he's taking care of."

"What did he do before you hired him? Do you know?"

Victoria opened her eyes wide and stared at Rivera for several seconds, then laughed. "Of course I know. You think I would let a stranger into my house to take care of the dogs without vetting him every which way and a few more? Jeez. You know me better than to ask that. I did a comprehensive background check."

"So what did he do?"

"Ned is a veterinarian. He was just a year out of vet school when he moved here. He started his own practice but didn't have enough clients to make ends meet. He has some hefty school loans. That's how I managed to get him. Okay, dad?" She sighed. "I've got enough people questioning my personal decisions already."

"Hey, you have a serial killer suddenly very interested in you. Strange notes left on corpses and strange footprints on your property. Your security cameras weren't working the other night. Time to rethink everyone and everything."

Victoria lowered her eyes and her voice. "Yeah. Okay. I get it. You're right."

Rivera moved his hand toward the center of the car. She thought he was about to reach for her own, but then he dropped it back on the wheel. "I want you to be safe more than I want to be right."

Chapter Twenty-Eight

Two loose ends remained: Jason and Kelly Smith.

They were gone.

I wasn't fast enough.

Beth had their home address. They had seen her close up, not once, but twice. Just like Todd Meiser had seen her inside the hotel. His name hadn't been listed with the other hotel occupants, but she recognized him immediately when she traced his Range Rover's license plate to a registration, then to a photo of him.

First things first. She had to get rid of Horrigan's truck in case they found his body. She turned into the shopping center where she'd first tried to kill the happy-go-lucky singing Smiths. The Walmart parking lot was bustling with cars. She parked the pick-up and hopped on a nearby bus to the airport where she rented a car with the last of her "borrowed" credit cards and fake IDs. She was grateful she had them, but worried about having run out of alternate identities and sources of payment.

She returned to the Vista Hotel. She didn't want to stay there too much longer on Sylvia Malone's newly opened credit card. There was more than one way to end up in prison. But she couldn't go home either. Not with Danny still hounding her.

Inside her hotel room, she pulled a blanket off the closet shelf and wrapped it around her shoulders. The news reports would be starting in a matter of seconds. Plopping onto the pull-out couch, she clicked on the television and found one of the major networks. She bit her lip through a car dealership commercial. A drug

189

commercial for a disease she'd never heard of came next. She chewed on her nails through the long, ridiculous list of side-effects. When the music signaling the news started, she lowered her hand, staring intently at the female newscaster sitting behind the studio desk.

"Breaking news. Another murder committed by someone the police are now calling the Numbers Killer. What are authorities doing to prevent someone else from falling victim? Stay with Channel 14 for the latest."

The other reporter went through his list of what was to come, but Beth tuned him out.

"What? How could they know about my counting? Danny must have told them!"

She jumped up, pacing the length of the room and back. *Two, four, six, eight . . . two, four six, eight . . .* She grabbed a water bottle off the dresser and gulped from it. The newscaster had sensationalized the murders, like Beth was some crazed killer going after people with no rhyme or reason, and no one was safe. She laughed, quick and sharp. Her amusement didn't last long. Danny had betrayed her. To hell with him. She didn't need him. Had she ever? No!

She needed to turn her new-found notoriety and skills into money. Maybe she should contact Raymond Butler and collect a little reward for her efforts? After all, as she now understood, she had inadvertently done him quite a favor. He owed her. But what did she have to hold over him? The deed was done, it wasn't like she could threaten to bring Meiser back to life if the Butlers didn't pay. Perhaps Butler could offer her a job, before he was carted off to jail. Not everyone could hack into an FBI agents' video camera feeds and shut them down. Not everyone could hack into hotel registries and the DMV, matching hotel guests to their rooms and cars. It might have been relatively simple, if some of them hadn't used fake names. She was pretty amazing and deserved a job with a guaranteed paycheck every week. That would be nice for a change.

190

The news report returned, jolting Beth back to attention. The tall brunette woman she'd seen earlier on TV spoke from an outside location.

"The violent killing spree that began yesterday morning with Todd Meiser now includes Robert and Anne Cossman, and Arnold Gomez. Channel 14 news just learned that all the victims had numbers written on their foreheads."

Oh. Of course! That's why they're calling me the Numbers Killer. She laughed with relief. Danny hadn't told anyone about her counting compulsion after all.

The camera view drew back, revealing the parking lot where Beth had left Gomez to die.

"Then, just yesterday afternoon, Arnold Gomez, also visiting the area, was murdered here at the Hampshire Apartments, where he was visiting his nephew. Police say the killer wrote the number six on Gomez' forehead, after he was shot. None of the other victims appear to have any connection to Raymond Butler and the trial that starts in just a few days. But the numbers appear to correspond with the order in which the victims were killed."

Hmm. No mention of Horrigan and his ugly fish shirt because she'd forgotten to write something on his head. But wait . . . That was a good thing! They couldn't know it was her that killed him. Grinning, she focused on the news.

"Channel 14 will stay on top of the investigation as authorities track down the killer. If the numbers really do represent the order in which the victims were killed—." The reporter frowned, like she was the one who had to solve these crimes, not Agent Heslin and Agent Rivera, "—where are victims number one and five?"

Victim number one? Beth's knees shook, and the room spun. *What's happening to me?* She reached for the wall to brace herself. Fear spiked her adrenaline and she desperately wished she wasn't alone. Being alone made her situation so much more frightening. Where was Danny when she needed him? She fought the wave of nausea rising from her stomach, dropping her head into her hands.

191

She managed to lower herself to the floor before she fell unconscious.

The news was still playing when she woke up. Lifting her head off the carpet, she rubbed her forehead. The nausea had passed, but her ears throbbed with the onset of a headache. She dragged her purse off the desk and onto the floor. Removing the gun first, she rummaged through the mess of useless junk in search of aspirin. *Where the hell is it?* The bottle wasn't there, but her fingers closed around two lint covered pills at the bottom of her bag. Those would have to do. She trudged off to the bathroom to wash them down with water, then returned to the television.

"Channel 14 News has just learned that the Numbers Killer left a threatening note for an FBI agent at the murder scene of Arnold Gomez."

"What?" Beth sat up, gasping. "A threatening note? No. No. No. I would never do that." Her hands flew up to cover her mouth. "I didn't threaten her! How could they think that? I was trying to protect her. I told her to be careful. I told her to watch her back!" She slumped against the wall, tearing at her hair. This was awful! How could she have been so misunderstood?

She had to see Heslin and clear up the terrible misunderstanding. It couldn't wait another second. But how? How could she get to her with those crazy dogs guarding her mansion?

Squatting on the floor next to the coffee table, she woke up her laptop. Waiting on the hotel's internet service was like watching grass grow, but within fifteen minutes she had intercepted the feed going from Heslin's home to the security firm who monitored her videos. This time, instead of shutting them down, she watched.

The house was huge, so on her screen, each live feed was smaller than the size of a postage stamp. Clicking on an image enlarged it. She needed to find where Heslin kept the dogs. She clicked on all the outside views. Finding no fenced kennels or pens, she switched to the interior views. Many of the rooms were almost empty of furniture, but covered with large stuffed squares, giant circles, and bean bag chairs. Some sort of contemporary decorating trend? A room with a sectional couch and a large television had the same squares and circles, but there, almost every stuffed shape had a dog on it. How many beds did those dogs need? Some of the creatures were laying around with their ridiculously long legs sticking straight out like poles, their mouths lolling open. A few were laying half-on and half-off the giant square beds. Some were curled up inside bean bag-looking chairs, their legs tucked beneath them. What a life they had!

Beth enlarged the view of the kitchen and her jaw dropped. What the—? A bolt of anger shot her to full attention. There was a tall man in Agent Heslin's kitchen, opening cabinets and drawers, acting like he was right at home. He had light brown hair and looked like he was in his late twenties, or early thirties. His muscles rippled under his jeans and form-fitting quarter-zip top, one of those silky athletic shirts. From all the pictures Beth had studied of the Heslin family, she would have recognized Victoria's brother, who had blonde hair just like his sister. This was not the brother. "Who the hell is that?" If Rivera was Mr. Sexy, then this guy was Mr. Sexier. But what was he doing in Heslin's house? He didn't belong there. And did Rivera know about him?

Beth quickly searched through the other feeds, clicking like mad to see if Heslin was somewhere else in the house. She didn't find her or anyone else. Unless the agent was in one of the bathrooms, this guy was alone in her house.

She returned to the feed from the kitchen. Mr. Sexier stood against the large, white-marble topped island in the center of the room. He was busy doing something, but Beth couldn't see what because his back shielded her view. She leaned closer to her laptop. Mr. Sexier moved to the side. Syringes lay spread across the counter. *What was going on there?* One by one, he filled them from a glass bottle. Beth squinted. The front of the bottle had a prescription label, it wasn't something from a store. Whatever he was doing, it was extremely suspicious.

He opened the refrigerator and removed a square, plastic container. Then he called to the dogs. *The video has sound!* They flew from their beds and surrounded him. He opened the container. Without a trace of hesitation, they gobbled down the food he handed them. The man grabbed the collar of a big dog, striped brown and tan like a tiger, telling the animal he was a good boy. Behind the man's back, his other hand held a syringe. Slowly, he moved his hand toward the dog's thigh. Once there, in one swift movement, he jabbed the dog with the syringe and depressed the plunger.

Beth gasped.

What the hell is he doing? Is he trying to kill Agent Heslin's dogs?

Chapter Twenty-Nine

Rivera picked the short straw on updating Murphy, so Victoria arrived at the Sonesta Hotel before him. She parked her SUV in the back corner of the parking lot, away from the main entrance, to survey the area without being on display herself. From the cooler in her backseat, she grabbed a yogurt and spoon. The yogurt wasn't exactly cold, but it wasn't quite warm yet either, so she went ahead and opened it. She only had a few minutes to finish eating and pull up her video camera feeds to check on her dogs. Before too much time passed, she wanted to be sure there wasn't another "glitch" with the system.

Four of her dogs were in the family room, three of them on dog beds, and one on the couch. All slept soundly. Leo and Bella slept side by side next to the picture window. Victoria tapped the screen to change rooms and found Eddie by himself in the kitchen. With his butt up and his tail wagging, he swatted his toy and then hopped after it. Izzy trotted into the room, her tail wagging like mad, attempting to join in his game.

Victoria smiled, eating her yogurt and watching her happy dogs. A year ago, Izzy was found malnourished and dehydrated, tied to the back of a house in Seville in the blazing sun. Victoria had pictures from when Izzy was first brought to the shelter. The vet had pulled more than fifty bulging tics off the pup's ears, treated her for mange, worms, and burns from God only knew what. The playful dog with shiny fur romping around her kitchen looked nothing like the despondent animal who had been rescued from a hellish life of neglect and abuse.

Eddie and Izzy froze in unison, ears up, and muscles tensed. After a few seconds of standing frozen like statues, they raced out of the room.

Ned's voice sang out. "Who wants to go for a walk next?"

An unfamiliar pang resonated inside her. She had become used to the concept of Ned being around whenever she needed him. The threat of him being with somebody else bothered her more than she would have thought.

Ned stepped into the entryway carrying leashes and wearing a Vanderbilt zip top and jeans.

The passenger side door opened with a sudden click and the interior lights came on. "I've got the folder with—"

Victoria gasped. The spoon dropped and clattered against the cup holder. Her hand flew to her sidearm.

"Oh, sorry. Didn't know I would startle you." Rivera sat down next to her and pulled the door closed.

She laughed, placing her hand over her chest. "Good thing you're not the perp."

Rivera frowned, watching the image on her phone. "That's Ned?"

"Yes. Jeez, I'm still trembling, here."

"What's he doing?"

"I don't know. I just turned the video on. He was supposed to give the dogs their shots today. Not sure if he remembered."

Rivera reached for her phone. "Can I see him?"

"Sure. You can even hear him." After handing him her phone, she collected her spoon from the floor, wiped it off with a paper towel, and dropped it back into the cooler with the empty yogurt container. She leaned in to see what Rivera was seeing. A smiling Ned attached leashes and spoke to the dogs while they jumped up and down, weaving around him like it was the best day of their lives.

Rivera's expression concealed any emotion.

"Let's get out there before it storms again," Ned said to the dogs. He began singing *Thunder* by Imagine Dragons, substituting in a few of his own lyrics.

"Here, give me that," Victoria held out her hand. "I feel bad that we're spying on him."

Rivera returned her phone.

"Did I tell you he agreed to go to Spain with me next month?" Victoria shifted in her seat. Her lips were pressed together, she didn't have the heart to smile.

"For another one of those dog group visit things?"

"Yes." She frowned and mimicked his deep raspy voice. "For one of those dog group visits."

"Don't you ever vacation at a resort, like normal rich people? And why Spain? Aren't there plenty of dogs here in the US that you can rescue?"

"Yes. Absolutely. And I do help . . . financially . . . It's just that some breeds really touch your heart. My mother had a thing for greyhounds, and the dogs at these shelters are all suffering, or they were, I mean. At the end of the hunting season, hundreds and hundreds of them are discarded by hunters like they're pieces of garbage. And few will find forever homes if they aren't sent to other countries for adoption." Victoria took one last glance at Ned leashing up her dogs before shutting off her device and pocketing it. "So, what's the plan?"

"Interview the staff again." Rivera placed his hand on the door handle.

"Good idea." Victoria turned away from Rivera. They both opened their doors and got out. "And first, let's take another look around inside."

"In case there are bodies stuffed in the cleaning supply closets
. . ."

"At this rate, I wouldn't be surprised." The doors clicked shut
and Victoria pressed the key to lock her car. "And I want to know
why we didn't know about Gomez staying here until we found the
key in his wallet."

They went straight to the front desk to introduce themselves
and took down the names of the employees currently working the
desk and on the floors. There had to be at least a dozen other
detectives and agents working the Numbers Killer case from every
angle, but Victoria and Rivera were the only ones at the hotel.

Victoria's phone rang. She glanced at the screen, frowned, and
held up a finger. "Sorry. It's Ned. Just give me one minute."

A frown appeared on Rivera's face.

Victoria wandered a few feet away from him to answer her
phone. "Hey, Ned. Everything okay?"

"No. Sorry to bother you on the job, but Sasha is acting really
strange."

"Sasha?"

"Yeah. Sasha is pacing and panting. I think she's sick and uh,
you should take her somewhere. Can you come home now?"

Victoria froze. An icy chill skittered down her back. "Sasha?"
Sasha passed away a few months ago from osteosarcoma. Ned
administered her chemo for months and eventually put her down
while Victoria held her and sobbed. Was he just getting her dogs'
names confused? Impossible. He wouldn't forget her name. He
knew all her dogs and everything about them. And if one of them
was ill or injured—something beyond what he could handle—he
was to rush them to the emergency vet hospital. Victoria didn't
take any chances with their health.

"Um, okay. I'll be there soon." Her voice wavered as the
phone went dead on the other end. What was he trying to tell her?

Was this code that another one of her dogs had broken a leg due to osteo, and he just didn't want to deliver the terrible news over the phone? A dull, heaviness crept into her chest. Did he have to put one of the dogs to sleep immediately, and wanted her to come back to say goodbye?

Rivera's dark eyes met her own. "Everything okay?"

She clamped one hand around her waist. "Um, I don't know. Look—I'm sorry. I hate to do this, but I have to leave. I'll be back as soon as I can. Okay?"

He narrowed his eyes, crossing his arms over his chest, and studied her. "What's going on?"

"I'm really not sure." Would Ned pull some sort of stunt to get her home because she had cancelled their date? Was this his way of showing her she could make the time? If that was his plan, she would be furious. Beyond furious. But it didn't seem like something Ned would ever do. No, something terrible had happened to one of her dogs. Already, her heart ached. Her limbs felt numb. She couldn't bear to consider which one was hurt.

Rivera's phone buzzed from inside his coat pocket. He slid it out and looked at the screen. "Murphy. I better take it."

Victoria waved over her shoulder and hurried off. In search of clues, she tapped the icon to view her security cameras and clicked the page with the video feeds.

They were all blank again.

A tendril of terror traveled down her neck and into her toes as her mouth went dry. She picked up her pace and called Ned back. His phone rang until it went to voicemail. She ran the rest of the way to her SUV, got in, and peeled out of her spot.

When she drove past the entrance, Rivera held his hand up and mouthed something. She didn't stop. She could call him later, once she knew what she was dealing with. At this point, all she could tell him was that something strange was going on at her house. Something that required her immediate attention.

The timing could not have been worse. They were closing in on the killer, had to be. The secret to everything was somewhere locked inside the Sonesta Hotel. She'd come back as soon as she could. She swallowed the lump in her throat and sped down the street, driving 70 in a 50 mile per hour zone.

Chapter Thirty

Rivera ran his hand over his head as he watched Victoria's taillights disappear into the night. What had Ned told her that made her spooked? Whatever it was, she hadn't wanted to share it with him.

Rivera did not consider Ned as a competitor—until he saw him on screen. In the past, every time Ned's name came up, he'd pictured a goofy-looking, skinny guy in a big baggy T-shirt and loose pants. Like Shaggy from the Scooby-Doo cartoons, or the hiker who found the Cossmans. The live video proved he'd been way off. The dude was good looking and had the run of her house. Maybe there was something more than their employer and employee relationship. Guess he and Victoria weren't as close as he thought. But when he pushed Ned and his emotions aside, he was even more uncomfortable with Victoria's sudden departure. She had never left work at a critical moment before. So, whatever Ned told her had to be a big deal. Putting that together with the notes she'd received from a killer, and alarm signals went off in his brain.

I should go after her.

Murphy's ranting broke through his thoughts. "Can you hear me?"

"Yeah, boss." Rivera forced himself to unclench his jaw and focus.

"Cops just found Horrigan's truck. Abandoned in a Walmart parking lot. Another dead end."

"Hmm," was all Rivera could think of in response. "I'm at the hotel. I'm going to find out what happened here if it kills me."

"Agent Poloski figured out why Gomez paid cash for his hotel room and checked in under a false name. His stuff is still in his room, by the way. I thought it might be our biggest clue yet, that Gomez knew someone was after him. But Poloski discovered that Gomez owes money to his ex and this follows a trend of not wanting her to know he had money for a pseudo-vacation and a hotel."

"Jeez. Okay. Let me know if he finds out there's more to it." Rivera ended the call and started walking back to the hotel with the folder of photos and sketches under his arm, cracking his knuckles. He stopped, turned toward his car in the parking lot, took a few steps, then turned again. With a loud, heavy sigh, he walked inside to the center of the three-story lobby and looked up at the upper floors. He closed his eyes and took a deep breath, taking in the faint smell of must, the muted sounds of shuffling feet, and a few murmurs coming from behind the reception desk. He opened his eyes. Behind the registration desk stood an overweight young lady in her early twenties wearing glasses. Her name tag said Betty. Next to her stood a bearded man who looked slightly older, also wearing a black blazer with black pants. The man kept his focus on something behind the counter. Betty tucked a stray hair behind her ear and smiled at him. "Hi. You checking in?"

Rivera held up his badge. "FBI."

"Oh. Again." She blinked and squared her shoulders. The male worker beside her straightened up and leaned forward against the desk. "I'm the manager on duty. Can I help you?"

"Aren't you supposed to wear a name tag?"

"Can't find it today. My name is Alex."

"Where can we speak privately, Alex?"

Alex lifted his hand toward the door behind the desk. "Come this way." He raised a movable piece in the side of the counter, so Rivera could walk through.

"I need you to come, too," Rivera told Betty. "I know you've already spoken to detectives, so I apologize for putting you through this *again*, as you say, but it's important."

Alex nodded. "Sure."

Rivera glanced out through the office window toward the front desk. "Have you seen anyone suspicious here? Any unusual behaviors that stick out these past few days?"

Betty pushed on the arm of her glasses. "We already told the detectives, and the agents, but there was one guy who left a few days ago."

"The one who wanted a specific room number, right?" Alex grinned. "Said he knew it was ridiculous but just to 'work with him.' It was just . . . strange."

"Yes. That was him." Betty's eyes had lit up with excitement. Or maybe she was just nervous about the investigation being focused on her place of employment. "He was wearing a baseball cap, can't remember what it said now, but I'm pretty sure he was wearing a cap. He's gone now, but he never checked out. Left a few days earlier than he had the room reserved for. I heard that the credit card he used wasn't his. It was some sort of identity theft thing. But you know what? I'm just remembering this—I'm pretty sure he asked for two key cards."

Two? The guy posing as Thomas Wilson and whoever he was with—were they the couple Olivia saw running out the back door? Was his companion the mystery killer? Or did they have absolutely nothing to do with the murders? Rivera opened his folder and showed Alex and Betty the pictures of their killer compiled by the police artists. "Have you seen this woman?"

Betty picked up the photo and drew it closer to face. "No, I don't think so."

203

Rivera pressed his lips together and silently sighed. Just because the staff hadn't seen her, didn't mean she hadn't been there. He trusted Olivia and what she claimed to have seen. Her "that might be her" response to the Smith's sketches was the most hopeful testimony they had so far.

He scanned the memos hung on a bulletin board next to his head. "Any kind of get together or meeting being held here?"

Betty shrugged. Alex shook his head.

The agent picked up the pictures and put them back in his folder. "A sales opportunity? A reunion of any kind? A hiking or fishing club?" None of the things he mentioned would be a fit for all the victims, but there had to be some commonality that hadn't occurred to them yet.

"Not that I know of. And I've worked every day this week." Alex's eyes flashed toward the door, then back to Rivera. "We're more likely to have guests who pay with cash and don't want anyone to know they're here than we are to have business meetings, if you get my drift. This place isn't . . . you know what I mean, don't you?"

"I understand. I've got some pictures for you." Rivera opened his folder and set down the same photos he'd shown to Olivia earlier. "Did you see any of these people together? Talking? Coming or going together?"

Betty stared, covering her mouth with her hand. "I recognize some of them as the people who were killed."

Rivera saw the fear in her eyes. The hotel's guests were more at risk than the witnesses for the Butler case. The police should be guarding them instead. But none of the victims had been killed at the hotel. Should the hotel close until the killer was apprehended? The media didn't know about the connection yet, but surely once the word spread about the victims' sole connection, everyone would flee and cancel reservations as quickly as they could. Once word got out, the hotel wouldn't be able to give rooms away. "Can you get me the names of everyone staying here for the past four days, with their room numbers?"

"Yes. We've already done that for the FBI and the police, like five . . ."

"I'd like to see it again."

"It will just take a few minutes." Alex shook the mouse on a nearby computer and woke it up.

Rivera left the office and walked to the far corner of the lobby where he had a view of the entire space. He called Victoria. There was no answer.

Alex returned and presented Rivera with several printed pages. The agent set them down on a coffee table. He jotted down the names and room numbers of the victims in order of their deaths. He also wrote down the Smiths' names, since it was possible, even likely, they had twice been targeted and followed.

Meiser, aka Jason Bourne: room 267.

Cossmans: room 383.

Gomez, aka Jim Johnson: room 145.

Horrigan: room 125.

Smiths: room 123.

And the still missing Thomas Wilson: room 332.

The hotel employees hovered nearby, ready for another request. Rivera stared at the information and rubbed his chin. The victims' rooms weren't in consecutive order, nor were they even on the same floor. He handed Betty his list. "I'll need access to these six rooms."

"Sure. Just . . . I'll be right back." She pivoted around and returned to the office.

Five minutes later, carrying room keys in six different labeled sleeves, Rivera headed to the room occupied by the Smiths. It had already been cleaned and made ready for the next occupants. He

205

didn't expect to find anything there, but he slipped on gloves and searched every corner, shelf, and drawer for possible answers. His eyes traveled the room one last time searching for anything that didn't belong. He moved the drapes aside and peered out the window into the dark woods. Beyond a large berm, twisted branches bent and straightened in the wind.

A glance at the bedside table clock told him Victoria should have made it to her house by now.

He walked down the hall, poked through Horrigan's belongings, and found nothing of interest. He took the stairs to the second floor and the room Meiser and Olivia had used. The room had already been cleaned, occupied, and cleaned again. But in room 225, Gomez's belongings were still inside. Again, nothing in the room struck Rivera as significant.

On the third floor, in room 383, the Cossmans' stuff had been cleared away since his last visit with Victoria. By request of the authorities, the hotel had been told not to give the room to any new customers yet. Rivera took another quick look. He didn't expect to spot anything new, and he was right.

Thomas Wilson's room, 332, had also been cleaned before the hotel had been instructed to leave it as is.

Except for room 332, each of the other rooms shared the same layout and the same view on one side of the building. The only other common thread between all was being in close proximity to each other between three floors of the Sonesta Hotel last Friday night. The same night Olivia saw the mystery couple fighting.

What are we missing?

Rivera parted the curtains and stared outside toward the woods again. Nice enough as a backdrop, if you didn't look too closely. Not a forest exactly, but enough trees for teens to hide in and guzzle beers. A place to toss trash into for those too lazy to make the trek to the dumpster. Big enough for small creatures, the ones who occasionally ventured out onto the highway for an unplanned game of Russian roulette. From his current angle, he spotted the start of a narrow trail, snaking haphazardly through overhanging limbs.

Removing his gloves, he checked his phone again for a message from Victoria. Doing something was better than doing nothing.

He walked down to the first floor and left the hotel through the backdoor. Outside, a dampness hung heavy in the cold air, descending with the gloom as if it meant to creep into every corner, every crevice. He crossed the parking lot and stopped somewhere between the building and the edge of the woods. Looking back at the hotel, he scanned the roof and the exterior walls. He located the rooms he'd just explored by their dark, unlit windows. Had all the victims seen something behind the hotel that put them in danger? After a few seconds of staring, he pivoted to face the woods. He'd have a quick check, and if Victoria still hadn't called him back, he was heading to her house.

Intermittent gusts of wind cut through his sports coat. A faint, unpleasant smell wafted from somewhere close by. A dead squirrel maybe—the little creatures didn't only die on the highway. He rubbed his neck. Something about the woods bothered him.

He scanned the edge, where the woods met the patchy grass, found the trail opening, and headed in. Tall, wet weeds slid against his pants. With each step deeper into the canopy of tangled trees and fallen branches, the smell grew stronger and more repulsive. Surprising that the hotel staff hadn't received a request to do something about it yet. Or maybe they had.

The swishing of sodden, fallen leaves accompanied his steps. It took stumbling over a bumpy root for him to get with it and turn on his phone's flashlight. Broken foliage indicated someone or something else much larger than a raccoon or possum had been through recently. His heart beat faster as he stepped slowly, alert for anything unusual.

The electric whoosh and the clickety-clack of an approaching train cut through the silence. The horn blasted, the noise steadily building to a roaring crescendo. Olivia's claim that the train blocked out all other noise rang true. He took another step forward. A metal can crunched under his foot. A few more yards ahead, a piece of white fabric floated above the ground, glowing like a ghostly apparition in the small circle of light emanating from his phone. Rivera peered toward the fabric. The smell was strong. A few steps closer and the outline of a torso became visible under the white fabric. A man with pale bloated skin and dark hair was lying face up. A single word covered his forehead. Not written in black ink, but in deep pink strokes of color. Lipstick.

Rivera edged closer, struggling to decipher the letters. B. E. T. R. He couldn't make out the rest. He looked away, cleared his head of assumptions, and tried again.

Betrayer.

He'd found victim number one.

Chapter Thirty-One

The time for medical attention had long passed. The man had been dead for several days. If the smell wasn't enough of a giveaway, the damage from scavengers—tiny missing chunks of flesh—made it certain. Rivera pulled a pair of gloves from his pocket and crouched down, disturbing as little as possible around him. The man had been shot at least twice. Black stains circled his collar bone, stomach area, and the grass and leaves around him. He had died right there in the woods. Rivera put the gloves on and searched the dead man's pockets for identification. He found a wallet with a license inside. The name on it meant nothing to him.

The train had passed, but the wind was starting to howl. He called the medical examiner's office and Rebecca answered.

"It's Rivera. I found another gunshot victim."

"Hello, Rivera. Where did you find him?"

"Sonesta Hotel. Can you come out?" He put Rebecca on speaker and moved his flashlight beam slowly over the ground, looking for shell casings or other evidence.

"It just so happens that I can, for you. I can be there almost immediately." The sound of movement and metal clinking came through the phone, like Rebecca was putting away her tools.

"You know where it is?"

"Yes, I do."

"Good. Drive around the back. Look for the dumpster. I'll meet you there." He glanced at the time and at his messages. Still no word from Victoria.

"Hold tight. I just have to clean up here and grab my bag. Then I'll be on my way."

"Not sure what you'll find. He's been there awhile and with the rain . . . It's starting again now. Sounds like a storm coming."

"Whatever there is to see, I'll do my best with it. I'm also good at my job." She chuckled. "I'll call Forensics on my way."

"Thanks, Rebecca."

The rain was just a cold drizzle, but the wind was cold and biting when Rivera called Murphy to give him an update.

Murphy huffed into the phone. "Why the hell didn't anyone find that body before?"

"Don't know, boss."

"I can't come out there. I'm up to my neck in this other thing. I'll call the Chief of Police, so he doesn't feel left out. Glad Rebecca and forensics will get there first."

On the verge of shivering, Rivera called Victoria next. Still no answer. She'd always answered his calls before, no matter what she was doing, even when she was out walking her dogs. Once she'd even picked up in the middle of taking a shower. He left a message asking her to call him immediately and told her he had found another body. Victim number one. He bit into his lower lip, his concern for Victoria escalating; his bad feeling about her situation growing worse. He had to wait for Rebecca to arrive. But then he was getting in his car and driving straight to Victoria's house.

His call to Sam went to voicemail. He left a message with the victim's name. "I'm going to text you an image of his license. Tell me anything you can about him." He ended the call and sent Sully a text, then read case updates in his email until the ME's familiar white van appeared. The drizzle changed into a light but steady shower as a young man stepped down from the driver's side and Rebecca emerged on the passenger side.

"Over here." Rivera waved from the edge of the woods. He was pleased Rebecca brought someone with her. He didn't intend to wait until she was finished, but also wouldn't have felt right about leaving her alone.

"What have we got?" Rebecca carried a bag of data collection tools. Her assistant walked behind her carrying an umbrella and lighting equipment.

Rivera wiped water from his forehead with the back of his hand. "Hey, Rebecca. Hi—"

"Eric. I'm an assistant. Just started last week."

"Hi, Eric. You got here fast." Rivera walked toward the path. "The vic is back here. He's been dead a few days."

"We hustled to get here before the rest of the cavalry arrives and tramples the scene. You think this one is also a victim of the Numbers Killer?" Rebecca asked.

"I'm sure." Rivera lifted a branch to avoid getting hit in the face.

"I hope he's the key to stopping the killer." Rebecca ducked under the branch.

"So do I." Rivera led the way to the body, staying off the path and walking right through the brush to preserve evidence. "There he is."

Rebecca followed Rivera's gaze to the corpse. "I smell him already. He's dead. You got that part right."

Eric set up the lights while Rebecca removed items from her bag. "You need a hat to keep the rain out of your eyes," Rebecca said, talking to Rivera but studying the scene before her. "I've got an extra one in the van you can have."

"I can't stay." Rivera glanced over his shoulder toward the parking lot. "Unless you need me for something specific."

Rebecca chuckled. "Nothing I need you for here." She glanced at him sideways. "Everything okay?"

"Yeah." Rivera rocked back on his heels. "I've got to go check on . . . a situation. I'll call and either meet you back here or at your office."

"Okay. No problem. Forensics is on their way. I'll give you a personal update as soon as I'm done. And good luck with your situation."

Rivera raced through the rain to his car, threw open the door, and sped out of the hotel parking lot with the rain battering his roof.

Chapter Thirty-Two

For the last few miles to Heslin's house, Beth drove her rental behind a small red car. Large magnets advertising *Farm Fresh Meals* decorated the back and sides. The car's brake lights came on as it approached the large iron gates. It stopped in Heslin's driveway. Beth pulled up alongside it, hopped out of her sedan, and walked up to the driver's window. "Hi. You're delivering?"

"Yes." The woman smiled sheepishly. "A little late. I got behind."

"I'll take that for you. I'm a friend of Agent—a friend of Victoria's. I'm going up to the house."

"Oh, okay. Are you sure?"

"Of course I'm sure." Beth forced a smile.

"All right. That will help. I'll get the bag." She removed it from the trunk. "Thanks."

"You're welcome." Beth maintained her fake smile. *Now drive away.*

She returned to her rental and waved the other woman away. Once the red car had disappeared down the road, she drove past the entrance and parked around a bend on the side of the road, where the car wouldn't be seen by anyone entering at the front gate. She dropped her gun in the delivery bag, hustled back to the gate, and pressed the buttons to announce her presence. "Hi. I have the—" Oh crap. What is it called? She glanced down at the bag. "The Farm Fresh Meals delivery for Victoria Heslin."

213

"Kristen?" said a deep, masculine voice. *Figured Mr. Sexier would sound like that.*

"No. Kristen is sick today. This is Beth. Are you going to open the gate? Food is getting cold." *Two, four, six, eight, ten, twelve . .* .

"The food is supposed to be cold."

"Oh. Fine. No one told me what's inside." *Two, four, six, eight, ten, twelve, fourteen . . .* "I have other deliveries to make." She swallowed hard, her mouth dry.

The gate inched open, swinging in a slow arc across the fancy pavers. *Yes! I'm in!* Beth hurried forward carrying the bag. She didn't know where the delivery people usually took the bag of food and she didn't care. Somehow, she would get past the guard dogs. Perhaps Mr. Sexier really had killed them today and she had nothing to worry about. Although what would that make him? Someone to watch out for, at the least. She walked around to the shadowy area at the back of the house. She'd just set foot on the edge of the stone patio when the dogs came rushing out, barking.

"Damn! No! Stay back! Bad dogs!" With her heart pounding and fear threatening to paralyze her muscles, she grabbed her gun from the bag. She violently shook the bag upside down, dumping its contents to the ground. Kicking at one of the boxes, she sent it flying up into the air, scattering roasted vegetables around the patio.

The dogs immediately forgot about her. They scarfed up the food like live vacuum cleaners. All except for the two smaller mutts who didn't really fit in with the others. Something about them was familiar. They stood together, away from the rest of the pack, barking, and snarling at Beth like they had their own set of rules.

Sweating and breathing hard, Beth yanked the tops off two other boxes of food and tossed their contents away from the house. The dogs scrambled after it.

With her gun cocked in front of her chest, and not taking her eyes off the animals, she hurried away. Grabbing the back door—*please be unlocked!*—she swung it silently open, jumped inside, and pulled it shut behind her. She slumped her back against the tall windows. On the other side of the glass, the dogs were eating and sniffing their noses over the ground. She sighed with relief. They were out and she was in.

She took a few quiet steps across the floor. Nothing creaked or groaned. Of course it didn't. Everything in the fancy house looked perfect, but not that it mattered, the dogs had already made enough of a racket. She stopped in the kitchen to admire the room, her mouth hanging open. The space was big and open but warm and inviting at the same time. Beautiful wood floors gleamed, and stately marble covered the counters. The high-tech stainless appliances—*a computer in the fridge?*— looked like something from a future decade. The tiny video feed images hadn't done it justice. Did it get any better than this? Actually—yeah- same set up but without the faint, lingering smell of dogs. Still - just wow! And if what Beth suspected was true, Heslin didn't deserve to live there.

A framed picture hung on the wall—the same family Beth saw online. Except in this photo, they were relaxed and laughing instead of formal and posed. She was reaching to touch it when an angry voice blasted through the silence from behind her.

"Who are you?"

She jerked around to see Mr. Sexier, a towering presence with his arms crossed.

She lifted her gun, aiming it at his chest. His eyes grew wide. He took several steps back.

Beth swallowed and cleared her throat with a sharp cough. "Listen, Mr. Sexier, I've killed people, and I won't hesitate to do it again. Do what I say, and don't you dare try to trick me."

"Ahh, yes ma'am. What is it you want?"

"Ma'am? What the—? I'm not an old lady!" She forced her anger out through her stare.

"I know." He opened his palms toward the ceiling. "I was just being polite."

Beth shook the gun. "First, I want to know who you are and what you're doing here."

"You want to know what *I'm* doing here? Shouldn't—"

Beth gritted her teeth and screamed. "Answer my question!"

"I'm Ned McCallister. I take care of the owner's dogs." He looked past her, out the glass door. "And since you dumped dinner on the ground, looks like I'm going to be her chef tonight as well."

Beth sneered. "Glad you can find humor in this situation. But let me tell you something, there's nothing funny about it. And it didn't look like you were taking care of them today. Looked like you were trying to kill them."

"Kill them? Why would you think—and how would you know anyway? Were you watching me?"

"Since I'm the one holding the gun, you don't really get to ask questions." She scanned the kitchen and gestured toward the leather bar chairs. "Go sit down on that chair thing over there."

The dogs swarmed back into the house, a caravan of twisting and turning, sniffing and snorting, hyper creatures.

Beth jumped back. "What the hell?"

"Dog door." Ned tilted his head toward a giant rectangular hole in the wall.

"Get them out of here right now. Get them out!" She kept the gun pointed on him. "Or I'll finish off what you started today."

"What I started?" He walked toward one of the doors leading out of the kitchen. "Come on, dogs. This way. Come on."

Beth followed close behind, keeping his body in the range of what she could hit without missing. "Don't try anything."

216

The dogs followed him. He shut the door and turned around to face her. "What's going on?"

"That's exactly what I'm here to find out. But not without Agent Heslin. Call her and tell her to come here."

"Tell her to walk into a potential ambush? I'm not doing that."

Now what? Without taking her eyes off him, she paced the floor. "Listen, Ned. You might be so stupid and brave that you're willing to sacrifice your life so your girlfriend doesn't get hurt, but are you willing to sacrifice one of her dogs? Seems to me she really cares about them. What would she think if all her dogs died because you wouldn't cooperate? Guess she wouldn't need you anymore if that happened. In fact, maybe that's a great idea. Maybe that's what's best for everyone. If I kill them all now, you can go before you've ruined Heslin's whole relationship with Rivera."

"Wait. Calm down. There's no reason to hurt the dogs. And I really have no idea what you're talking about." Ned shook his head.

"Don't look at me like I'm stupid. Make the call!"

Frowning, Ned reached for his phone on the counter.

"Wait! Let those dogs back in."

"Now you want them back in?"

"Just let them in! Some of them."

Ned opened the door and called to the dogs. They all rushed in. Beth took a step back, cringing at their exuberance. "Not all of them!"

"Oops," he said, not sounding one bit sorry that he hadn't done exactly what she told him to do.

Beth shifted the gun's aim to the pack of dogs bouncing and leaping around Ned. "Now call Agent Heslin and tell her to come home because one of the dogs is hurt and you need her help. Do not say anything else. Do not tell her I'm here. Do not mention anything about a gun. One wrong word and I will start shooting these dogs. I will. I really, really will. Is that understood?"

Ned's face hardened. He moved his gaze over the dogs. They were all looking up at him like he was royalty, although they occasionally eyed Beth in a way that bothered her immensely. The two smaller ones resumed snarling at her.

Ned glared at Beth as he picked up his phone.

After thirty minutes, Beth's arms ached with exhaustion, tired from holding the gun raised for so long. "Where is she?"

"She said she was coming." Ned sighed. A big white dog rested its head on Ned's lap. Ned stroked its neck. "You know she's a federal agent, right?"

"Of course I know that. Where was she when you talked to her?"

"I already told you. I have no idea."

Through the floor to ceiling windows, a bolt of lightning illuminated the sky in shades of deep purple. With a backdrop of ghostly black branches, shadows moved around the patio. Beth wasn't sure if there was really something out there, or if it was just an illusion. In the corner of the kitchen, the two little dogs hadn't stopped barking and snarling since she arrived. "Shut up, shut up, shut up," she hissed at them. Their yapping only grew louder. "What the hell is their problem? Why are they doing that to me?"

Ned shrugged. "They've been nothing but friendly and submissive, until you came along."

With no warning, all the big dogs jumped up and ran toward the back door.

"Why did they do that?" Beth kept her finger on the trigger, lest Ned forget who was in charge.

The backdoor opened with a soft, almost undiscernible crick. The dogs' panting and huffing escalated. A repeated slapping noise echoed into the room. Someone was moving slowly toward the kitchen.

"Ned?" came a female voice from the entry way. Agent Heslin.

"Finally," Beth whispered. She gestured to Ned with her gun. "Stand up slowly and turn around." She twirled her hand to get him going, keeping enough distance so that he couldn't grab the gun, but close enough that she could still shoot him without missing. When he was facing the entry, she stood behind him, pressing the gun into the back of his neck. "Tell her you're in here."

"Don't come in here," Ned shouted.

"That's not—damn it!" Beth whipped the back of his knee with the gun.

Ned groaned. His knees buckled from the blow.

"Get up." Beth grabbed his T-shirt, peering around him, suddenly nervous about catching her first real-life glimpse of the FBI agent. "You're going to be sorry if you don't do what I tell you." She cocked her weapon. "And don't you worry about Agent Heslin. She can take care of herself. Let's just hope she'll tell me the truth. I need to hear what she has to say."

Heslin crept around the corner, her gun stretched out in front of her, surrounded by all the dogs except the two littlest, meanest ones. Kudos to the agent for being so calm and well prepared. But what had Beth expected? Victoria Heslin was a real agent. She'd had actual training.

"What did you tell her, Ned?" Beth poked his shoulder with the muzzle. "How did she know I was here?"

"Because she's good at her job. And you better listen to her." He shifted his weight to one leg, favoring the one Beth hit.

Beth huffed. "Aren't you a brave man for someone who could have their brains blown out at any second. How many warnings do you need?"

"I'm a federal agent. Drop your gun. Let him go and we can talk." It was the same voice from the news interviews. And the agent was even prettier and more polished in person.

Beth gripped her gun tighter. "Oh, I know exactly who you are. But do you know who I am?"

"I'm not sure that I do, but I'd like to know. Put your gun down so we can talk." Heslin took a few steps forward.

"I'm the one who tried to warn you. I told you to watch your back. I was protecting you." Beth angled her body sideways, making herself as small as possible behind Ned's body, keeping the muzzle of her gun on his back. "You never know who you can trust, and who wants you dead. But little did I know that it was you who couldn't be trusted."

"I can be trusted." Heslin came closer. "Put the gun down."

She looked so calm and yet so serious. How did she do it? Beth squared her shoulders and leaned into Ned's body. She was completely shielded. "I want the truth from you, Agent Heslin. Only the truth."

"You've got it, as soon as you put the gun down. Whatever it is you need to know, I'll tell you. Only the truth. What's your name?"

Beth had to admire the agent's intense focus. No freaking out. She acted like they were having a normal conversation. Well, if that's how it was done, Beth could do the same. "I'm not going to let go of my gun because I don't know who deserves to live yet. Maybe Ned does, maybe he doesn't. You see, I thought we could be friends, Heslin. Now, well, I just hope you aren't about to disappoint everyone. It's not fair to Rivera. And I won't let him suffer."

"Rivera isn't suffering. Rivera and I are colleagues. Nothing more."

"Oh, really? Is that what you want me to believe now? Don't patronize me. Do you think I'm that stupid? Do you?" *I'm shouting. I need to calm down, not lose my cool.* She took a deep breath. "I need to know who this man is, and what's he doing here at your house. But first, make those dogs shut up."

Heslin didn't respond. She moved slowly forward, her progress so slight, Beth wouldn't have noticed if she wasn't so astute. *One step, two steps, three steps, four . . .* "Stop right there. Don't come any closer or I will kill this man. I swear to it, I will blow his brains out just like I did with Meiser and the Cossmans and the rest of them. Where is your partner?"

Heslin's eyes flickered away from Beth's for a nanosecond to look at Ned.

"He's out trying to catch the Numbers Killer, right? He is, isn't he?" Beth snorted. "How about that. Well, he's in the wrong place."

The agent's phone rang from inside her coat pocket. She ignored it.

Beth let go of the gun with one hand to wipe her sweaty palm on her pants. "So—who is he?"

"His name is Ned. He's a vet. He takes care of my dogs."

"Ha! A vet? At least your stories line up, but I'm not sure if I believe them. So, let's say your GQ model boy-toy really is your dog walker and a vet . . ." She trailed the butt of her gun up Ned's back between his shoulders until it was pressing against the back of his neck.

"He is." The agent's gaze didn't waver.

"Does Rivera even know about him? I wonder how he feels about you hiring someone so handsome? I don't think he likes it much. Now he always has to wonder. Why would you do that to him?"

Victoria didn't respond.

"I've never even met Rivera," Ned said, sounding exasperated instead of terrified, which made Beth very angry. "I think I'd have met him here if they were a couple. Don't you?"

"Shut your mouth." Beth snarled. "You're the cause of all this. You don't belong here, and I know what you're planning. Don't think I'm going to believe anything you have to say about Rivera."

Heslin took a step closer.

Why isn't she putting down her gun? Doesn't she care that Ned could get killed right in front of her? What do I have to do to make her cooperate? She lowered her gaze. All the dogs were lined up in front of Heslin, staring at Beth. Their skinny, half-starved muscular bodies creeped her out. And the little ones were still doing all they could to drive her off the edge. Sharp intermittent yaps, coming at her in odd numbers, like screeching fingernails on a blackboard. She tried to find a pattern, a way to add the barks together in a rhythm that ended up even. They were fraying her nerves with their yapping, yapping, yapping.

From somewhere beyond the kitchen, she heard the voice she did not need to hear. *Not now. Oh, God. Not now!*

"You're losing it, Beth." Danny laughed. "You're counting, aren't you? I know you are. Better drop the gun. You're no match for her."

Beth cringed. She didn't know how he'd gotten there, but it was just like Danny to show up right when she was starting to really stress out. She gritted her teeth. He was trying to mess with her confidence, like always. *Wouldn't he just love to see me fail.*

"Agent Heslin is not going to put her gun down, Beth. FBI agents don't do that. You're the one who needs to do what she says." Danny's tone was mocking, like he was enjoying her anguish.

"Get out of here," hissed Beth through clenched teeth. "I mean it. I do not need you here right now."

"You want us to leave?" Heslin still sounded calm, like everything happening in the kitchen was normal. Like Beth was no big threat.

"I'm not talking to you." Beth shot daggers through her eyes at Heslin.

"She's going to beat you, Beth. You're going to jail," Danny said.

From behind Ned, Beth cocked her head toward Danny's voice. "Get out! I don't need you. I never have. You've ruined everything, and I know what you were planning! You thought I'd get caught, didn't you? That's why you wanted me to kill them."

"I don't know what you mean," Heslin said. "But drop the gun and we'll talk about it. You can explain everything. I'm a very good listener."

"Listen to the lovely, calm agent and drop your gun, Beth," Danny said. "I'm damn sure she has more experience than you, in spite of your little killing spree this weekend."

Beth grimaced, her face contorting with rising anger. "Shut up, Danny! Just get out of here! I'll never trust you again. Never!"

Victoria and Ned exchanged glances. "With whom are you speaking?" Victoria asked.

The agent's snooty arrangement of words sparked a flame of anger inside Beth. *What the hell?*

"Do you think I'm someone named Danny?" Ned's voice had the bite of being placating. There was an edge of condescension, not just fear. *He thinks he's better than me.*

"He's asking who you're talking to, Beth. Are you gonna tell him?" Danny's voice rose. "He feels bad for you. He thinks you're crazy. Can't you hear it in his tone? He thinks you're a nut case who hears voices."

"Go back outside!" Beth shouted.

Victoria moved her eyes slightly to the right, just over Beth's shoulder.

"Is there someone with you?" Victoria's tone was even calmer now. She spoke as if she was consoling a child.

Why were they acting so strangely now that Danny was here? Was he hiding behind something so they couldn't see him? She didn't dare risk turning around to look. She was not going to take her eyes off the agent for a second. Were they trying to trick her? Of course they were. Everyone was out to trick her. It was Beth against the world. Always had been. Well, she wasn't going to fall for it. Not for a second.

The little dogs kept barking. Barking and barking at the top of their stupid, puny lungs. Beth pressed her lips together so tight her teeth dug into her lips. "I'm going to kill those dogs if they don't shut up."

Victoria's lips quivered, but her voice remained steady. The gun didn't waver. "If you hurt one of those dogs, I will shoot you. So that's your decision to make. I hope you do the right thing and choose wisely."

Beth laughed, a high-pitched frightening sound that surprised her. "But you don't mind if I shoot your boy-toy?"

A muffled sneeze startled Beth. She stepped backward, pulling Ned with her. "Who's there?"

No one answered.

"Danny? Is that you? For once in your life, help me out for a change. Go outside and tell me what's going on."

Rivera entered, his gun also drawn in front of him.

Beth laughed again. She sounded unhinged, even to her own ears. "Oh, now it's really going to get interesting."

"Ma'am, please set the gun down and let's talk." Rivera spoke calmly, politely. He kept his eyes locked on hers. "You're outnumbered. If you shoot at any of us, you will die. We don't want you to die. We want to hear about what you did and why you did it."

"I'm here for you, Agent Rivera. You!" pleaded Beth. "I know how much you love her! I've seen it with my own eyes. I'm here to warn you that you can't trust her."

"I appreciate that, Elizabeth." Rivera took a step closer. "And I want to hear your advice, but it's hard to talk when we're aiming weapons—"

"How did you know my name?" Beth shouted.

"You're famous now. Really." Rivera's nose twitched, his face contorted, and he sneezed but went on as if it never happened. "I want to hear what you did, and why you did it. Everyone does."

"You know what I did, then. I killed all of them who saw me. Almost all of them. Jason and Kelly Smith got away. But not for long. And that Butler guy had nothing to do with any of it."

"We know. We know it was all you," Rivera said, as if she had done something wonderful. But did he really appreciate what she'd done, that she'd had the strength to do it all by herself, identifying them and tracking them down, or was he placating her so he could put her in jail?

"You killed Todd Meiser, the Cossmans, Steve Horrigan, and Arnold Gomez?" Heslin asked.

"Yes. All of them. By myself."

"No wonder their dogs despise you," Ned muttered.

"What was it they saw you do?" Heslin was still watching Beth closely.

Beth lowered her gaze for a second, but the gun against Ned's back didn't waver. "I—I had to do it. Danny said they saw me."

225

"Who is Danny?" Agent Heslin asked.

"Tell her who I am," Danny shouted. "Tell her what you did."

Beth's hands were cramping around the gun. She'd been holding it in a death grip since Agent Heslin came in. "You said they saw me!"

Danny laughed and slapped his leg. "That's not what I mean, and you know it. And you really are the stupidest woman on this earth. No one saw you! You killed them because I told you to. No other reason. You didn't want to go to jail. Guess you really wanted to do it, didn't you? You wanted to know what it was like to have the power."

"That's not true! The first one, Todd Meiser—before I killed him, he begged me—said he wouldn't tell what he saw if I let him live."

"He was about to testify against the mob, Beth. Surely, with all your insane counting, you can put two and two together. Or can't you?"

"Who is Danny?" Victoria asked again.

"You want to know who he is? You want to know who Danny is?" Beth screamed. Her face contorted in anguish. "He's my worthless cheating husband. But why don't you ask him who he is for yourself." She laughed, a high-pitched crazy sound. "I'd love to hear what he has to say."

"We can't ask him." Rivera edged toward her. "I found your husband, Elizabeth. I found him in the woods behind the Sonesta Hotel."

Something snapped inside Beth. Again. And this time, she felt it happen. A giant dam broke inside her mind, spewing forth a torrent of filthy memories. An ache spread through her chest, her lungs, her throat. The truth left her shocked and gasping, with nowhere to hide from it, no way to avoid the drenching in pure heart-breaking nastiness.

226

Chapter Thirty-Three

Last Friday night. That's when it all happened. Just four days ago, but it seemed like ages. Beth had been innocent and stupid. Well, maybe not innocent, but certainly unaware.

She and Danny hadn't talked much during the long drive to Virginia. Danny said he was tired. He slept most of the way while Beth drove. They checked into the Sonesta Hotel long after sundown. He went to the front desk to check them in, since they were using Thomas somebody or other's credit card. Once they had their keys, they drove the car around to one of the side doors and went in with their stuff. There was nothing special about the hotel, but their room was clean, with windows offering a view of the woods. Beth gazed out. In the varied degrees of blackness and shadow, it was nice enough, but barely.

Danny yanked the curtains closed. He stepped on the back of his shoes to pull them off and tossed them into the center of the room. He plopped himself back on the bed like he wasn't going anywhere for a while. "Damn!" He lifted his head off the pillow, his voice taking on the edge of irritation she knew so well. "I forgot somethin'."

"What is it?" Beth picked up his shoes and lined them up side by side in the closet. "Maybe it's something we can buy here."

"No. Nothin' from home. I left my gun in the car. I can't leave it there, in case someone breaks in." He didn't make a move to get up. Beth knew what was coming. "Go get it, will ya? Bring it inside."

She had been about to open his suitcase and put away his clothes but stopped. For the vacation to be any fun, she had to make sure Danny stayed happy and didn't run out of beer, but also didn't drink too many at once. She picked up the car keys he'd tossed onto the desk. "Sure. I'll be right back."

"Wait. Throw me a beer before you go."

She opened the cooler they brought from home, got the beer, and handed it to him. "Here you go, hon. And I'll be right back." She smiled suggestively, but Danny hadn't taken his eyes from the television, except to open the beer. Leaning down, she kissed him gently on the edge of his mouth, just a fleeting kiss where the scar on his cheek met his lips, her hand resting on his chest.

Dutifully, she left the room carrying her purse, so she had a place to conceal his gun. She didn't know why he had the gun, or what it was used for, but he'd always had one. She went through the empty lobby and out across the dim parking lot. Opening the driver's side door, she glanced around. Seeing no one close by, no one paying attention to her, she scooped the gun out from under the front seat.

A couple holding hands walked toward the front entrance and a man stood just inside the automatic doors. She was wary of carrying the gun. Danny didn't have a permit for it and neither did she. She didn't want to get in trouble for something so insignificant, didn't want to take any additional risks that might ruin their vacation and the surprise he had lined up. Despite all the illegal activities she'd participated in, above all, she was terrified of going to jail.

Making a split-second decision, she walked around the side of the hotel toward the woods, shivering in the cold. She used her key card to open the back door, where no one would see her. The entryway was dark and smelled slightly of ammonia. On the other side of the stairwell, someone she couldn't see was having a one-sided conversation. She stopped to make sure her purse was zipped shut.

There was something familiar about the voice coming from around the corner. The deep gravelly sound reminded her of Danny, but the tone was off. Too accommodating, too charming, and there was soft laughter.

"I miss you too, kitten."

Beth's skin turned clammy. A feverish chill raked through her body and settled in her bones. The voice was too much like her husband's to belong to anyone else. But who was he talking to? Who was he calling 'kitten'? She stood still, holding her breath.

"She went out, but I'm in the stairwell because she'll be back in a minute." Danny spoke in the coaxing voice he used when he wanted something he couldn't get with force. "Don't get all panicked on me, now. It's gonna work out. Just trust me. Do what I say. And remember, I was with you all weekend working on the plans for remodeling the inside, we went to the—" Beth flattened herself against the side of the staircase and craned to hear him, she missed a few words because he was practically whispering.

"There'll be no trace that I was ever with her here. No video cameras. That's why I picked this dump. So stick with the plan."

Beth clenched her hands into tight fists. A terrible sickness threatened to rise out of her throat and spill onto the floor.

"Use my credit card tonight at a drive-through and a few times tomorrow, but make it all seem business related, during the day, nothing too private. You know what I mean? And nowhere with video cameras. Got it?"

There was silence and then Danny laughed.

"After she's gone, just a few months more, and then we can do whatever we want. One million dollars buys a lot of everything, baby."

Another pause. Another deep, soft laugh. "Wish me luck. Love you, gorgeous."

229

An icy current snaked through Beth's chest at the same time she felt like she'd been slapped hard, knocked off balance. The scraping of shoes on the concrete told her he was coming closer. She froze, fear and anger forming a tight ball in her throat, choking her.

Just a few steps away, he switched direction and walked up the stairs. At the top, a door opened and closed.

She waited another minute, trembling, her mind racing, her stomach rolling with nausea. She swallowed hard. She slapped her cheek, hoping to wake up from a horrible, ultra-realistic nightmare. Surely, she had misunderstood. It couldn't be what it sounded like. It couldn't, because if it did, that would mean . . . *Oh, God!* It meant she was a pathetic, misguided fool. She had no one. She had nothing. Her whole life was worthless.

She crept up the stairs, the last three years of her life flashing through her mind in sharp snippets, the best and the worst of it all: meeting Danny at her sister's wedding, his proposal the following Valentine's day, the first time he'd slapped her when they were on their honeymoon.

Slowly she opened the door to room 234, afraid her face would give her away. How could she possibly hide her hurt and shock? She stuffed her hands in her pockets to keep them from trembling.

Danny was stretched out on the bed again, head propped on all the pillows – having left none for her—watching a game on television. He glanced at Beth—as if she was an annoying mosquito who buzzed inside when the door was open—then back to the screen. In that brief instant, she saw the coldness in his dark eyes, darker than usual. Her heart ached. How could she have been so stupid? Mini vacation? So close to hitting the jackpot with his business venture? She shuddered. She had trusted a cheater, a man who would rather she was dead than alive. She finally averted her gaze from him, feeling painfully alone, more alone than she had ever felt before.

In the wall mirror, she caught her reflection, ashen skin and worried eyes. She wiped at the tears spilling down her cheeks. Her gaze dropped to her suitcase. A new sick feeling of shame and stupidity arose inside her like a sudden wave of violent illness. Inside was the present she had bought him, her own surprise. A power station charger and Wi-Fi hotspot he could use when traveling. Something he said he needed.

"Did you get my gun?" he grunted.

"Yes. I'll just keep it in my purse." Trembling inside, she sat down at the tiny desk, grateful it was positioned in a hideaway around the corner, away from Danny's line of view. She shoved off one shoe and then the other.

"What took you so long?"

"I um, I got something from the vending machine." Her voice came out thin and weak. She reached for her laptop.

"What are you doing now?" The volume on the television increased.

"Nothing." She opened her computer and powered it on.

"Nothing?"

"I'm uh—I'm checking a site with things to do in the area."

"We're going to hike to the top of the waterfall. Rain or shine."

"Uh, huh." She typed furiously.

"I can barely hear this show. You're making too much noise."

"Sorry. I'll be more quiet."

Quickly, as if her time was running out, which apparently it was, she logged into their checking account expenses and searched through the charges. She hoped and prayed for some sort of mistake, some crazy misunderstanding. Danny snored loudly on the bed, sounding like a fat and congested hog.

Most of the recurring payments belonged to Danny. A video game subscription, a music subscription, the internet, and cable. Only one monthly payment stood out as something she didn't recognize. It went back several years, starting a few months after their marriage. She traced the payment to an insurance company, didn't even have to hack into their system because dumb-ass Danny used the same login and password—baddanny1—for everything. She entered his email and password. There it was—the insurance policy she didn't know they owned. One million dollars to be paid to Daniel Dellinger in the event of Beth Dellinger's death.

Scenarios flashed through her mind, each more terrible than the next. How did he plan to do it? Push her off the waterfall when she was admiring the view? Or shoot her first and then push her? Was that the big surprise? Because if she hadn't overheard him downstairs, then yeah, it would have been the mother of all surprises.

Staring at the screen, the cold, hard pang of her sadness wrestled with the hot fury of her rage. *How could he do this to me?! How could he?!* Then came more anger, directed at herself. *How could I have been so stupid and unsuspecting? How could I have almost let this happen?* Part of her perched on the brink of exploding, part of her threatened to crumble and break like old brittle bones. *Confront him? Or run?*

One overriding urge emerged through her tumultuous, warring emotions—the fierce need to survive. He was not going to kill her. She was not going to die.

She pulled her pocket book closer to her side. The hard muzzle of the gun pressed through the material and against her hip. She opened a new browser and typed: how to shoot a revolver. She read the first set of instructions and clicked on another. How hard could it be?

"You're acting strange, Beth."

He'd gotten off the bed and snuck up behind her. She slammed her laptop closed and jumped sideways in her seat. "What? No, I'm not."

"What's going on?" Hovering over her shoulder, his hot, beer breath warmed her neck. "What are you doing?"

"Nothing." She wrapped her arms around her chest instinctively. "I wasn't doing anything."

He eyed her with an intensity she now recognized as hatred. "I'll be the judge of that." He pushed her out of the way and grabbed for her computer. He lifted the top. The screen flashed to life and he clicked on the tabs she hadn't closed.

Clutching her purse, she made a dash for the door and ran out. Tears stung her eyes. She flew barefoot down the back stairwell, taking them two at a time, without looking back over her shoulder. Yanking the hallway door open, she ran through the corridor and straight into the hotel lobby, gasping for breath. She stopped for a second, eyes darting from the exit to the front desk. The office door swung shut on the backside of a man in a cheap black suit. There was no one else in sight. Jumbled thoughts raced through her mind. She could scream for help. Surely the employee, or someone, would come out and help her, or call the police. But what good would it do? If Danny didn't kill her tonight, he'd be even angrier after a run in with the cops. What proof did she have that he was going to kill her? "Kitten" wasn't going to back up Beth's story. And even if she did, Danny wouldn't be the only one taken to jail. Identity theft carried a longer sentence than domestic abuse. Danny would see to it that Beth would pay for their crimes. She could count on that.

Decision made, she kept her mouth closed and sprinted down the hall to the back of the hotel. Had she made a conscious decision to run to the woods behind the hotel? She didn't know then and she didn't know now. The will to survive superseded all else. She flung open the back door, barely even registering the man who stood aside to let her pass and the attractive woman with dark hair who hurriedly leapt out of her way.

Danny breathed heavily behind her. "Come back here! You don't understand. What you saw—the insurance thing—it's not what you think."

She ran. Her violent entrance into the woods was echoed by branches cracking and snapping close behind her.

"Stop! Come back here!" Danny yelled.

An approaching train barreled down the tracks like it was coming right at them.

He wanted her dead.

He would kill her.

But not if she killed him first.

She yanked the gun from her bag. She aimed. She fired.

The incessant barking and growling of the two littlest dogs snapped Beth back to reality. Her hands were shaking so hard it looked like the gun was vibrating. *Danny is dead. I killed Danny. I killed my husband.* A muscle below her eye began to spasm.

"We don't want to hurt you, but I'm counting to three and if you don't put the gun down, you leave me no choice. One."

Heslin let the odd number hang in the air, as if she knew what it would do to Beth.

Danny laughed again, a cruel, mocking sound. "You got yourself in a real doozy now, dumb ass. How are you getting out of this one? Can't wait to see how this works out for you."

"How could you? How could you do that to me?" She screamed, and the gun jerked up and down in her hand.

"Two."

"Guess you're going to prison after all, Beth." Danny's laughter grew louder.

"No! I'm not!" Beth shrieked. In one swift movement, she whipped the gun toward her head.

"Nooo!" Victoria shouted.

Three shots rang out. One from each gun in the room.

Chapter Thirty-Four

Trembling inside, Victoria lowered her gun. Four of her dogs raced away, tails underneath them, terrified of the gun shots.

Beth lay motionless on the ground, blood spewing from her shoulder and neck. Rivera crossed the room. With a swift kick, he sent Beth's gun spinning across the floor and away from her.

Victoria hurried to Ned's side, followed by the remaining dogs, and gripped his upper arms. She gazed up at him. "Ned! I was so worried I might lose y—." She removed her hands and took a quick step back. "I mean—are you hurt?"

Ned shook his head, closed his eyes for a second. "No, I'm fine. Shaken as hell, but fine. That might be an everyday occurrence for you two, but not for—"

From the floor, Beth let out another moan.

Rivera shouted, "She's still alive," and pulled out his phone.

Gasping, Ned ran to Beth and kneeled by her side. He tore off his shirt and pressed it against her neck. "I don't think the bullet hit the jugular. Get me some towels."

"This is Federal Agent Dante Rivera. We have a serious gunshot victim who needs immediate medical assistance. The address is—Victoria!"

"1406 Arbor Way," Ned answered.

As Rivera repeated the information to the dispatcher, Beth's lips moved rhythmically.

"What's she saying?" Victoria asked.

"I think she's counting," Ned answered.

Beth's eyes flew open and rolled back into her head. She fell silent.

"Go!" Ned yelled to Victoria.

Victoria rushed away with dogs trailing after her.

"Wait," Ned hollered. "Get a tie, or a scarf, too! And get tampons!"

"Okay," Victoria shouted from the hallway.

"And gloves if you have them!"

With her breath coming in fast gasps, she hurried to the master bedroom. She yanked a scarf from a rack in her closet, snatched tampons from under her bathroom sink, and grabbed a tall stack of crisp white towels from the linen shelves. She rushed back with her arms full. She'd been involved with life and death emergencies before, but never in her own kitchen. With Ned, Rivera, her dogs, and so much blood. . . there was something surreal about the entire situation.

The dogs surrounded the spreading pool of blood and lapped at it. She swung her leg toward them. "Out! Get away!" They scattered, spreading bloody paw prints across the floor. "I still have to get gloves."

"I've got some." Rivera grabbed them from his pocket and held them out.

Ned's hands were already soaked with blood. "You put them on," he told Rivera. "Then grab a towel and put your hand where mine is. Press down like you mean it."

Victoria dumped the load she was carrying onto the floor and tossed Rivera a towel. He took Ned's place.

Ned straddled Beth and began chest compressions. He glanced up at Victoria for a fraction of a second, just long enough for her to know he was telling her what to do. "Tie the scarf or—whatever you brought—tie it around her shoulder like a tourniquet," he said breathlessly. "Then plug each of those holes with a tampon." He did another series of compressions. "Then one of you needs to get behind her and stabilize her neck, don't let her head move at all. Damn it! We should have done that first."

Victoria knelt and tied the scarf around Beth's shoulder and pulled it tight. Sweat slid down Ned's temples as he continued pumping Beth's chest. Her blood spread across the floor, soaking through their pant legs as they knelt around her. The dogs returned and licked at the blood while Victoria yelled, "No. Get away," in a futile attempt to make them stop. Rivera sneezed violently, four times in a row.

Ambulance sirens wailed in the distance as Ned continued compressions.

"I have to let them in." As Victoria keyed the code to open the gate into her phone, and the approaching sirens grew louder, Ned and Rivera worked furiously to save the killer's life. Rivera's lips moved silently, and Victoria knew he was praying. The woman bleeding out on the ground was a dangerous killer with severe psychological problems. They would do everything they could to save her.

Epilogue

Victoria looked forward to getting home early. It was only a matter of time before something would happen and she would be called away by the FBI for a new case. She hated not knowing how much time she had—an hour, a week?—but that was part of the job. It was in her best interest to relish the downtime while she had it. She was only a few miles away from her house when her father called. After exchanging a few pleasantries, he got right to the reason for his call.

"Fenton is always keeping watch for our names in the media."

Victoria coasted the Suburban to a stop sign. "I know he is."

"Well, you'll never guess what he dug up."

"What is it?" She looked right and left before easing the car into motion.

"He found an online newsletter for a shelter in Seville Spain. It's called the Abigail Heslin Foundation for Animals. It's a large facility built to house over 700 dogs at a time, with an onsite Vet."

"Wow. Really?" She gripped the wheel tighter. "Sounds just like something mom would do."

"Yes, I thought the same. Except the shelter didn't exist until a few years ago, Victoria. Your mother didn't do this."

Victoria sighed. Bracing herself for the questions that would follow—exactly how much did she spend? Did she know that the money was being used wisely, etc.

"But she would be very, very proud of you."

Victoria smiled, and a warm feeling radiated through her. "Thanks, Dad. I hope she would. I'm going to visit the shelter next week. I'm taking Ned with me. We'll fly back with some dogs and help them find homes here. Can I mark you down to take one, or two, or three? Three is a good number."

Her father laughed. "I admire what you're doing, but I think you know the answer to that question."

The dogs greeted Victoria in the mudroom with a flurry of huffing, puffing, and smacking their tails against the walls. She stroked their heads as they bounced around her. "That's right. I'm home, babies." Izzy shoved her head into Victoria's shopping bag.

"No. That's not for you," Victoria said, gently pushing the dog's head away.

Ned walked in from the direction of the guest wing. With him came the slight scent of a fresh, sporty aftershave or deodorant. She liked that smell. His hair was wet. His skin glistened from his shower.

"You're early." He slid his phone from his pocket. "Did I miss a call?"

"No. I didn't call. I had mountains of paperwork to do today. I could only take so much of it, so I left early. I was hoping you could hang out for a while and talk about our trip." Victoria lifted the bag. "I brought dinner. Hope that's okay and you haven't made anything yet."

"No. That's great."

She set the bag on the counter. Ned walked forward to open it. "Wow. Is this just for us or do you have friends coming?"

Victoria laughed. "Just us. I wasn't sure what you wanted, and I know you've been training hard. Thought you might eat a lot."

Ned chuckled. "I'm always hungry. Izzy and I just had a long run."

"No one else is coming for dinner, but someone is coming to get Leo and Bella."

"Oh." He crouched down and scratched Leo behind the ears. "Hear that, little guy. Hope wherever you're going is almost as good as this place."

Victoria pushed the bag further toward the center of the counter where it was safe from the dogs. "I just need to change my clothes." She walked to her bedroom and stripped down to her underwear and sports bra. She replaced her work clothes with jeans and a long sleeve t-shirt and went back out to the kitchen. In the short time she'd been gone, Ned had set out plates, silverware, and napkins. He'd transferred salmon, rice, and grilled vegetables from boxes into bowls. He smiled when she entered the kitchen and pulled a chair out for her.

"Thanks." The wonderful aroma of the food filled the kitchen as she sat down, feeling warm and relaxed. "So. Only a few more weeks. Have you ever been to Spain? I can't remember if I asked."

Ned tipped the bottle of wine to fill Victoria's glass. "I spent half my junior year of college studying in Barcelona."

"Oh! That's wonderful. I had no idea. So you speak the language fluently?" She took a sip of wine and set her glass back on the table.

"Well . . . I used to speak it well. But it's been awhile." Ned scooped up a spoonful of rice and ate it.

"I'm sure it will come back to you once we get there. We'll check into our hotel and freshen up. Then it's straight to the shelter."

"How do we get all the supplies there?"

"They'll be there already. I shipped them last week." Victoria took another sip of wine. "They're so glad you're coming. There are always dogs who need surgery. Many of them were hit by cars. We've had a few where their owners didn't need them anymore so they broke their legs then dumped them far from home so they wouldn't get back." Victoria closed her eyes and shook her head.

"Holy crap." Ned let his spoon clatter onto his plate. "This is going to be tough."

"Yes, it is. And it's going to be exhausting, but everyone will be so grateful, especially the dogs."

Ned smiled. "My dad used to do mission trips to Haiti every two years with some of the physicians from his hospital. That's what this seems like to me."

"That's exactly what it's going to be like for you, except your father probably didn't take any of his patients back to the US with him." Victoria took a bite of her food and sighed. It was delicious.

"After the first time he went, he couldn't wait to go back. Even though a lot of what he saw was heartbreaking."

"Yes. Same," Victoria said.

The intercom buzzed. Someone was at the front gate. Victoria tapped the code to open it and walked to the front door.

A woman wearing running shoes, jeans, and a sweatshirt stood on the other side of the door. "Hi. Are you Victoria?"

"Yes." Victoria smiled warmly. She liked the woman already.

"I'm Sarah. I'm Ann's sister."

Leo and Bella ran to Sarah and sniffed her.

"They know you?" Victoria asked.

"Oh, they know me all right. I take care of them whenever my sister and Robert need help." She dropped to her knees and let the dogs lick her chin. "You're coming home to live with me now." She stood up and wiped the tears from her eyes. "Being with them will help me cope with losing my sister. This is a good thing."

Victoria smiled. "I'm glad you feel that way. I'm sure your sister would be so grateful if she knew."

Sarah sniffed and nodded. "Thank you for taking care of them." She looked around, taking in the beautiful home, and laughed. "They might not want to leave."

"Dogs don't care where they live as long as someone there loves them," Victoria said. "I'll go get their leashes."

Ned introduced himself to Sarah. "We're going to miss them."

Sarah petted Eddie and Myrtle, her eyes roaming over the house, the dog beds and toys. "I guess you and your wife are really dog lovers."

Ned smiled. "Oh. I'm just—"

Victoria walked back in carrying leashes and a dog food bag. "Here they are. And this is the food your sister was feeding them."

"Thank you." Sarah attached the leash and they watched her leave with the dogs. When she was inside her car, they closed the door and returned to the kitchen.

"How about a walk?" Ned asked. "After we clean up here."

"Sure. Who should we take?"

"Let's try and take them all. Three for you. Four for me."

She laughed. "Really? This will be a first."

They put on their own jackets, and then put sweaters on the dogs to protect them from the chilly air. They headed across Victoria's backyard to one of the main trails.

"There's something I'd like to talk to you about. Something from, you know, the other night." Ned said, walking with two dogs on one side and two on the other.

"Sure. It's normal and healthy to talk about things like that— the fear, the stress. It's important to talk it out with someone who will understand."

"I was afraid, yeah, I mean, Beth Dellinger was disturbed, but I'm dealing okay with what transpired."

"She might be in a coma forever. The doctors aren't sure."

"I know, and I have to admit I feel bad for her, she was not healthy, talking to her dead husband like he was really in the room

243

with us." He shuddered. "But that's not what—it's about something you said."

"Me?" Victoria swapped Eddie's black leash with Myrtle's pink one as the dogs crossed in front of her.

"Well, I'm guessing you've handled situations like that before, hostage situations. But maybe not where the hostage is someone you know, right?"

"True. That was a first."

"So—I'm going to be direct here—when you said, 'I was so worried I might lose you,' were you worried about losing me as in, now I have to find someone new to take care of the dogs? Or was there something else?"

Victoria smiled, their eyes met. Her heart skipped a beat. "A good dog walker is hard to find, Especially one who . . ."

"Especially one who?"

"Maybe I'll wait until we get to Spain before I fully answer that question."

He smiled. "Can't wait to hear your answer."

They couldn't clasp hands, not with seven dogs between them. Victoria slipped the leash loops up her forearm and reached her free hand over to squeeze Ned's.

The End

READY FOR BOOK TWO?

Pretty Little Girls

Book 2 in the Agent Victoria Heslin Thriller Series

Until you know who you can trust, you trust no one.

The mysterious discovery of a young, unidentified girl in the woods, and the disappearance of a prep school girl from an affluent family lead to a shocking world of hidden secrets.

Agent Victoria Heslin investigates, but the mysteries only get deeper. Why aren't the girl's parents cooperating? And why are local authorities resisting her help?

When her efforts uncover a complicated sex trafficking operation, Heslin enlists friend and fellow Agent Dante Rivera to go rogue and try to save the girls, before it's too late.

An excerpt from the first few chapters of Pretty Little Girls follows.

PREVIEW: PRETTY LITTLE GIRLS
Chapter One

Ava trudged up the hill towards the woods behind her apartment complex, following her dog. She glanced at her watch again as she tugged the leash, pulling Max away from whatever he was sniffing. "Crap, why did you let me hit the snooze button five times, Max?" Puffs of white breath formed in front of her as she wrapped his leash around her wrist and picked up her pace. "Because a warm bed is heaven, Ava. That's why."

Max trotted straight through a mud puddle; Ava jumped over it. "You have an answer for everything, don't you, boy? Can you give me a good one for Mr. Parker when I'm late for the third time this month?"

Wearing a large puffy coat, Ronald drove toward her on the maintenance golf cart, brooms and shovels bouncing along in the back. She waved at him. He was nice enough, but as she hurried onto the trail into the woods, she hoped he wouldn't follow like he did that day last summer.

The blanket of crisp leaves crunched under her feet. Max strained against the leash, flung his head into the bushes, and nuzzled his nose into a mound of decaying vegetation, going after every strange and wonderful outdoorsy scent. Ava peered back over her shoulder and was relieved to see Ronald driving in the opposite direction. Groaning against the cold, she jogged in place, one hand in the pocket of her coat. She had to admit, the chilly air was invigorating, and it would make her morning coffee so much more enjoyable, even though she'd have to take it to go. Why did Mr. Parker care so much about her being late anyway? She always got her work done.

Wheezing, Max hauled her forward, deeper into the woods. Once he caught the scent of something interesting in the wild—a deer or its droppings, a discarded hamburger wrapper—he was determined to get to it.

"No, come on. Are you trying to get me fired? Max, stop! We need to turn around."

He lurched ahead, ears erect and nose twitching, dragging her off the worn path.

"Max, no!"

A large tree trunk stretched alongside the trail, covered in moss. Max lunged to inspect it, his entire body wagging with excitement.

Ava's phone buzzed from inside her coat pocket. *Don't be Parker, don't be Parker.* She reached for her phone. *Please let this be one of the days when he has a doctor's appointment for his weird skin condition.*

She glanced at the screen. Jared. She didn't have time for ex-boyfriend's antics right now.

The leash went slack. Max whimpered. His front paw was lifted and his tail pointed. Ava moved closer to see what he'd discovered on the other side of the log.

Ava blinked. Her mouth dropped open. Her phone fell from her hand as she screamed. She stumbled backwards, tugging on Max, unable to tear her eyes away.

Is she . . .? Is she . . .?

The young girl didn't belong there, underdressed, unmoving, alone on the ground.

She had dark brown hair and pale skin. Her gray sweat pants and pink flannel shirt were wet from the morning's frosty mist. Leaves were tangled in her hair and strewn across her body. But it was her beautiful brown eyes staring blankly at the cold, gray sky that shook Ava to the core.

Ava screamed again as Max stretched forward and licked something off the corpse's chin.

◆ ◆ ◆

FBI Medical Examiner Dr. Rebecca Boswell didn't care if it was still November. As soon as the Thanksgiving dishes were washed, Christmas was on. An acoustic version of Deck the Halls blasted through the autopsy room as she studied the slender girl on the steel gurney. No identification on her—another Jane Doe, number 2537 to be exact—and this one was unusually young, sixteen at most. The ME lifted the girl's eyelids, revealing bloodshot brown eyes. A linear ligature mark circled her neck. Even before doing an internal exam, Rebecca was confident that the girl was a victim of foul play. No doubt she had been suffocated.

She pressed a button on her recorder.

"Jane Doe. Caucasian female, possibly of Eastern European descent. Very slender. Height five-foot-four, weight one hundred and two pounds. Long, dark hair."

An exceptionally lovely, symmetrical, face. Would have grown up to be a stunner.

"She's wearing eye makeup and blush. Aside from ruptured capillaries—consistent with asphyxiation, will confirm—her skin is smooth and clear. She has pink gel polish on recently groomed nails and matching polish on her toenails."

Youth today—in such a rush to grow up.

"Blood trailing from the corners of her mouth and over her chin, suggesting an internal injury."

She leaned over the table and gently pulled open the girl's lips. "Examination of the mouth indicates…" Rebecca's gut wrenched as she jerked backwards, gasping. In ten years of autopsies, she'd never done that before. Rebecca squeezed her eyes shut, letting her sadness turn to rage and then back to professionalism. She opened the girl's lips again and continued her examination. "The subject's tongue…" The ME swallowed hard. "…has been cut out." She turned off the recorder and took a deep breath, gazing at the child. "You didn't deserve that, honey. No matter what you did."

Rebecca removed her gloves and filled a cup with water. She gulped it down, crushed the cup, and slammed it into the trash can. She took another deep breath, wiped her forehead, donned new gloves, and returned to her work.

"Bleeding minimal, no inflammation, indicating the tongue was removed post-mortem." That, at least, offered Rebecca a small morsel of relief. She'd seen tongues cut out before, although never in such a girl. Whoever did it could be a unique kind of messed-up and wanted a souvenir. However, there was a more likely, uglier explanation. Someone was sending a message—keep your mouth closed, don't talk. But to whom?

What were you involved with before you died?

Rebecca cleared her throat. "Healthy, straight teeth, but no signs of previous dental work." *No fillings or caps to trace.*

After making dental impressions, she turned Jane Doe over to study her backside. At first glance, because the back of the girl's neck was covered by an array of silky hair, she thought she saw a brown tattoo. When she swept the hair away for a closer inspection, she frowned. It wasn't a normal tattoo.

"Dark, well-defined scar, two inches in diameter, at the base of her neck at her T1 vertebrae—a circle with marks around the perimeter and an infinity symbol inside, most likely made by a small branding iron."

The brand was unusual, but could mean anything—an impulsive pact made with girlfriends, a boyfriend's favorite symbol—but seeing that the girl had likely been murdered, Rebecca wondered if the marking was gang related.

Serenaded by *Carol of the Bells*, Dr. Boswell pushed her braids over her shoulder, snapped digital pictures, and measured the bruises across Jane Doe number 2537's arms and neck. She collected scrapings from under the girl's finger nails, combed through her hair, and applied tape over her body to collect fibers. After she finished collecting external evidence, she washed the girl's body. She'd been found in urine and feces, a sign she'd lost control of her bodily functions. Might have been sick, or terrified, or a result of dying. It's possible Rebecca wouldn't be able to discover which. Lastly, before beginning the internal exam, Dr. Boswell printed the girl's fingers.

The internal exam took her over an hour. With a tap of her foot she recorded the summary of her findings.

"Abnormal findings in the internal exam included evidence of healed fractures, minor, but on multiple bones. Vaginal bruising and tears indicated recent, rough sexual activity. No semen found."

Rebecca neatly stitched the body back together, minus its vital organs. She exercised her lungs belting out *Gloria in Excelsis Deo* as she returned Jane Doe to cold storage.

"Jane Doe Number 2537 is only a temporary designation. Mark my words, poor girl, we're going to find out who you are and who did this to you." Dr. Boswell slid the heavy, steel drawer into place.

The ME washed up, anxious to load the photo of the brand into the computer and hopefully find a match in the FBI's database of tattoos and symbols. After the search had run its course, nothing turned up that looked like the mark on the back of the corpse's neck.

Curious, the ME called Special Agent Dante Rivera. A quick glance in one of the mirrors confirmed her full lips still held a hint of shimmer and her hot pink scrubs were great with her skin color. No reason not to look and feel good when she spoke to him, even over the phone. They hadn't been on a date yet, but she was a patient woman.

"Good afternoon, Dr. Boswell," Rivera answered, always the gentleman.

"Good afternoon, Agent Rivera. I just finished the autopsy of a teen-aged Jane Doe. She was suffocated. Her tongue was removed post-mortem."

Rivera grunted. "Such a nice world we live in."

"Isn't that the truth?" Rebecca sighed. As much as she wanted to flirt with him, the circumstances of their interactions rarely allowed for it. "What prompted my call was an interesting burn mark on the back of her neck. A brand."

"Like cattle?"

"Unfortunately, yes. I was hoping it might help identify her or give us a clue as to who killed her. I checked in the FBI database, and there wasn't a match. I also sent a picture to your phone. In case there's a chance you've seen something like it before. I know you've worked with some gang cases in the past."

"You know that, huh?"

Alone in the autopsy room, she smiled. "Yes."

"Okay." She heard the echoey noises of being switched to speaker phone, and a few seconds passed before he spoke again. "I'm looking at it right now. Can't say it looks familiar, but I'll ask around."

"Thanks, Rivera. I'm sending her prints and her dental images out. Such a young girl. And the final indignity is that as far as we know, no one has reported her missing. No one is looking for her."

Chapter Two

Sofia was a beautiful, graceful girl. She had vivid blue eyes and thick, dark lashes. Her mouth held a natural pout, even when she was terrified. In her petite, red dress, she stared out through the floor-to-ceiling window, squinting. She couldn't see the skyscrapers, only thousands of tiny lights blurring together in the darkness.

Anastasia joined her at the window. She was just as stunning. Light brown hair, emerald-green eyes with specks of copper, full lips, and an upturned nose. "Sexy and childishly innocent," according to their boss. The childish part wasn't hard to accomplish, especially not when she started working for him. She had only been thirteen.

Anastasia placed her hand against the glass and leaned into it. "Big view city skyline. I wish you see it clearly." She often dropped her articles and mixed up a few words when she spoke English. The girls were forbidden to speak their native language.

They'd worked in many nice homes, and this condo with its enormous televisions, sleek furniture, and modern art was no exception. A buzzed exuberance vibrated through the home along with the bass in the sound system. A new group of men burst in, all wearing Panther jerseys.

"Super Bowl bound, baby!" shouted the loudest, slapping a big bald guy on the back. "I knew they were going. I called it at the beginning of the season, did I not?"

The bald guy draped his arm over his friend's shoulder. "Don't jinx them, man. There's lots of games left."

With big smiles, and long swigs of beer, the hardcore fans broke into a chant. "We're number one! We're number one!"

"Are they some of the players?" Sofia asked Svet.

Her bodyguard huffed. "Hardly. They're just a group of traders who probably take roids."

Sofia sat on the couch and stretched one of her long, slim legs over the lap of a guy who could have passed for an NFL lineman. She gently stroked his bulging biceps with her light pink nails. He was an ugly white dude with a crooked nose and a neat, close-shaven beard, clearly intended to cover his acne scars. Even though he was much older than her, he was younger than most of her customers. Best of all, he was having a hard time making eye contact, focusing on his drink instead. It didn't happen often that a man was uncomfortable, but when it did, she appreciated it. He would be gentle. Chances were good he wouldn't hurt her.

The man patted her behind. "She looks really young, Mikey."

Mikey, just as large but not as ugly, responded with a laugh, his hand cupping Anastasia's breast. "Don't worry about her." He finished his beer and set the iced mug on one of his fancy glass tables. "They cost a small fortune. They probably take home more than we do."

Sofia cringed inside. He was wrong. So very wrong. She made nothing. If she had been earning money to send back to her mother and siblings in Ukraine, there would have at least been an upside to the miserable circumstances of her life. Yet, she knew better than to correct him. She couldn't trust any men with the truth. She'd tried before. Just because someone seemed kind, didn't mean they could be trusted. The last time she'd thought she could trust someone, he'd betrayed her. She'd been locked in a closet for days with only water to drink and a pot for relieving herself. So, no matter how sensitive the huge man with the bent nose seemed, she had to assume he was just like all the rest— stone-cold and uncaring to her plight.

She shrugged it off, forcing her sweetest, most genuine-looking smile. Batting her eyelashes, she shook her head slightly, pretending she couldn't understand his words. He offered her a drink, pointing to his own bottle and then the mini-bar across the room. "No, thank you," she said, adding an extra thick layer to her existing accent.

Svet carefully surveyed the rooms from a corner, wearing a silk suit and a scary, stern expression. A giant man, he had a thick neck, square jaw, and puffed out chest. He would force a quick stop to anything or anyone that might permanently scar the girls' faces or bodies, but that wasn't his real purpose. He followed them closely at every party as a constant reminder that there was no escape.

With guards, constant threats, no money, and little idea of how things worked in America, the girls believed they had no chance of successfully getting away. Meanwhile, there was a never-ending stream of men ready and willing to hand over cash and take advantage of them.

The ugly man took Sofia into a bedroom. Closing her eyes, she moaned softly in the practiced way she'd been taught. It helped each ordeal end quicker. She put her actions on autopilot and let her mind travel to another place. She asked herself the questions that had been circling through her mind since her best friend Sasha disappeared two days ago. Where was she? Locked inside a dark closet with only a bottle of water and a bucket? Had she been taken to a different city? Would Sofia ever see her again? Sasha was too brave for her own good, and that might be the reason she had disappeared. Sofia said a silent prayer that her friend was still alive . . . somewhere.

She closed her eyes and moaned.

If Sasha didn't come back, Sofia would have to be the brave one.

Chapter Three

Magda pulled her employer's Lexus up to the South Charlotte Mall behind a Porsche SUV and a flashy BMW Coupe. Tiny white holiday lights were already strung around the bare trees on each side of the mall's main entrance. In the center, a tall pine with silver and gold ornaments the size of bowling balls rose to the roof line of the building.

A valet parking attendant rushed toward her car. Magda held up a finger. "One second, please. I don't need parking. I'm only dropping off."

Emma brushed another coat of gloss on her lips and bared her teeth in the visor mirror. Her thorough once-over finished; she opened the passenger side door.

"Wait." Magda placed her hand on Emma's arm. "I don't see your friends. Where are they?"

Emma shook off Magda's hand and rolled her eyes. "They're inside. Waiting for me."

"Are you sure? I shouldn't drop you off until I know they're here."

"They're here. See? Emma shoved her phone in front of Magda's face, then pulled it away just as quickly. "I'm already late."

"You're meeting Tiffany and Nicole?"

Emma sighed, heavy and loud, as she got out of the car. "Yes. I'm meeting Tiffany and Nicole."

"All right. Be safe."

Emma slammed the door.

Magda lifted her eyes skyward, silently asking God for strength, before watching Emma walk away. The teen wore tight stretchy red pants and a draping black top with cut-outs in each shoulder. Magda wished she could reverse the girl's age back to when Emma was sweet and friendly and enjoyed spending time with her nanny. Despite Magda's best efforts to help raise a decent human being, Emma's attitude was turning out to be more like her mother's and father's. Magda had evolved into a personal assistant and chauffeur, while the sweet Emma had become a sullen teen who grew a bit more disrespectful every day.

"You can't stay here, ma'am." The parking attendant frowned at her. "You have to move." She held up her hand and offered a slight smile. "Sorry. Going now." She put the car in gear and drove off. Maybe Emma was simply angry with her parents again. That was probably it. The constant threat of divorce hung heavy in the air at the Manning home. It made sense that Emma was taking her frustration out on Magda, who was always available.

♦ ♦ ♦

Emma strutted to the center of the mall, past the big Christmas tree and the Santa station and straight to the bathroom near the food court. She had to pee, even though she'd just gone before leaving her house. Nerves did that to her. After exiting a stall, she stopped at the mirror. Pulling her long, straight, reddish hair forward on her shoulders, she slowly turned to her right and then to her left, studying herself again. She pursed her lips and sucked her cheeks in, so her face looked thinner, more angular. She was pretty, everyone told her so. Her newly straightened and bonded teeth looked amazing. She had long dark lashes and beautiful brown eyes that popped thanks to expertly applied eyeliner and eyeshadow. But she wanted to look *really* pretty, and she needed to look older. If Damian found out how young she really was, he might be angry. And worse, he might not be interested in her any more.

She gripped her phone. Only a few more minutes before she would finally meet him in person. This was it. She squared her shoulders and marched out of the bathroom with the saunter of a runway model, shoulders back and neck extended. Her stomach fluttered and her legs were a little weak, but years of performances at the Children's Theater had taught her how to conceal nervous excitement. She passed the Coppa Coffee and Tea store. Maybe she and Damian would come back and have a latte together. She really liked the Chai tea lattes there. If Damian didn't already have a plan for hanging out, she would suggest it. But probably he did, since he was older and seemed so confident and sure of himself. Would he look the same as he did in the pictures he'd sent over the internet? Or had he photoshopped those to make him look like a movie star? In a short time, she would know for sure.

She slowed her pace so as not to arrive early. But what if she was late and he left because he figured she wasn't coming? She sped up again.

The escalator took her down to the parking garage where they had arranged to meet. She hadn't thought twice about the odd choice of a location. Despite her nerves, she had to look nonchalant and cool, like meeting Damian was no big deal. Wouldn't it be great if one of her classmates saw her with him—

maybe some of the older girls from her school? They would be impressed.

With her coat wrapped over her hands, she leaned back against the wall, then stood up straight, then leaned back again, unable to decide which pose was better. Fidgeting with her hands, she pretended to read a mall directory. What if he blew her off? What if he'd never intended to come? She shifted her purse to her opposite shoulder. It was a little heavier than usual because Damian had asked her to bring her MacBook along. She had no idea why. Maybe he wanted to show her some new game.

"Emma?"

She turned around at the raspy voice and her stomach flipped over. Damian walked toward her. Hard to believe, but he was even more handsome in real life.

"Hi." She giggled as her nerves threatened to turn her into a silly child.

Damian's skin was the color of Emma's perfect spray tan. He had a beautiful smile, and his hair was cut in a cool way, neat and not messy. His outfit was perfection—olive-colored jeans, a navy shirt, and a North Face jacket—and it looked *so* good on him. He looked like he played football or rugby. Not too big, but strong enough to protect them if necessary.

She expected him to walk over to her, but he stopped a few yards away and glanced around. He had one hand inside his coat pocket. For a second, she worried he had changed his mind about hanging out with her. But then his smile grew bigger. "How are you?"

"I'm fine. And you?" Her answer was automatic, the same response she would offer a teacher or one of her parents' friends. She needed to do better, but her mind was racing, part of it wondering why he hadn't come closer. She walked toward him until she was a more normal distance away. She cocked her head and batted her eyelashes until she could think of something clever to say.

"Hope you haven't been waiting long." He glanced up toward the escalator as he spoke. There was no one coming down.

"Me? No. I just got here, like seconds before you did."

He nodded. "You look really nice."

His smile made her tingle inside. There was nothing creepy or immature about the way he looked at her. She could tell he approved, and his gaze made her confidence soar. "Thanks," she said, shifting her weight, and moving her coat into one hand so she could put the other on her hip.

"I forgot the mall would be so nuts with Christmas shopping starting already. It took forever to find a parking spot."

"Yeah. Me, too." Heat rushed to her face with her lie.

"Since it's so crowded, what do you say we go to the Starbucks down the street? That one usually has booths and tables open around this time. We can jump in my car, it's a little cold for walking."

The Starbucks was close to her neighborhood. What if her mother went to the grocery store and then grabbed a latté and saw them? Nah. Her mother never did the grocery shopping anymore,

Magda did it. But here's who did visit that Starbucks—Emma's friends. She would love them to see her with Damian.

"Sure," she said, in as natural and confident a manner as she could muster, already imagining how she would casually wave to any of the girls from school who might see her. How great would it be if a few girls from her field hockey team were there?

Emma headed toward the exit.

"Wait. This way." Damian gestured to the other end of the entry with one hand, the other hadn't left his pocket.

"Why? There's an exit over here."

He smiled. "Just come this way."

"Okay." She caught up to him, walking alongside him as he led her on a roundabout route through the garage.

"Sorry. Forgot where I parked." He laughed, occasionally looking up toward the corners of the parking structure as they weaved through and around dozens of cars.

Strange that he'd already forgotten when he only arrived minutes ago, but he must have been nervous, too. Emma barely gave it a thought, so concerned was she with her walk and her hair, worrying about looking old enough, and feeling grateful her orthodontist had taken her braces off a few months earlier than planned.

Pretty Little Girls is available on Amazon in print, kindle, audiobook, and kindle unlimited. If it's not on the shelves at your local library, you can request that they purchase it.

NOTE TO READERS

If you have the time, I would deeply appreciate a review on Amazon, Goodreads, or wherever you purchased the book. I learn a great deal from them, and I'm always grateful for any encouragement. Reviews help authors like me to sell a few more books. Every review matters, even if it's only a few words.

Jenifer Ruff

BOOKS BY JENIFER RUFF

The Brooke Walton Series

Everett

Rothaker

The Intern

The Agent Victoria Heslin Thriller Series

The Numbers Killer

Pretty Little Girls

When They Find Us

Lake Lucinda

The FBI & CDC Thriller Series

Only Wrong Once

Only One Cure

Young Adult Suspense

Full-Out

ABOUT THE AUTHOR

Jenifer Ruff is a USA Today bestselling author of thriller novels. She writes in three series: The Brooke Walton series, the Agent Victoria Heslin Thriller series, and the FBI and CDC Thriller series.

Jenifer grew up in Massachusetts, graduated from Mount Holyoke College, and received her Master's in Public Health and Epidemiology from Yale University. An avid hiker and fitness enthusiast, she lives in Charlotte, North Carolina with her family and dogs.

Sign up to join her newsletter for special giveaways and promotions like free books and free audio books. Be the first to hear of new releases. The newsletter only goes out a few times a year. Visit Jenruff.com to join.

Made in the USA
Monee, IL
31 December 2020